# THE LION'S DEN

## ANNIVERSARY EDITION

Coventry Press Ltd.

# THE LION'S DEN

## THE CURSED BY BLOOD SHIFTERS

MARIANNE MOREA

*"My son, there is a battle between two wolves inside us all. One is Evil. It is anger, jealousy, greed, resentment, inferiority, lies and ego. The other is Good. It is joy, peace, love, hope, humility, kindness, empathy and truth." The boy thought about it and asked, "Grandfather, which wolf wins?" The old man quietly replied, "The one you feed."*

*~Cherokee Proverb~*

# ONE

"Lily, maybe you should hire a wedding coordinator. I'm not cut out for this kind of thing." Emily slumped onto a wooden folding chair, crushing some of the white flowers and delicate vines decorating its beveled edge.

People bustled in and around the clearing all day, each working to help prepare for the evening's festivities. Spring was in full bloom and the Compound was awash in color adding to the festive feel. Pale, green leaves not yet at full flush, capped the trees lining the immense property. Clusters of early wildflowers covered the landscape, replacing the gloomy haze of winter with the luster of rebirth. Insects and butterflies buzzed and fluttered around the flat wooded area, mimicking the hum of anticipation for the sunset ceremony.

Lily turned, clipboard in hand. "Nice try, Em. As my maid-of-honor and future sister-in-law it's your moral imperative to be here. You cover society events and promote fundraisers every day for the Chronicle. If you were organizationally inept you wouldn't have landed the job, so don't tell me I need to hire professional help. I have you."

"That's exactly what you need. Professional help. After everything that's happened how can you still want to be a part of this insanity?"

Lily's gaze flicked toward the flurry of nuptial activity before shifting back to Emily. "It is a bit over the top, I admit, but Rissa insisted. I wanted to elope to Vegas, but she practically went into early labor when I mentioned it."

Emily made a face. "I wasn't talking about the wedding. I mean us." She crooked her fingers in mock quotation marks. "Supernaturals." She sighed. "As a group we are pretentious and volatile, and as fickle as the weather, or haven't you figured that out yet. I may be a shifter by blood, but I would trade human places with you in a heartbeat."

Doing the best she could not to laugh, Lily considered her future sister-in-law's glum face. "I doubt that. Trust me, Em. Proving your human worth on a daily basis gets old fast. Especially when the majority of who you're proving it to are a giant *collective* pain in the ass." Lily glanced down at the beautiful heirloom gracing the third finger of her left hand and smiled. "I'm sure Sean could say the same about me and mine, but that's the whole point. Why would you want to trade places when our worlds are as similar as they are different? I want to be part of this world because I love Sean. His crazy is my crazy, and together we make it sane."

Wide blue eyes met Lily's gaze. "If you say so."

Putting the clipboard down, Lily moved closer to where Emily sat, considering her more closely. "What's going on, Em? This is more than just wedding aggravation. Parties are your stock and trade, but lately you've been acting aloof and unavailable. Almost as if you're sorry you ever came home. What gives?"

Emily shrugged, shaking her head. "Nothing. I'm just a little out of my element here. I've been on my own a long time, Lily. I'm glad to be back, but old habits die hard."

Lily's gaze tightened. She wasn't buying it. "This..." she interjected, letting her hand sweep the clearing and the set up around them. "... none of this should surprise you. You grew up with this kind of fanfare, and yes, I get you were gone for a long time, but my gut is telling me your stress is more than just my wedding pinging your protective wall." Lily hesitated, but then plunged ahead. "Something's not right. Something way beyond your normal aversion to being home. You didn't even come back when Rissa had the baby. A quick phone call to make sure they were both okay, and then nothing. If Sean hadn't sent Gehrig to San Francisco to bring you home you'd have missed the wedding, too."

"Gehrig." Emily snorted. "Yeah, I guess he's the new Jack."

Lily stiffened. The subject of Jack and his betrayal was still very raw, but now wasn't the time to get into it. The position was a toss up between the younger shifter, and his older brother, Dash. The Collier brothers were like bookends, but Sean knew what he was doing testing them both.

"So you think the grass is greener on the human side of the fence, and keeping yourself apart from what you know, and who you love, will insulate you from heartache."

Emily twisted and untwisted a few strands of sweet grass plucked from the decorations. "I was just saying."

"Just saying, huh. Well, this is me calling bullshit. So much has happened in the last six months, both before and after you visited for the holidays. You mentioned how gossip kept you up to date on what was happening here, but hearing about it is different from living it. You were removed from the sickness, the worry and the death affecting anything with a supernatural pulse. Or without one for that matter. You knew about the betrayals that put more than just my life in danger, but according to you, pretense is just shifter business as usual. If that's what you need to tell yourself so you can close your eyes at night, that's fine. But I can't."

"I lost the life I knew. I've had to kill or be killed," Lily continued. "I've been lied to, misled, threatened, kidnapped, and rescued. All by shifters. So to say I'm nuts to want to be part of this is a fair assumption. Nevertheless, after all I've suffered and lost, I've also gained, and not once did I have to go through any of it alone. For the first time in my life I feel like I truly belong."

Emily was quiet, almost contemplative, and it was more than a moment before her eyes met Lily's again. "You're right. Staying away was my choice. After my father died and Sean took over as Alpha, I heard about the changes he implemented. I could have come home. He even asked me to, but I ignored his letters and emails. I told myself I was better off alone. Then Rissa got sick, and when I didn't come home I knew it was too late."

Lily slid into the chair next to Emily and slipped her arm around her shoulders. "Sean's right, you're as stubborn as I am. It took me a long time to realize it's never too late. Terri taught me that."

"Terri?"

"A friend who died. It was her death that led me here. She was the one who taught me to let go and to listen to my heart."

"Ha! Now who's talking bullshit."

Lily laughed. "What. You've never done something stupid and impulsive because your heart told you to?"

"No."

Lily let go of Emily shoulder, chuckling as she stood to retrieve her clipboard. "Now, that's a laugh."

"What?"

Lily's lips slid into a sideways smirk. "After our weekend in Boston you came back looking like the cat that swallowed the canary. You never said a word, but it was clear you met someone. Someone who rocked your world."

Emily shrugged. "That? I hooked up, so what? It's not like I signed a marriage contract in blood. It was just sex."

Lily dropped her chin, letting her smirk spread even further across her lips, making Emily shift in her seat. Her cheeks tomato red.

"Oh, come on. Not fair! You promised you would never use your psychic ability on me. We agreed. Only in case of emergency."

Lily laughed out loud. "You make me sound like a medical alert pendant. Help! I've fallen and I can't get up," she mimicked.

"Lily!"

She put her hands up. "Relax, Em. I'm no voyeuristic mental peeping tom. Your sexcapade was written all over your face, not to mention how Stephanie ran around telling everyone how happy you smelled."

Emily grumbled in reply. "And what does that mean or don't I want to know."

Lily chuckled through a half sigh. "It's just Stephie's explanation for how happy Rissa was once she and Mitch started having sleep-overs." Lily made bunny ears with her fingers. "Stephanie is a smart little girl, and she clearly picked up on the after-scent of consensual sex but is too young to understand what it means."

Emily groaned.

"Don't be like that. It's nothing, and we all thought it was funny."

"Thought *what* was funny?"

Lily grinned. "How based on Stephie's outbursts you were *very* happy when you came home that weekend."

Emily threw the mangled grass strands at Lily. "Nice. X-rated scents. We should go into the perfume industry. We'd make a killing."

"So, who is he? Are you still seeing him?"

Emily sighed and shook her head. "It's complicated."

"Now you sound like me trying to explain Sean and the Compound to Beverly and Carl. You should have seen the tap dance I did trying to make them understand that a handfasting was a legitimate wedding ceremony."

Emily brushed stray hairs from her forehead and looked away, regret stinging the corners of her eyes. "The guy from Boston was amazing. We had an instant connection. I know it sounds corny but being with him felt like coming home. In a good way. Like I had known him forever. Then again, he was here, and I wasn't. Simple."

"I don't understand."

Em turned back with a shrug. "What's there to understand? I've been on my own for a very long time. Success or failure was on me and me alone. I knew I was up for the society desk promotion when I came home in January for the Wolf Moon Ball. I had everything I wanted and more at my fingertips, and then I met him. I made a choice. The increased pay wasn't something I could ignore, not to mention the connections I'd make. I wasn't willing to blow something certain for something uncertain. I worked too hard to just let it go on a whim, and a whim that had plenty of odds stacked against it from the get-go."

"I still don't follow? What odds? Was he married?"

Emily smiled. "No, nothing like that. I would have kicked him to the curb with his underwear still around his ankles if that was the case. I meant the odds were stacked against the relationship because of distance. He was geographically undesirable."

"Seriously? Geographically undesirable?"

Em shrugged again. "Long distance relationships are hard. We tried it by phone, even facetiming each other, but it wasn't enough. You of all people should understand. You went home to New York and left Sean behind while you both figured things out. Phone calls. Phone sex. It's just not enough."

"I never had phone sex with your brother."

Now it was Emily's turn for skepticism. "Really? And the telepathy thing you've got going on is completely different, right?"

Lily grinned. "Okay, you got me on that. But is geography the only thing about this guy that was undesirable?"

Heat crept up Emily's cheeks at the memory of just how *desirable* he was. She sighed. "Yup. Other than that, he seemed perfect."

"Seemed?"

"Look, you and Sean have a special bond and a relationship that's built on more than just heat. You've been through hell and came out on the other side closer than ever. Between you and Sean, and Rissa and Mitch, the constant love fest is enough to make me ill." She shifted in her seat again, but this time to face Lily eye to eye. "Why else do you think I haven't been home since January? It's too much of a reminder of what I don't have."

Lily took Emily's hand. "Okay, Debbie Downer. You can stop right there. I'm not buying this poor me stuff. While there may be a kernel of truth in your words, I know you well enough to know you're the type that always goes for what you want. You wanted this job, great. Now you have it. Maybe it's time to stop making excuses and reach out to this guy and see where it goes. Take a chance, Em. What have you got to lose?"

"Oh, I took plenty of chances with him that weekend," she said with a wink.

Lily laughed. "Oh really. Maybe you should take another chance and give him a call while you're here. Boston isn't that far away."

She shook her head. "He's not from Boston. He's from New York. He's a cop. A detective, actually, and from what I gathered he's damn good at his job because he's also half-shifter, not that he knows it."

Lily's eyes narrowed. "A half-shifter NYPD detective?"

Emily nodded, her stomach knotting at the guarded look on Lily's face. "Yeah, I'm guessing he's part cougar or something along those lines. I got a distinct feline vibe, and his scent was definitely big cat. Why?"

"When's the last time you saw him?"

Emily dragged in a breath and let it out in a melancholy sigh. "Two months ago. Like I said, we tried the whole long distance thing, but I let it drop. I haven't spoken to him since."

"I see."

Confused, Emily searched Lily's distracted expression. "Well, I'm glad *you* see, because I sure don't."

"Hey you two!" Amilynn waved from across two rows of chairs. "Lily, what in heaven's name are you still doing here? The ceremony is in six hours! You need be at the manor getting ready," she scolded.

"Perfect timing, Ami. I was just going to hand the rest of this over to you and the girls," she replied, picking up the clipboard and handing it to her friend. "I'm sure you, Patricia, and Celia won't mind handling the check list for me, right?"

The dark haired girl practically squealed. "Of course! I'll corral the girls and get right on it..." She stopped mid-sentence watching Emily's confused frown. "Em, I know you're coordinating the decorations, but Rissa sent me to find you as well, so you'd better get going, too. She's a sleep-deprived new mom. Trust me you don't want to tangle with her. The only one who's got immunity today is Lily."

Ignoring Ami's reproving chirp, Emily stood, her gaze never leaving Lily's face.

"Did you get a chance to check out the bride's tent?" Ami asked, pointing to the Moroccan style tent right out of 1001 Arabian Nights. "It's very Scheherazade, don'tcha think? You can do the bulk of your prep upstairs at the manor, but according to tradition, you have to enter the circle from the eastern woods. The groom's tent is on the opposite side." She gestured to a much smaller, less extravagant tent across the clearing.

Lily smiled at the girl's infectious enthusiasm. "I haven't yet, but it looks amazing. And thanks for taking care of the rest of this." She gestured toward the clipboard. "You're a lifesaver." Giving her a quick nod, she hooked elbows with Emily. "We'll see you at the ceremony later, Ami."

Tugging Emily by the arm, Lily steered them toward the main lawn and Rissa's impatient beauty regime. "Things are really coming together, aren't they?"

With a frustrated exhale, Emily jerked Lily's arm hard enough to stop them in their tracks.

"Hey! What was that for?"

Emily opened her mouth and gaped. "You tell me. You're the one being all cryptic with your, *hmmm, I see,* and no follow up. You may be the psychic in the family, but I don't need ESP to know you're hiding something."

"I'm not hiding anything, Em. It's just we now have a happy, yet awkwardly unexpected set of circumstances at the wedding. That's all."

"What the hell does that mean?"

Tightening her arm in Emily's, Lily pulled her into an unhurried pace along the gravel path. "Let me put it this way. Remember the pep rally scene from the movie Grease, where Rizzo arranges for Sandy to run into Danny Zuko at the bonfire..."

CHAPTER
# TWO

"Hurry up, Rissa," Lily moaned impatiently.

"Relax. It's not like they can start without you. Besides, I'm almost done," her friend assured, buttoning the last of a long line of pearls running the length of Lily's antique wedding dress.

Lily turned to look at herself in the mirror. The creamy satin of Sean's mother's gown looked wonderful against her skin.

Like a porcelain doll.

That's how Sean said she'd look, and he was right. Her thick, chestnut hair hung in loose curls, and when Rissa fitted the sheer fingertip veil and accompanying silver and rose gold circlet to her head, the picture was complete.

"You look beautiful," she said, standing next to Lily in front of the mirror. "I'm so glad you decided to put your hair back to its natural chestnut color. The honey blond was nice, but this is you."

The past six months had been hard for both women. Full of sadness and sacrifice, but also unbelievable joy. Turning, Lily gave her friend a hug. "Thanks for everything, Rissa."

"Are you kidding? It's my pleasure. Especially after all you've done for us." Rissa took Lily's hand in hers and squeezed. There was no need to say anything else.

The dress was exquisite ivory silk, with a square neckline cut low over the swell of Lily's breasts. A whalebone corset built into the bodice fitted the creamy fabric tight around her small waist, tying at the back with a crisscross pattern of satin ribbons. Bell sleeves accented the rest of the gown as it fell in a full A-line skirt with a cathedral length train. A panel of red silk flowed at the center of the train, embroidered with silver thread in an intricate Celtic pattern.

The same red trimmed the bottom of each sleeve and the center panel of the bodice, also embroidered, but here with both silver and gold threading to symbolize the god and the goddess of the ancient religion. The entire design came together in a beautiful representation of the phases of the moon.

The embroidered detail on the gown's waist dropped to a *V* pattern over Lily's hips in medieval style. Rissa fastened a delicate silver chain around the bride's waist, attaching a small silver dagger to be used in the blood oath the new alpha female must swear during the ceremony.

"I've never seen a wedding dress trimmed in red." Lily swished in the mirror. "It's beautiful. Does it signify something? A royal color, maybe?"

Rissa snorted. "Royalty now, is it? Would you listen to herself giving airs, and the blood oath not even spoken." She feigned a brogue, mimicking the women of old.

"Rissa!"

"I'm just teasing, but yes the red symbolizes the blood the alpha female spills in fealty to the Alpha of the Brethren."

"Ha. That sounds almost medieval."

"And you're surprised? Look at the dress, Lily. Look at the decorations, and the set up for the ceremony. It's called a handfasting, for chrissake. You do remember what you're supposed to do, right? You enter from the east where the sun rises, and then circle around to the south, west, and north, where Sean will then take your hand and circle the perimeter again with you. The two of you then stop at the stone altar, make your request to marry and only then say your vows."

"Got it. I hope."

"After all that, Sean will take the dagger from your waist and then hold his out hand for yours. You make your blood oath, and then together you and Sean light the ritual fire."

"Will the blood oath hurt much?"

Rissa rolled her eyes. "This from the woman who escaped Edward Parr's rogue shifters, and their bungled kidnapping attempt. Not to mention you shot a diseased vampire, fought Jack before he got the better of you, and..." She stopped short at the pained look on Lily's face. "I... I'm sorry, honey."

Lily lifted one shoulder and let it drop, sparing Rissa what she hoped was an apologetic look. "It's okay, Ris. It is what it is. Jack is dead, and nothing is going to change that or the fact he betrayed us."

Rissa didn't reply.

Lily turned toward the mirror again. In the reflection she saw Rissa's face tighten, and Lily knew she was mentally taking herself to task. "Ris, it's okay, really. And I was kidding about the blood oath. With the way people around here want to kill me every time the wind changes, I'd better be able to take a little knife prick." She absentmindedly ran her fingers over the scar on her left hand. "It's ironic you know."

"What is?"

"Terri and I made a similar blood oath when we were little girls. We'd seen something like it in an old movie. We thought if we did it too, it would make us real sisters. We didn't know then our sweet, innocent act would eventually save my life."

Lily inhaled, refusing to let the thought of Terri or the fact she was no longer here ruin the day. "It's strange, really. In the end it seems as if being part of this pack was pre-ordained."

"Seems that way to us too, sometimes."

"Well?"

"Well what?"

"Will it hurt?"

Rissa laughed out loud. "You are asking the wrong girl. I wasn't an alpha female when I married Jerard, remember?"

Lily smirked. "Yeah, but you will be when you marry Mitch."

Hmmm.

Lily fastened a pair of tiny pearl studs to her ears. "To tell you the truth I am a little nervous. Not about the blood oath, of course...but let's face it, when it comes to formal shifter occasions my luck hasn't exactly been stellar. I don't want another unexpected surprise.

Rissa's eyes narrowed. "Please don't tell me Delia Monroe has been seen skulking around."

Lily shook her head.

An unladylike noise left Rissa's mouth. "I didn't think so. She's arrogant, but she's not stupid. After her involvement with Edward Parr and his biological warfare, she'd have to be an idiot to show her face here, especially today of all days. I can't imagine any pack offering her sanctuary. It would take something unconditional, something our laws couldn't ignore to circumvent a universal shunning." Rissa waved her hand as if clearing away an unpleasant smell. "Enough about her. Today is all about you and Sean."

"So, what do you think?" Lily turned from the mirror to model the full effect.

"It's perfect," Rissa breathed, stepping back to take in the full effect. "You look like you stepped out of Camelot."

Lily paused, her eyes searching Rissa's in the mirror's reflection. "Are you sure Emily won't be insulted I'm wearing her mother's gown?"

Rissa shook her head, giving Lily's shoulders a quick squeeze. "Relax. Emily is the one who suggested it, otherwise I would never have taken the box out of storage to show you the dress. Besides, with her height she would need to add about two feet to the bottom hem."

"I'll have to remember to thank her for being so generous." Lily made a face. "That's if she shows up."

"Why would you say that? She would never miss her own brother's wedding."

Lily shrugged. "It's nothing really. She was distressed about someone we invited to the wedding."

With a dismissive wave, Rissa bent to gather Lily's train and move it to the side. "That's silly. What happened with her and Connor is ancient history, and the Abenaki know better than to start anything today. Mitch even warned his mother to behave."

"It's not Connor or the Abenaki. It's Ryan."

At Rissa's questioning look, Lily shrugged. "I wasn't going to say anything, but it looks like Emily hooked up with him when she was here visiting for the holidays. It didn't work out, and she had no idea he was involved with me and everything that happened afterward with Edward Parr and the vampires."

"Does she know now?"

Lily exhaled, her hand smoothing the back of her dress to sit on the bride's chair beside the full length mirror. "Yes. I filled her in."

"And?"

"I don't know. I've seen flight or fight responses before, but this was unreal. Em was almost panicked."

"That doesn't sound like Emily. She's made hiding her feelings an art form. Especially when she's scared or feels trapped. It's how she managed to run five years ago. No one suspected a thing."

"Believe me, she did her best to keep her appearance passive, but she couldn't fool me. Her body language screamed bolt."

Rissa sat in a chair opposite Lily, her mouth pressed into a line. "You should've said something earlier. If Emily isn't at the ceremony, people are going to view this union as tainted. As in taking place without the Alpha's family blessing."

"But you're here."

"In this instance, I don't count. I'm not of the bloodline, and Stephanie and the baby are too young. Emily needs to be here to give approval. It's tradition. It's superstition. It's all of the above, but without it..." she let her words trail off.

Rissa stood, smoothing the front of her own lavender gown. "Well. There's nothing we can do about it now. What's done is done. Your relationship with Sean has never been an easy go, so why should your wedding be any different. Whether Emily is here or not doesn't change a thing. Maybe it won't matter. Her history doesn't exactly endear her to the Compound as reliable." With a shrug, she turned to straighten what was left of their bridal prep.

"Ris."

"Hmmm?"

Lily stood, pulling the other woman into a hug. "Thanks."

"Hey. That's what friends are for, right?" She stepped back, keeping Lily's hands in hers as her eyes swept the bride's elegant frame. "There's only a few minutes before we start. I'd better check on Mitch and grab our bouquets. Stephanie is dressed and waiting with him, but he's got the baby, too. Clara is there as well, but Mitch has it in his head it's his responsibility to do everything."

"Typical hunter."

She sighed. "I asked Clara to stay on as our nanny because I knew the kids were going to be a handful. If I know Mitch, he's probably reached his breaking point but is too stubborn to admit it."

A genuine smile spread across Lily's face. "Mitch in daddy mode. I had a feeling he'd take to it like a fish to water. How's it going with you two, though?"

Rissa blushed, disengaging her left hand from Lily's so the oval diamond on her third finger twinkled in the chandelier's light.

"Oh my God! Rissa! When?" Lily pulled her friend's hand closer, practically jerking her forward. "I can't believe I didn't notice it earlier! I'm a horrible, self-absorbed friend! When did he pop the question? Sean never said a word!"

Rissa chuckled. "Sean said plenty. He and Mitch went out for a run, and when Mitch got back he was sweating and nervous with a funny look on his face. I was in the middle of making dinner and had egg and breadcrumb up to my wrists. I knew something was up when he told me to stop what I was doing and wash my hands. That we needed to talk."

"Romantic."

A huge smile spread across Rissa's face. "I know it doesn't seem so, but he was too cute. He stumbled over his words, trying to explain his big plan. First he wanted to wait for Braden to be born. Then he didn't want to intrude on you and Sean and your plans. Finally, he just stopped and blurted out, 'Oh hell, woman. Are you going to marry me or not?' I swear I had to bite the inside of my cheek not to laugh at him being so comically sweet."

Lily pulled Rissa into a hug, the soft fabric of her wedding dress rustling between them "All I can say is it's about time."

Stepping back, Rissa laughed, wiping her eyes with the back of her hand. "I never thought I could find this kind of love, but I have. He's wonderful, and I'm so happy." She paused. "You know, this wedding is more than just our Alpha taking a mate. It's a symbol of us moving on yet honoring the past. In a way Braden is, too. I'm moving on from my past, but the baby is my link to what was good, bad, or otherwise.

"Even his name is symbolic. Braden Joshua Leighton. I named him Braden because the name is traditional in Mitch's family. My way of honoring him for taking on the role of father to my children. The name Joshua is for the baby Jerard's mother lost. To honor her and the rest of the Leighton family." She grabbed a tissue to dab the corner of her eye. "Listen to me blubbering about my past and future when it looks like we both have a chance at being happy."

Lily smiled, handing her another Kleenex. "I'm thrilled for you. Mitch too. Just as long as he doesn't get it in his head to kill me again."

"If he does, he'll have more than just Sean to answer to," she said tossing the crumpled tissue into the trash. "I'd better scoot before it's too late. Be right back. You look amazing!"

The tent's flap wafted in cool breeze, and Lily closed her eyes wishing that slight chill could was Terri.

"She's right, you know. You look stunning."

Lily whirled around, her dress a cloud of ivory. She paused for a millisecond. "Oh. Hey, Em."

"Just me." She tilted her head. "You look as if you were expecting someone else."

"No, not really. Where have you been? I was starting to worry you wouldn't show up."

Em shook her head. "Just giving you a little space. That's all."

"Ha. You mean giving yourself a little space."

Emily shrugged, a bittersweet expression on her face. It didn't take much for Lily to recognize the sadness edging her future sister-in-law's eyes.

"What happened in the past six hours, Em? Are you not happy for me and Sean, or is being here really too much for you?"

Emily laughed, her eyes shining with tears. "Oh, Lily. I couldn't be more thrilled for you. I love how happy you've made Sean, and I know you'll be great together. It's just..." she paused, struggling to find the right words. "I can't do this." Her words trailed off, barely a whisper.

Lily hesitated. Then picking up her lipstick, she waved it dismissively. "All this angst because of Ryan, right?" She wasn't being callous. Em needed to snap out of her funk.

Emily's nod was hardly discernable.

"So you had a fling. Big deal. Is the situation awkward? Sure. But we're all grownups, and from what you've told me about your new job, you're not about to let anyone or anything get in the way of your career."

Emily didn't say a word, just stared at Lily's reflection in the mirror.

"The truth is hooking up with Ryan makes sense in a bizarre way. This family's entire connection to him is inexplicable. Yours. Mine. The Compound. The pieces that link him to us, and us to him, are astonishing on so many levels. Levels I haven't even told you about, but none of them would have come to light if I hadn't been called in to help solve the bloodbath murders in New York. He's my partner and my friend, and he helped your brother save my life.

"Whatever happened between you two, you can handle it. I know Ryan pretty well, and he's not the type to do or say something awful. I wish Sean and I had known of your relationship beforehand, but we can't very well disinvite him at this point. Nor would we consider it. I'm sorry Em, but the choice is yours. You can either suck it up, or you can run. If you run, I'm telling you now, no one will track after you and beg you to come back."

Emily stood stunned. "Wow. Is there anything else you want to throw at me?"

"Emily, I'm not trying to be cold. I'm trying to understand and put it in perspective. Does this have anything to do with the guy you were supposed to marry? Or because members of his pack are here tonight."

"No." Em shook her head. "It doesn't have anything to do with Connor."

Lily turned around completely, the dress's long train twisting with the motion. "I hate games, Emily, and your timing sucks. If you won't talk to me, then maybe talk to Rissa."

The tent flap opened, and Rissa bounced into the bride room a little out of breath. "Talk to Rissa about what?"

Rissa's gaze tracked to the tall blonde standing at the back of the tent and gave her a quick once over. "Wow, Em. You finally decided to show up. I guess we should be grateful you're dressed and ready."

She put her armful of bouquets down on one of the plush chairs. "Far be it for me to say anything, but Lily's had enough black clouds following her around for the past six months to have something go wrong last minute. At least now no one can say Sean is marrying her without his family's blessing."

"Where's Mitch?" Lily asked. "Everything okay with the kids?"

"Better than okay. Mitch is finally letting the nanny do her job. He left the kids with her, and he and Sean are in the groom's tent having a beer, thank God. I don't know who's more nervous. Him or the groom." She moved to the mirror, motioning for Lily to stand still. "Let me fix the back of your veil. It's not smooth beneath the circlet."

Soft tears trickled down Emily's cheeks, and Rissa froze midway. Her eyes traveled from Lily's stunned expression to Emily's quiet sobs and back again. "What just happened?"

Neither one answered.

"Will someone please tell me what is going on?" Rissa's voice raised an octave.

Lily took the comb from Rissa's hand and tossed it onto the vanity. "I don't know, and Emily's not in a sharing mood."

The music swelled outside, and Rissa glanced toward the tent flap. "Oh for God's sake. Emily, pull yourself together and wolf up. Whatever is causing this drama, it needs to wait. If you can't or won't compose yourself for Lily's sake, then step aside."

The new mom turned, steering Lily toward the door. "It's show time, lovey. One hundred people are waiting to see if you can carry off this ritual without falling on your single-natured butt."

Emily and Lily stared at the petite martinet. Both their mouths open.

Rissa handed Lily her bridal bouquet, sweeping Emily's up as well and holding it out to her. "Don't look so surprised. You learn a lot about strength and true perspective when you face losing a child. Plus, pushing a ten pound baby out of your hoo-ha is enough to turn anyone into a consort battleship."

Emily took her bouquet from Rissa's hand.

With a steadying breath, Lily squared her shoulders. Both she and Rissa eyed Emily and the woman stood holding her bouquet in front of her in proper maid-of-honor fashion.

"It'll be fine, I promise." Lily reached out and brushed Emily's cheek with her fingertips. "Besides, you've got the strategic edge and the element of surprise on your side. You know about him, but he has no clue about you."

Emily laughed, wiping the last wetness from her eyes. "Don't worry. I've got it together. Today is all about you and Sean. I'll sort it, eventually."

"White dress or not, I've got your back." Lily hugged her, squeezing her shoulders lightly.

Two of Sean's hunters held open the tent flap, and Carl poked his head in. "It's now or never, sweetheart."

With Rissa and Emily leading the way, Lily stepped out of the tent to take Carl's arm. "Wow, Carl. You clean up good." she said, admiring the cut of the older man's tux, and how he'd cut his hair and trimmed his beard for the occasion.

"Thanks, kiddo. Beverly made me shave up a bit. She told me I needed to stop puttering under the truck and get my butt to the rental place. You should see her, though. She looks almost as beautiful as you." He pressed a kiss to Lily's forehead.

Her throat tightened and her eyes stung. Beverly and Carl. They were her family, and she had kept them at a distance for too long. She once told Jack that she and Terri were sisters in everything but blood. The torrent attached to those words came back in a rush, but this time her chest clenched with warmth instead of pain. Her family. And now she had Sean's, too. A small smile tickled her mouth, and Terri's voice echoed at the back of her mind saying I told you so.

"You okay, honey?" Carl eyed her, a worried look puckering between his eyes. "If you have any doubts, the three of us will get in the car and head for home. No questions asked."

Lily smiled, pressing her fingers to the outside corner of her eyes. "I'm fine. Just trying really hard not cry and to ruin my makeup."

Carl slid his arm around her shoulders. "This is the shortest and longest walk you'll ever take, kiddo. Enjoy it."

Lily stepped back to look at the man who raised her, and a million emotions squeezed her heart. "I wish Terri were here."

"She is sweetheart."

Loving memories, long forgotten blurred her vision even more than the tears that threatened. "I love you... Dad."

The older man's craggy smile spread across his lips. "I've waited sixteen years for you to call me that. I love you too, Lils."

"Come on, you two!" Rissa called from her place at the beginning of the petal-lined walk. "The sun is setting. It's time."

"Ready?" Carl asked, with a wink.

Lily linked her arm into his elbow, holding tight. "Don't let me fall, okay?"

"Never."

# THREE

S oft white twinkle lights dotted the trees. Their gentle glow adding an air of mystery to the enveloping twilight. Sean waited just out of sight, his gaze noting the last minute flurry of activity as people took their seats.

The soothing melody of Claire de Lune played in the background. Everyone invited had come, including the vampires from the New York council. Sébastien caught Sean's eye and inclined his head. Rémy did the same. A quick smile playing on the vampire's lips. Probably from the surrealism of their presence at the Compound.

Sean nodded once in deference, the tenuous truce between the supernatural factions fresh in his mind. There was no need for worry, though. Tonight was for celebration, and the vampires appreciated the gesture of a twilight ceremony ensuring public solidarity with the Alpha of the Brethren and his chosen mate. A new air of separate but equal had taken root in both camps, and tentative glances from both sides were more curiosity than anything else.

The remainder of the audience was a mix of shifter and human, including those shifters who expressed doubts about Lily. This was the defining moment for which Sean had waited. The validation necessary to ensure Lily's place in his world. Their world.

Emotion welled. His chest aching with the knowledge she was finally his without question or doubt. The overwhelming feeling wisped across their intimate mind path, and Lily replied in kind with an answering kiss and the scent of orange blossoms. Wrinkling his nose, he sneezed, and the feel of Lily's laughter filled his mind.

*See you in a bit. I'll be the one in white, in case you forget...*

A possessive growl left his throat in response. Sean choked at the minister's raised eyebrow, realizing he'd let the sound go audible.

"You okay there, big guy?" Mitch asked, stifling a laugh.

Sean fixed his tie, clearing his throat. "I'm fine."

The minister stepped forward positioning himself in front of the stone altar, and Sean took his place with his hunters by his side. He looked at the men flanking his left and a sense of pride washed over him. They were an unflinching line. Loyal and trustworthy. Except for one melancholy reminder. Jack.

Anger and melancholy warred for a moment. Jack was supposed to occupy the place where Gehrig and Dash Collier now stood beside Mitch. Mitch was his right hand. His second in all things. Jack had been the runt of the litter, making him the little brother of Sean's heart.

The young man had committed the worst offense in their world. He betrayed his Alpha and his pack to a sociopath for personal gain, but even that Sean could have forgiven. That Jack used Lily in the process and caused her harm was the ink on the man's death warrant.

Mitch's hand on his shoulder helped dismissed the unpleasant memories, and Sean returned the gesture. Never was there a moment clearer. Mitch had proven himself more brother than anyone else, and with the ring he gave Rissa it would make it official soon enough.

The last notes of music drifted into the dull hum of the gathered audience. Everyone stood as the first violin strains of Handel's *Air from Water Music* floated through the clearing. Lily appeared behind Rissa and Emily. She held Carl's arm and was more beautiful than he ever imagined. His mother's dress clung to her as if meant to be. The shimmery fabric hugging her small waist and highlighting the full swell of her breasts. Every other thought left his mind, and one word filled him. *Mine.*

Her eyes were down as if counting measured steps through the rose petals swirling alongside her gown. Unease edged its way into Sean's mind. Why were her eyes downcast? Did she have second thoughts? How could he blame her after everything his kind had put her through?

Carl leaned toward Lily and murmured something in her ear as they walked. Her answering smile was brilliant and full of love. It was then she lifted her eyes.

Unshed tears stung as their gazes held locked, and the liquid honey of her eyes melted any fleeting worry. It was never purer than in that one moment. She loved him as much as he loved her.

"She's beautiful, Sean. Absolutely stunning," Mitch whispered. "Looking at her now, you'd never guess how deadly she can be."

Sean grinned, his eyes never wavering from Lily's. "Smart, beautiful, and dangerous."

Gehrig chuckled. "And never boring."

Sean's grin spread even wider. "You said a mouthful, little wolf."

LILY FIDGETED with the end of her bouquet. She and Carl followed Rissa and Emily as they rounded the clearing, marking the directions of the circle of life and the elements.

Now it seemed like centuries before Carl answered the minister's question, "Who gives this woman in marriage?" A choked, "her mother and I do," left his lips as he wiped his eyes with the back of his hand. A bittersweet moment later, he kissed Lily on the cheek and then placed her hand in Sean's. "Take care of my girl," he whispered before taking his place beside Beverly.

No one mattered but Sean. Not the well-wishers whose presence barely registered as she and Carl moved up the aisle. It was Sean's face. His expression of love and pride that filled her with such hope it nearly broke her heart.

"You look gorgeous, love."

"You clean up pretty well yourself."

Sean looked every bit the gentleman in his tuxedo. His wide shoulders and narrow waist gorgeous in the double breasted suit.

"You okay?" he asked squeezing her hand.

Lily nodded, flashing him a brilliant smile. "More than okay."

Her body's reaction to his clean, masculine scent feathered across their intimate mind path until the quizzical look on his face spread to a full on knowing grin.

"Hold that thought, love." He lifted her hand to his lips. "We have a few formalities to take care of first."

Feeling her cheeks flush, Lily dropped her eyes to her bouquet. He steered her towards the south, grateful for the chance to compose herself as they rounded the four directions together before stopping again in front of the stone altar.

The minister nodded, raising his hands. "Welcome everyone to the joining of two lives. Sean Leighton and Lily Saburi. Two people of one heart and one soul. For those unfamiliar with the term handfasting, it is nothing more than an ancient term used to describe the ceremony of marriage. In days of old, precious metals were dearer than they are today, and even harder to come by. So a bride and groom would bind their hands with a symbolic cord. A thick braid woven with the colors of each clan in a symbol of love and fidelity. Today, the term handfasting is symbolic, but no less binding. Both in the eyes of God and in the eyes of the law."

The minister turned to Sean. "Sean Michael Leighton, declare your intentions before your clan and kith."

Sean turned and joined hands with Lily. "I, Sean Michael Leighton, do solemnly declare my intention to take Lily Ellen Saburi to my side, together in all things now and forever."

Ritual lances struck the ground followed by whistles and cat calls until the minister cleared his throat. The man fixed Sean's hunters with a withering stare before he turned to Lily and asked for the same declaration.

"I, Lily Ellen Saburi, do solemnly declare my intention to take Sean Michael Leighton to my side, together in all things now and forever."

The minister stood silent, waiting for the onslaught of cheers to subside before raising his hand. "Now that you have declared your intentions before this congregation, I ask you to join your hands, right over left, and recite your vows."

Emily stepped forward to take Lily's bouquet as Mitch reached into his pocket to hand the minister two gold engraved bands.

He stepped back, but then hesitated, his eyes darting to the young hunter to his left. "Gehrig. Where's the cord?"

The young man's face fell, his hands patting down his pockets before a sly smile spread across his face. He pulled the red and silver braid from his inside pocket, not quite dodging a shot to the back of his head from Dash.

"Ow!"

"Time and place, little brother."

Shaking his head, Mitch yanked the silken length from the young wolf's hand and gave it to the minister.

"There's always one monkey in every bunch," the minister tsked.

Red faced, Gehrig stood dwarfed by Mitch and Dash in more than just height.

With the rings in his palm and the symbolic braid draped neatly over his arm, the minister nodded for Sean to begin.

Sean took the smaller ring and held it inches from the third finger on Lily's left hand. "This circle of gold has no beginning and no end. I give it as a symbol of my love. As this simple band circles your finger, I pray my simple words will forever circle your heart."

The delicate gold slid onto Lily's finger, and Sean's voice echoed full and clear as the ancient words fell from his lips. "Le mo chroí is breá liom. Le mo chorp a chosaint mé. Le mo shaol déanaim trádáil ar do shon, a choinneáil go deo." With my heart I love. With my body I protect. With my life I trade for yours, forever to keep."

A round of applause spread, and even the minister grinned.

"Not bad for the man who swore he'd mangle the pronunciation!" Mitch chuckled, slapping Sean on the back. "Now let's see if your lady can manage it."

Lily answered with a smirk, but a quick wink earned warm smiles from the hunters. Sean's eyes twinkled with laughter as well, and she went up on tip toe to peck a kiss to his lips but earned a well-timed cough from the minister.

"There's time enough for that, missy. We're not done, yet." His tone was scolding, but his eyes shined, and Lily responded with a sheepish grin.

The clearing quieted, and Lily took Sean's ring from the minister's palm. The feel of the gold stunning her with the significance of the moment.

"Sean, with this ring I take you as my husband. I take your world as my world. Whatever mountains need climbing, whatever rivers need crossing, as the stars follow the moon I will be your partner, your friend, your lover, and your wife. Forever."

With a deep breath Lily's eyes locked with Sean's, and his steady gaze gave her courage. She slowly pushed the gold ring onto his finger. "Le mo chroí is breá liom. Le mo chorp a chosaint mé. Le mo shaol déanaim trádáil ar do shon, a choinneáil go deo." With my heart I love. With my body I protect. With my life I trade for yours, forever to keep."

The moment seemed suspended in time, as if everything waited on a precipice. Sean gently removed the dagger from the chained sheath at Lily's waist. He took Lily's left hand and turned it palm up.

With the point of the dagger he made a small slit along the third crease closest to her fingers. Doing the same to his own, he then returned the dagger to its sheath and joined his hands with Lily's, cut palms together, left over right.

This was the defining moment, and Lily realized everything else was embellishment. All the promises made with words meant nothing in the eyes of the shifters, but the joining of their blood was the physical manifestation of her bond with Sean and with them.

Sean paused for an instant, his eyes serious and full of meaning before he spoke. "Blood of my blood, soul of my soul, as was done by the ancients, so I do now. I am given."

Lily's heart squeezed as the words slipped from Sean's lips. The minister wrapped the silken cord around their wrists, nodding for Lily to repeat the words.

"Blood of my blood, soul of my soul, as it was done by the ancients, so I do now. I am given."

The clearing exploded into cheers and no amount of throat clearing from the minister could calm the crowd.

The hunters howled and Sean and Lily laughed, both looking at the minister in anticipation. The man then raised his hands and yelled above the din, "According to the laws of God and the State of Maine, I now pronounce you man and wife. You may kiss your bride!"

Hands locked between them, Sean pulled Lily in and kissed her. "Hello, wife," he growled.

She grinned against his lips. "Hello, husband."

Without pause, Emily untied their wrists handing the braided cord to the minister and she, Rissa and Mitch gleefully flanked the two and steered them toward the ritual pyre. The hunters brought the torch forward, and Dash handed it to Sean.

Holding the flare for the gathering to see, Sean dropped the torch into the pit, igniting the ceremonial herbs and white cedar and sending their clean scents into the air.

Emily took her place between the bride and the groom, taking their hands in hers. As Sean's sister and only blood relative of age, it was necessary she be the first to introduce them as man and wife.

The hair on Lily's neck prickled and her guard went up, at least until she tracked the source. Ryan. The full weight of the man's scowl fell on Emily, but Lily wasn't about to worry about him or her new sister-in-law. There was time enough for the two to sort things out, though it was clear from his expression the man's attention had been on Emily and not the ceremony the entire time.

As if reading Lily's thoughts, Emily winked and raised her arms. She faced the crowd, her eyes purposefully ignoring Ryan. "Ladies and gentlemen. I give you my brother and his wife. Mr. and Mrs. Sean Leighton!"

CHAPTER

# FOUR

T he reception was in full swing. The atmosphere merry and relaxed as Emily looked across the dance floor. With a sigh she let the tension in her shoulders drop a tentative notch. Maybe Lily was right, and everything would be okay.

"Lily and Sean look good together, don't'cha think? Then again, if halloween monsters are real, then maybe fairytale endings are, too. Or maybe it's just the full moon. After all, that seems to be the way things work with you wolves."

Emily whirled around.

There he stood, unbelievably striking in his streamlined tux. A glass of champagne in his hand, and condemnation on his too handsome face. Her eyes scanned the immediate area, but no one was around to deflect the inevitable. Sean and Lily were on the dance floor with eyes for no one else but each other, and Mitch and Rissa were busy showing off the baby to Beverly and Carl.

The rest of the party was, well… partying. Even the vampires had melted into the background, their own personal waitstaff ensuring their satiation with a curiously thick crimson liquid served in Sean's

35

finest crystal. She was alone beside the dais in the one moment she dreaded all day.

"Hello, Ryan." Her voice cracked despite the squared set of her shoulders.

He tilted his head, lifting his glass of champagne in salute. "Surprise." He downed the amber liquid placing the empty flute on the table behind them, his arm inadvertently skimming Emily's in the process.

The unassuming touch should have meant nothing, yet live current cascaded through her and she jumped, spilling her own champagne. She cursed the sudden dampness between her legs, and her inability to fight the overwhelming attraction toward this man.

Ryan reached across the dais for a cloth napkin and blotted at the spill. "You know, at first I was stunned to see you. Then after a minute, I realized you didn't seem at all surprised to see me. I spent most of the ceremony trying to piece it all together, and then it hit me. Leighton. I realized then you had to be related to Sean, but his sister? Really? Never in a million years."

His eyes searched hers. "Leighton is a common enough name, so when we first met I didn't put two and two together. Didn't you think to tell me? You knew what was happening in New York with Lily and the Dracula contingent." He gestured toward the vampires sitting in the back.

"Ryan..."

He held up his hand. "You know what? I don't want to hear your explanations. Anything you could say would be a little too little and a little too late. You made it clear you wanted no part of me except my dick. You kept our relationship on a need to know basis. Except it was you who chose what I needed to know."

Emily bit her lip, but only to stop it from trembling.

"Don't give me that look. You knew what I was from the first night we met. That whole, *you smell familiar,* line. Was that some sort of fishing expedition trying to find out if I was like you? I didn't know a shifter from a Won't at that point. It was Lily who helped me figure things out and Sean who helped me accept it. But from you I got zip."

"Ryan, please."

He shook his head, hard. "No, Emily. You don't get to say anything. You wouldn't return my calls, my emails, nothing. I tried to work things out, and instead I found myself out on my ass. No explanation. Just the words, I don't have time for this, or you. You dropped off the face of the Earth without warning. Without a reason. Yet you expect me to listen now?"

He exhaled, running his fingers through his dark hair. His jaw clenched, making the dimples in his cheeks more pronounced. The liquid green of his eyes flashed in frustration and her heart squeezed.

"You're right. You don't have to listen to anything I have to say, but for the sake of my brother's wedding, can we at least pretend to be civil? For him and for Lily. I know the two of you got really close during that nightmare in New York." When his eyebrows shot up, she nodded. "That's right. Lily told me everything. Including how the full moon played games with your libido."

Ryan's lips pressed together. "I hadn't seen or heard from you in a month at that point. The last time was when I flew out to California to track you down, and all I got was a goodbye fuck."

Emily winced at his words. "Is that what you really think?" Her voice was barely a whisper, but she knew he heard her.

Ryan's face softened, and his eyes searched her face. "Isn't that all it was?"

She balled the napkin in her hand and went to throw it at him. "When did you become such an asshole?"

Catching her arm he yanked her forward, so close she smelled the champagne on his breath and the very masculine scent of his skin. Her breath caught in her throat and her mouth went dry, her knees weak. It was that first night all over again, and she closed her eyes.

He leaned in as if to reply but instead he inhaled, taking in her scent the same way he always did. He once said he wanted to bottle the way she smelled so he could take it everywhere with him.

Nuzzling the skin beneath her jawline, the rough edge of his chin scraped the delicate hollow beneath her ear. "And when did *you* become a coward?"

Her eyes flew wide, and she stepped back. The spell broken. "I'm no coward." Her eyes locked on his, daring him to say something else.

"Perhaps not. But you're still a runner." He picked up his empty glass and held it in mock salute before turning on his heel and walking away.

RYAN STOOD next to the bar, nursing a Jameson's and water. Swirling the single malt in the glass, he took a sip. His eyes followed Emily across the dance floor. She looked amazing in her dark lavender gown. The shimmery fabric hugged every curve. Curves that held a new lushness that wasn't there the last time he saw her. She moved in time to the music, her body swaying and he suddenly wished he hadn't been such a prick.

"She's quite a beauty." The voice was accented old French, and when Ryan turned he recognized the unmistakable profile. The scored and powder burned skin, scarred, and melted in places. Rémy.

He exhaled, tilting his glass to his lips. "Yes, she is."

"And her scent. *Incroyable.*"

Ryan's eyes narrowed and a low rumble echoed at the back of his throat.

"Very good, mon ami. You sound as though you are learning your own power. Big cats are a mystery. Did I tell you I spent a great deal of time in the wilds of what is now Western Canada? I came across many a cougar pride during my travels there."

Keeping his eyes on the vampire, Ryan shifted his position slightly. He leaned on the bar, but angled himself so that both Rémy and Emily were in his line of sight. Sean may have forged a tenuous alliance with the fanged and furious, but that didn't mean all bets were off as far as he was concerned.

"Okay, Rémy, what is it you're trying to say? Shifters in general are mysterious, at least to me."

"Indeed, mysterious and surprising."

"Well, I could use a vacation from surprises right about now. That said, I guess I shouldn't be shocked to see you and Sébastien here this evening, but I am. You don't seem at all surprised to have been invited."

"Au contraire. We were both honored as well as surprised to receive our little witch's invitation, but the nuptials were only one reason for making the trip north. As to my earlier comment, I meant no disrespect. I am gratified to see you coming into your own. You see, unlike wolves, cougars are solitary creatures. Except when, of course, they are looking to mate." Rémy signaled the bartender and gestured for a glass of scotch.

On the outside, the conversation with the vampire seemed benign, but Ryan had been a cop far too long not to see beyond the small talk. Not to mention his sympathetic nervous system blared red. Every shifter sense he could recognize, plus dozens more he couldn't identify were on high alert.

Perhaps it was the close proximity to a walking talking corpse that caused him to react. Ryan cleared his throat, trying to shake the edginess. "And who is this little witch of yours that sent the invitations?"

Rémy smiled, and the emotion crossing his face softened the ruined lines. "Lily. It is a private joke. My own, what is the saying? Fond endearment."

"Interesting. Lily usually doesn't like nicknames."

Rémy winked, tilting the edge of his glass toward Ryan.

They stood together in silence, watching the dance floor and the people milling around the various tables. The great hall had been transformed into an enchanted garden. Flowers and ropes of spring vines were strung from the center forming a canopy of fragrance, while small decorative lights shimmered with the colors of the blooms.

Round tables dotted the perimeter, glittering with crystal and fine china etched with a silver and gold braid. The bride and groom's dais crowned the back of the great hall. Two chairs stood on the raised plat-form like thrones, with the Alpha's crest inscribed on the leather adding to the regal feel.

Lily and Sean talked with Beverly and Carl, and the two seemed over the moon. A jealous knot formed in Ryan's chest as Emily took the dance floor with a young hunter. The guy was just as tall and blond as she, and for a moment Ryan guessed he was just a relative. That is until the man slid his hand toward the small of Emily's back, stopping only when her hand blocked his path.

A kneejerk hiss ripped from Ryan's throat. The sound was completely primal. Lily and Sean glanced across the room at him, them, and of course, Emily.

Embarrassed, he didn't acknowledge their concern. Instead, he downed his scotch in one go before turning on his heel to face the bar.

"My friend, you need to learn to control your animal. The pup dancing with your lady is barely weaned from his mother's milk. He is of no consequence."

Rémy's eyes shined with a little too much laughter for Ryan to swallow. "You don't know what you're talking about." He shot back another scotch, and then tapped the bar for a third.

"That is much more than a touch of the Irish, as the saying goes. A maxim that actually comes from the Gaelic, *uisce beathe*, meaning water of life. It is of life that I speak, and yes, I do know what I'm talking about." Rémy replied, commenting on nothing and everything at the same time.

Whether it was the Jameson's or jealous hormones, or a combina-tion of the two, Ryan turned to face the vampire. "What is it you want, Rémy? The undead aren't paragons of moderation, so spare me the lecture on temperance."

The vampire raised one eyebrow.

"And you can save the imperious act, as well. You wouldn't be standing here talking to me about nonsense unless you wanted some-thing. After everything that happened in New York, and how the shifters helped clean up the mess in your shadow houses, I would hope we would be beyond small talk and subterfuge."

Rémy was silent. He spared a glance at Sébastien still seated at his table toward the back of the room. The elder vampire's nod was almost imperceptible, but still not furtive enough for Ryan to miss.

"I apologize for the serpentine tactic." Rémy inclined his head. A show of respect among the undead. "You are correct. We need help."

"I'm listening."

"After our shadow houses were cleared of donors infected by the virus, we found our resources stretched thin. Cultivating willing donors takes time. However, there was one shadow house, more of a family, really, that allowed the council, and some of our key personnel at Les Sanctuaire, to partake of their abundance."

Ryan grinned at the vampire's polite squirm while describing their practices. "Don't sweat it, Rémy. I get the picture. This particular family loaned you their suppliers. Now you owe them a favor, and you need shifters to help you deliver. Does that about sum it up?"

"Succinct and to the point." Rémy took a sip of his drink at the blunt assessment. "It is no wonder you are successful in your chosen career, but it's not the shifters I am petitioning for help. It's you."

Now Ryan was all ears. He was top cat for the job, making this even more appealing.

"Someone has gone missing." The vampire didn't skip a beat. "Someone very dear to a former member of our council. You did not have the pleasure of meeting Carlos Salazar, though he and Lily formed an immediate attachment. He couldn't be here tonight as his new mate is still..." he paused, "rough around the edges when it comes to human proximity. She is unpredictable, and as such we thought it best for Carlos and Trina to make their excuses."

Ryan kept his face impassive and professional. "I can imagine. So, who is missing? If it's a fellow vampire, can't they be traced through a blood link?"

"You've been watching too many movies, my friend." Rémy chuckled. "Humans can be traced through a blood mark, but not vampires.

The missing person is a young woman by the name of Melissa Lindquist. She is very important to Julian Trevelyan. Carlos's oldest progeny."

Ryan bit back a frown. If the missing girl was human, then this case fell squarely into his personal moral jurisdiction, regardless of whether it was an official case or not. There was no room for stereotypes or prejudices. Just facts, and the pertinent questions that needed to be asked and answered.

"Rémy, pardon my ignorance, but there's an inherent urgency attached to this girl's disappearance. If she belongs to Julian, then she bears his mark. Surely, that gives her protection. If she's more than an intimate donor, then why is she still human? Also, the question needs to be asked, did she run because she wanted no part of joining the ranks of the undead, or was she taken?"

Rémy looked uncomfortable, and his cautious glances towards Sébastien's table sent Ryan's defenses into high gear. "Look, if you need permission from on high to discuss the facts of this case, then I'm not your guy. You said humans can be tracked by their mark. Obviously this girl was intimate with her vampire lover in every way. If they shared blood, then let him track her."

"We've already tried that to no avail. You, detective, are our last resort. Sébastien and I owe Carlos for his hospitality. Vampires take their oaths seriously. If you can't help us, I understand. The last place we were able to track Melissa is California. She was in the company of a female vampire headed west with her shifter lover."

Ryan's head spun. A vague memory sparked the image of a woman's face and the tiny bit of fang he tried to dismiss as drunken imagination. "This vampire. She wouldn't happen to be Russian with long sable hair and dark bedroom eyes?"

Rémy's head snapped around. "Yes. How do you know her?"

"Wow, talk about an unexpected and inelegant caveman vibe. You couldn't have broadcast it more if you yelled MINE at the top of your undead lungs. What is she to you, Rémy? An old lover?"

The vampire's face took on a look of pure violence, and Ryan swallowed hard. He put his hand up and delicately tried to play it off.

"Hey, you tweaked me about Emily, so one good tweak deserves another. Just between brothers in the supernatural world, if this vampire means something to you and she is connected in this case, then I need to know."

The vampire's face softened, but Ryan now knew what lurked beneath that polite, polished surface. He wondered if Lily, his 'little witch' also knew the violence that simmered under that veneer of calm and sophistication.

"We are not brothers, Detective. Make no mistake. For the sake of finding Melissa with all expediency, I will forgive your all too human gaffe. It is clear you do not understand the nuances of vampire society, nor do you understand our interpersonal relationships or our hierarchies. Jenya has been in the company of a single male shifter for some time now."

Ryan nodded. "I saw her once in Boston, and it was only for a moment. The shifter traveling with her may be connected to the Compound." He spared a look for Emily and Sean. "I suggest you to let the Alpha of the Brethren know."

"Of course, this sheds new light on what we need to accomplish this task. Julian is a hothead, to use twenty-first century vernacular, and as you would move heaven and earth to ensure the safety and well-being of those you love, it is the same for us. He is beside himself with worry and rage. Carlos has managed to restrain him, but only with the council's promise to use all means necessary to find the girl.

"Vampire ranks in New York as well as across the United States are in a shambles since the virus. Never before have we been vulnerable to disease. It has many of our kind running scared. So much so, there is a contingent calling for the unthinkable."

"What do you mean, unthinkable?"

Rémy didn't blink, and the undead stare nearly unnerved him. "They are calling for our kind to leave the complacency of our shadow houses, and once again embrace the violence of the hunt. In other words, to throw a yoke over humanity and reap from it what we will.

"I know Sean and Lily will understand the danger of this pestilential concept, especially as they just fought the same kind of insanity with Edward Parr and his dreams of a master race."

Ryan considered the vampire's words. He sniffed, finishing his drink. "You said the human female was tracked to California. Where?"

"Fort Ross."

"The state park?"

Rémy exhaled. "It may be a state park now, but the territory was once a Russian stronghold. The area extends far inland and to the north. It was an important part of the maritime fur trade, and the expansion into Alaska and the North American mainland sanctioned by Catherine the Great. Countless people died in the battles between Russian explorers and certain indigenous peoples. It was there that Jenya was sired. In the midst of the blood and mayhem."

Ryan was silent.

"It is also not far from where you were headed, I think." Rémy prompted. "Or am I mistaken, and you have not taken leave of absence from police work to go and find your... *roots?*"

Mouth open, Ryan started to speak but then thought better of it. "Your intel is remarkable. You said Jenya was with her shifter lover. I'm assuming you don't mean the human."

The vampire nodded.

Ryan's eyes turned to search for Emily among the party guests. When he found her, she turned in that exact moment and their eyes locked, making his heart skip a beat.

"Rémy, I think I know exactly who Jenya travels with, and if I'm correct, then you have no choice but to tell Lily and Sean. It was a mere suggestion before, but now it's imperative. If you don't tell them, I will."

The vampire's gaze followed Ryan's, and he nodded slowly. "Then we are of the same mind, my friend. Unfortunately for the bride and groom the timing as you say... sucks."

## FIVE

"Connor Stetson? Are you sure?" Agitated, Sean ran a hand through his hair.

"Pretty sure, Sean." Ryan avoided eye contact with Emily. Telling her brother how he knew the truth would drop her in deep.

The last of the wedding guests had made their goodbyes, leaving Sean and Lily alone with Ryan, Mitch, and Emily. Rissa had left to put Stephanie to bed. She needed to nurse Braden as well, giving their nanny the opportunity to relax for the rest of the night.

"We need to speak with "Rémy before we make any decisions. This might have nothing to do with us." Mitch watched the hunters close the doors to the great hall, leaving five of them free to talk.

Emily twirled the stem of a champagne flute, ignoring Mitch. He eyed her as if wanting her to agree.

"Em, c'mon." Mitch wouldn't be ignored. "Besides me, you of all people should want to be sure before reopen this can of worms."

Lily looked at Sean who gave his head a soft shake. She ignored him same as Emily ignored Mitch. "If Ryan's gut is correct, and this Connor is the same one your father arranged for Emily..."

"Just stop." Em's hands came down on the table. "I'm not a child in need of protection. I've been on my own for five years. If this shifter is Connor, what of it? His life has nothing to do with me. Acting as if it does only validates the Abenaki claim that Connor's life is still the responsibility of this clan. Of mine. And it's not."

With dawn approaching, the New York vampires retired with their entourage to feed before their death-like sleep took hold. Sean had placed them in the farthest wing of the manor, giving explicit orders for them not to be disturbed.

Mitch took another tack, his skepticism palpable. "No disrespect, Ryan, but Rémy didn't name Connor, did he? So how can you be so sure? You didn't even know you were a supernatural until two months ago. You're still coming to grips with your own abilities and the laws that govern our world. It's not like you can recognize another shifter by sight or smell."

Ryan's eyes flicked toward Emily. Her own were glued to her folded hands. High color stained her cheeks, and the set of her jaw told him she prepared herself for the worst. When Sean realized it was their weekend tryst affording all this intel, it was not going to be pretty.

"You're right, Mitch. I'm new to being a shifter, but I've been a detective for a long time and my blue hunch never misses. On the job they call me *the dog* because I sensed things no one else could. Now I know it was my innate abilities. You can chalk this situation up to that, as well."

Ryan gave Emily a heads up about situation before they all sat down. Regardless of how things ended between them, he would never toss her to the wolves. Literally. No one needed to know she was with him when those elevator doors opened at the hotel, and Connor stepped out.

"Fine," Sean acquiesced. "If your inner cat is telling you the shifter in question is Connor Stetson, then you had to have come into contact with him at some point. We need the when and how, if only to be sure."

Emily's fingers splayed on the table. The tension coming off her body was thick enough to assault a human nose, and he caught the look she shared with Lily. So the new alpha female of the Compound knew the truth of his clandestine weekend with her sister in law.

It didn't matter. Sean was still in the dark, and he needed to keep it that way. "If it's all the same, I'd rather not say how I know. I've proven myself enough over the past couple of months for you to trust my judgment. I may not know a lot about my dual nature, but like I said, I've been a cop for years."

Mitch considered Ryan. At the Alpha's nod, he spread his hands in invitation. "Okay, Cat. Respect goes both ways, so we won't pry. If you can, fill us in on what you know for sure. The rest we'll keep filed away until we know more."

"Fair enough." Ryan inclined his head, the same way Rémy had earlier that night. "Mitch's intuition is on the money. I was in Boston this past January. Why I was there and who I was with is immaterial. We met for drinks, and then decided to go up to my hotel room. I bumped into the shifter and the Russian vampire in the elevator at the hotel. My guard went up the minute our paths crossed. I didn't know then it was my supernatural sense kicking in, but the reaction was strong enough to make an impression, nonetheless. I dismissed the man and his fanged friend as weirdos with too much time and money on their hands, but still filed the incident to the back of my mind."

Ryan watched Emily's shoulders relax the minute he glossed over the facts of who, what, when, and where. Whatever happened, he was still a gentleman.

"Based on "Rémy's reaction when he spoke of the Russian vampire, it's clear they share a connection," Ryan continued. "We need to tread lightly. "Rémy didn't say, but there's history between them. I'm sure of it. I tweaked him about it a little, and he nearly bit my head off. Getting back to the missing girl, Rémy is pretty sure the she was taken off the street. She was previously a resident at the shadow house belonging to Carlos Salazar."

Lily's eyes widened, and she shifted her gaze to Sean. "I know Carlos. He was at the council parlay the night I was kidnapped. He wasn't there long, and I got the impression he was not on great terms with their supreme. We spoke for a short while, and he struck me as different from the others. Not so much Rémy, Sébastien for sure.

"It seems the two held philosophical polar opposites about their kind, and what the future holds for the undead. Sébastien dismissed Carlos from the council, but the dismissal didn't seem contentious. In fact, Carlos seemed relieved. Sébastien appeared unconcerned, as well, but then again, we had bigger problems to deal with that night."

At the word kidnapped, Sean took Lily's hand and kissed it. The determination behind the simple gesture screamed never again.

Ryan sat back in his chair, an aggravated exhale voicing his unease. "Well, kidnapping seems to be at the heart of this, as well. The girl in question was the human donor/lover of Carlos's progeny, Julian Trevelyan. Rémy only touched on the subject, but it seems Carlos considers his shadow house to be family, but his new mate took exception with the practice of keeping blood donors. Or at least she did while still human. The upshot is Carlos released the donors from their blood bonds."

Lily cocked her head, her lips pursed. "Rémy mentioned something when he made Carlos's regrets about the wedding. Seems Carlos turned his mate after an ordeal at the hands of a rival vampire. Considering her youngblood thirst level, I wonder if she's changed her mind about a keeping a houseful of willing blood donors."

Ryan waved his hand trying to get everyone back on track. "We could discuss the nuances of vampiric life until our ears bleed, but the point is when Carlos let everyone go, Melissa, bolted."

"Rejection?" Emily questioned.

Ryan shrugged. "We don't know. I want to find out if it that was the case, or if she ran because Julian wouldn't take no for an answer on his dark gift. My gut tells me that's not the case. From what I was able to gather, Carlos has rules about increasing vampire population. Turning a human must be as a last resort, and only with their full understanding and consent."

Emily's eyes dropped again.

"Em?" Suspicion and concern warred in Sean's eyes. "Do you know something about this you're not telling us?"

She nodded, looking up to meet her brother's gaze. "After Connor and I broke up, and I heard he'd gone rogue. Hooking up with vampires and becoming addicted to their blood through sex. His life, his choices, obviously, but that didn't stop the guilt from eating at me. I researched everything I could about the undead. It seems if vampires are turned against their will, the violence of the act strips them of all human emotion except the last ones they recall. Fear, pain, cruelty, vulnerability. That's all they retain, and what they carry into their new existence."

Lily was taken aback. "That's awful."

"I know, right?" Em continued. "At least when a human becomes shifter, nothing changes except the ability to tap into their inner animal. On a brighter note, the opposite is true if fledgling vampires are created with compassion and kindness. They retain the full spectrum of human emotion."

"Like the ability to love, right?" Lily asked.

Emily shrugged. "The whole emotional enchilada and everything in-between."

Ryan lifted his hand grabbing everyone's attention. "Julian wants Melissa back. If you ask me, I think he loves the girl. Or as much as a vampire can love something that's usually on the menu. Whether or not she reciprocates his feelings is immaterial. He is ready to rip the world apart to find her before she meets a fate worse than true death. Carlos has him in check, but it's only a matter of time before he goes postal, so we need to find her first."

"Whoa. Back up a minute, Ryan. If you want to head west and go on some vampire crusade that's your business, but you can't waltz in and ask us to join you," Mitch argued. "This past year supplied enough intrigue to last me a lifetime. Plus, I've got a plate full dealing with the Abenaki and Rissa's acceptance into my pack." He pushed his chair back from the table. "Sorry, dude, but I've got to sit this one out."

Ryan nodded. "I understand, but maybe consider helping from

behind the scenes. Since this may involve Connor, and by extension the Abenaki, you could keep the line open, so the situation doesn't escalate trouble for Sean."

"That's a fair enough request." Mitch looked at the Alpha, and then nodded. "That I can do."

Ryan's concern was reasonable, considering the bad blood between Sean's family and the Abenaki with Emily at the core. They had pledged fealty to Sean as the Alpha of the Brethren when the Compound of shifters was established, but that meant very little when one of their own was shunned. The only tie keeping a possible rift in check was Sean's relationship with Mitch, and the man's recent engagement to Rissa.

Mitch would become an alpha in his own right soon enough, but until that day anything was possible. If Connor resurfaced under questionable circumstance, Sean would be forced to act, and no one relished that idea. Especially not Ryan, since that meant Emily would suffer all over again.

"Thanks, Mitch." Ryan replied. "As for me, I was already headed to California to look for my mother's pride and learn about my cougar heritage. I already gave Rémy my word, so I'm going to help them. If the girl is still alive and still human, maybe she wants to stay that way."

"We'll go with you," Lily said before Sean could stop her.

Emily's head jerked around, her eyes flashing between her new sister-in-law and her brother. "Haven't you played in the dark with vampires enough? What about your honeymoon?"

Sean didn't say a word. Ryan watched the man weigh the options, clearly running the percentages and risk. He finally took Lily's fingers and kissed them before turning toward everyone else.

"Lily and I can have a few days honeymoon in San Francisco before meeting up with Ryan. We can hit the Caribbean when this is done and dusted. I know Connor has made his choices, but if he was party to kidnapping this girl, then the vampires can attach guilt to shifters in general, and to me, specifically as Alpha of the Brethren. I have to help.

You all know how ruthless vampires can be, especially when wronged. It's my duty to ensure our safety, and by our safety I mean all shifters. The undead are not the forgiving type, and they don't believe in extenuating circumstances."

Emily's face blanched.

"Worrying is wasted energy, Em. I appreciate the concern, but I know what I'm getting into, and Lily is more than capable of taking care of herself. Her psychic abilities may actually help. Plus, Ryan will need our backup when he introduces himself to the cougars. As far as searching for this girl, it's going to take Ryan a few days to collect leads and get acclimated to the northern climes. I'll make arrangements for a tracker to help get him started. There are a few good ones that cover northern California and the Sierra Nevadas."

She eyed her brother, resolute. "Ryan doesn't need a tracker."

"Em. Whatever your feelings, it's cruel to expect Ryan to do this blind. He needs a tracker."

"No, he doesn't, because I'll take him north."

Stunned, Ryan's head swiveled between the two. "That's a terrible idea. Sean and I can handle this on our own."

Lily sat back in her chair, squaring her silk clad shoulders. "Does that mean you don't want me along, either? I thought we put this whole you Tarzan me Jane thing to bed a long time ago. If Emily thinks she can be of help, we should hear her out. Everyone knows shifter women are protective as well as intuitive. She might prove to be as much of an asset as I am."

Sean opened his mouth ready to protest, but Lily shot down.

"*Let it be, Sean. You know there's history and unfinished business between Emily and Ryan. I may not be a full shifter by blood, but I've logged enough full moons since we left New York to sense the chemistry between them. Can't you smell it? They're electric.*"

She sent a mental caress down the crease of his inner thigh.

"*They remind me of us...*"

"Okay then. Emily is a full shifter, and she knows northern California like the back of her hand. Plus, Sean and I will be there before things truly get started. Remember, telepathy works both ways." Without missing a beat, she stood, taking Sean's hand. "It's settled. We leave tomorrow."

Sean swept Lily up with a grin, pivoting toward the door. "You heard my lady. Do what needs to be done. We've got a wedding night to get to."

He swept through the door, Lily's laughter fading as they headed for the manor. Mitch pushed his chair back, as well. "I'm calling it a night, too. I've got a family to attend to, and with Sean heading west in the morning, that means double duty for me as acting Alpha."

He yawned, rolling his shoulders. "Keep me posted, Cougar. I'm counting on you and your instincts to do right by us."

"Don't I always?"

Mitch left with a short wave, leaving Emily and Ryan alone at the table. Sean's hunters had left with him, and suddenly the large great room seemed cavernous and cold.

"Well, I'd better head upstairs, too." Emily scooted her chair back, the sound against the floor louder and harsher in the empty room.

"Emily, wait." Ryan stood quickly, a staying hand on her arm. "Maybe we should talk."

Emily let a tired breath out in a slow rush. "You're right, we should. But not tonight. I'm tired and there's a lot to say." She brought her hand up to cover his and their eyes met. "Tomorrow, I promise."

The feel of her hand was a punch to his gut. The liquid blue of her eyes combined with the silky feel of her fingertips was enough to bring it all back. The way she felt in his arms. The way she fit beneath him as if God had made her just for him, and her scent, her delicious scent. It was even more so now, and his mouth watered.

Without warning or hesitation, he pulled her to him. Everything that happened between them, the time, the distance, the isolation, it all melted away with his need to kiss her again.

Emily stiffened in his arms. "Ryan, don't."

He froze, pressing his lips to her temple instead of her warm, wet lips. "I know you feel it too, Em. I smell the want in you. I sense you still feel something for me. Let go for tonight the same way you let go before. You were so strong and wanton. So full of passion..."

Her body slumped against his and her head found his shoulder. "A lot has changed since then, Ryan. I... I don't know."

The tiny chink in her armor was all the invitation he needed, and he cupped her face, claiming her lips, her tongue, and her mouth with his own desire. "I want you, Emily. Like I've never wanted anyone before or since. It hasn't changed for me."

She pulled back. "I can't..." With no other words, she ran, leaving him alone in the empty room.

CHAPTER

# SIX

T he plane landed in San Francisco and taxied to the gate. When the fasten seatbelt sign pinged off, people stood, stretching in the aisle, and reaching for their bags in the overhead bins.

"You two head over to baggage claim," Sean jerked his thumb towards the end of the aisle. "I'll see about our rental car. If we're headed to where I think we're headed, we're going to need an all-terrain vehicle."

Emily tugged on her bag, trying to free it from the bin above her seat. "I'm so tired. Let's just grab our suitcases and go. There are a ton of taxis outside. I'm supposed to meet Ryan early in the morning, though why he couldn't fly out with us is beyond me."

Neither Sean nor Lily said anything, but the two exchanged looks. Ryan had filled them in beforehand. He needed time to himself to focus on what lay ahead. Emily was part of that equation, but he needed to put things in perspective so she wouldn't be a distraction.

"We need a car, Em. I don't plan on tooling around the Bay Area with Lily hanging on for dear life behind me."

Emily cracked a smile. "Did you really just say tooling around?"

"Haha. Go ahead, yuck it up. But I'm not the one who drives a scooter."

"It's a Vespa, and it's the best mode of transportation for San Francisco. You think New York has a monopoly on traffic and parking nightmares? Try doing it on a ninety degree angle and then talk to me."

They followed behind the crowd, stopping only for the bathroom before heading down the escalator to baggage claim. Three high pitched beeps gave way to a grinding whir as the luggage carousel turned, a methodic thump, thump, thump, highlighting each bag as it landed on the black rubber track.

"Over there." Lily indicated their bags rounding the far end of the circle. Sean reached over and snagged the three, hoisting them as if they were filled with feathers.

Two bags were large canvas duffels while the other was a brown and gold Louie Vuitton roller bag.

"Careful with that." Emily flinched. "It cost me nearly two weeks' salary."

Grumbling, Sean didn't reply, just dropped the bags near the door and walked to the car rental desk.

"Wow. You two really are siblings. I've never seen this side of Sean. How does it feel to know you bring out the worst in him?" Lily laughed, knowing full well it was a loaded question.

"The worst in him? Why would you say that?"

A knowing but doubtful shake of the head was Lily's only reply.

"No really—"

Lily looked at her new sister-in-law. "You've been moody and griping since Gehrig pulled the car around this morning. Since then, most of your guff has been directed at Sean. I don't know if it's because he's your brother and you know he won't say a word, or because you know better than to pull that crap with me, but you'd better cap it quick."

Emily's mouth fell open.

"And close your mouth, you look like a cod fish." Lily smirked. The shock on Emily's face was priceless. Especially since Sean had said the same thing to her once upon a time.

Emily snapped her mouth shut just as Sean walked back with the rental car paperwork and the keys in his hand. Emily huffed and wheeled her bag through the double doors to the curb.

"Jesus. Who peed in her cornflakes today?" he asked, giving Lily a quick kiss.

Lily lifted one of the bags and slipped it over her shoulder. "I have no idea, but I'd bet dollars to donuts it has everything to do with a certain cat we know. Maybe the two of them played in the kitty litter last night and the claws came out."

"Ugh, spare me the visuals, please," he said, hoisting the last bag onto his shoulder. He paused, shifting the strap a little higher. "Lily, please tell me you didn't." He stopped, cutting his words off halfway.

"No! Jeez what is it with you people! First Emily, and now you. I do not scroll through people's heads in search of sex scenes." She exhaled a disgusted breath before breezing out of the baggage area toward Emily and the cab stand.

With a sigh Sean adjusted his bags again and then stepped into the brisk air. "So, who's driving?" he asked, dangling the rental keys.

Emily snagged them from his hand. "That would be me. What did you get us?"

"That." He pointed to the Jeep Wrangler four by four parked at the curb. "Perfect for off roading."

Both Emily and Lily exchanged glances. "You reserved that yesterday, didn't you?" Lily asked with a wide grin.

"Nope. This morning. I know a guy who knows a guy," he said, giving her a love tap.

"You rock, Sean. I love this!" Emily tugged on the rear door to tuck her bag inside. "Come on, you two, we're burning daylight!" Opening the driver side door, she slid in, beeping the horn impatiently.

Both Lily and Sean burst out laughing.

"What was it Rissa said? Between our psychics and our psychos, it was getting hard to tell the difference?" he joked.

"Ha! Get in. If Em is driving, you're riding shotgun."

He put the other bags in the back and then slammed the door. "Oh, I plan on riding all right," he murmured pulling his wife close. "A long, hard ride."

She tugged his bottom lip lightly between her teeth. "Like the song says, when it comes to love if it's not rough it isn't fun."

He growled, spinning her around toward the rear passenger door. Without missing a beat, he walked around the car and pulled open the driver's side door. "Slide, Em. I'm driving. We're dropping you off, and then it's honeymoon go time."

Emily's apartment was the top floor of a Victorian Queen Anne style house. One of the colorful, gingerbread trimmed, painted ladies in the Pacific Heights section of San Francisco.

The views were amazing as she stood at the bay window. A cup of coffee in hand, she watched the gentle white caps on the water. The sky was clear and the temperature on the warm side. It was going to be a perfect day. Well, weather wise anyway.

Ryan was late, and for a moment she worried he decided to go without her after all. She'd been back in the Bay area for two days and had nothing but radio silence. She had rejected him at the Compound, but she hadn't done so for the reasons he thought. How could she allow herself to get caught up with him again knowing his life was so far removed from hers? He wanted so much from her before. More than she could give, and now it was too late.

There was so much she needed to explain. Things she needed to say, but she didn't know how or where to begin. The longer she waited, the harder it would be until telling him would be utterly impossible.

Perhaps that was what she was waiting for subconsciously. For her options to run out. Unfortunately, she knew in her heart there was no statute of limitations on telling a man he was going to be a father.

He called her a runner, and he was right. Most of her life was spent keeping people at a distance, even if it meant pushing them away. She'd done it so many times it was second nature. So much so she didn't know how to handle it when she finally wanted to stick around.

Only this was something she couldn't run from. She'd tried to convince herself that she could, that she *should*, but it wasn't right. Ryan deserved to know, and now an opportunity had presented itself and there were no excuses left.

Funny thing was he already sensed her pregnancy. When he told her at the wedding that she smelled amazing, she thought for sure he figured it out. But how could he? He wasn't raised as a shifter. How could he know the minute a shifter conceives, her scent changes. Her taste more intense. Not that she planned on letting him get that close again. If she did, she'd never have the strength to leave.

Ten a.m. As if on cue, Sean and Lily pulled up with Ryan. Of course they'd want to be here, as well. Sean was nothing if not thorough, and he probably wanted to satisfy himself she and Ryan had everything they needed to get this party started. If she knew her brother, he also wanted to make sure there was a truce in place, at least until he and Lily joined them.

She dumped the rest of her decaf in the sink and rinsed the mug before grabbing two bottles of water and two oranges from the fridge. She opened her pack and stuck in a bag of trail mix and a couple of bananas.

Barely eight weeks pregnant and she was already hungry all the time. Sliding her camping pack over her shoulder, she closed her eyes and issued a silent prayer Ryan wouldn't hate her too much.

Grabbing her keys and a baseball hat, she snapped off the light and closed the door behind her. She'd never get another opportunity to be alone with him again. It was now or never.

"Ready to roll?" Ryan asked taking the pack from Emily shoulder.

"As ready as I'll ever be," she replied, feeling fully well the double meaning attached to her words. She paused a moment, holding onto the bag's strap. "Wait a sec."

"I already stopped for water and snacks."

Emily shook her head, rummaging past the bananas and granola. "No, I downloaded a new GPS app to my phone. The rental didn't come with navigation, and we need a good one."

She located her phone in the pack's inside pocket, and then handed it to Ryan. "The dash screen should register the device once the phone is plugged into the USB. I already programmed in the address for Fort Ross. We can take it from there as we go."

"Thanks. Good thinking."

Sean slammed the Jeep's rear door closed, making sure it locked. "Lily and I will see you guys in three days. Once you get to the target area you can check out the perimeter, but don't head too far inland. We don't know much about the mountains or how far cougar territory extends. I don't want either of you in that wilderness without backup."

Ryan grinned. "Listen to you getting all *bad boys bad boys* with us. I'm a cop, Sean. I got it covered. Plus, I am locked and loaded. I would never take anyone into a situation like this without being prepared. I made sure the department cleared me for out-of-state carry, just in case." He pulled the side of his jacket back, revealing his standard issue 9mm.

"Just be careful, okay. Watch each other's backs," Lily interjected. "See you in a few days."

Ryan opened the door for Emily, and she slid onto the passenger seat from the running board.

"You two enjoy your honeymoon. You earned it," Emily added, blowing them a kiss. "Don't forget to water my plants."

Ryan climbed into the driver's seat and then put on his sunglasses. His faded blue jeans and weathered t-shirt molded his body so perfectly she had to look away.

He plugged Emily's phone into the USB and then queued up navigation before closing the door and starting the ignition. "Ready?" he asked.

"It's now or never."

Ryan honked the horn, pulling away from where Lily and Sean stood waving on the sidewalk. They made their way out of the city toward Route 101 north, neither saying a word. Music streamed in the background, and except for the dulcet tones from GPS voice prompts, they rode in silence.

Emily fidgeted with the cuffs of her denim jacket. Ryan was too quiet, but she knew it was because of what happened in the great hall after everyone left the wedding. He had put himself out there, and she had stepped on his heart, or maybe just his libido, once again.

The moon was high in the sky even though it was almost midday. Through the wispy clouds it was easy to see the lunar orb was as full as a saucer. Perhaps what happened in the great hall was just the waxing moon talking, but she knew better.

Ryan glanced over, and the weight of his eyes made her even more self-conscious. "What's the matter with you, Em? You're as nervous as a cat, and I should know."

Rewarding him with a half-smile, she crossed her arms in front of her chest and looked out the window. His lame attempt at humor was Ryan's way of breaking the ice. That was along shot considering the secret she carried.

His eyes went back to watching the road instead of her, but his body language said he wasn't going to let the situation go. "Em, I know you volunteered for this, but if what happened back at the Compound gave you second thoughts, I can turn around and head back to town. No worries."

"I'm good, Ry. I'm just a little queasy. Would you mind if I rolled down the window a bit?"

"Not at all." His eyes darted sideways again, taking a closer look at her expression. "Do you need me to pull over? If you're car sick, I promise I'll hold your hair back."

"No. I just need a little cool air."

The wind from the open window whistled into the backseat, and though Ryan was quiet again, his eyes left the road every few minutes to glance her way. "Feeling better?"

She nodded.

"Maybe it's the Jeep." He cracked his own window a bit, as well. "It might be great when it comes to off-roading, but its highway suspension leaves a lot to be desired."

When Emily didn't comment, his lips mashed in an uncertain

frown. "Em, I'm sorry this has made you so uncomfortable. I should have apologized as soon as I saw you this morning, but with Sean and Lily hovering—" he broke off, hesitating. "No. That's an excuse. I didn't apologize for a reason. I'm sorry I upset you, but I'm not sorry I told you how I felt. Now that I know you don't feel the same way about me, I promise I will never inflict myself on you again." He glanced at her once more. "Friends?"

Emily's throat went dry, and she swallowed the cotton in her mouth. She nodded, not trusting herself to speak.

"Good. Now that we've cleared the air, is there anything else you can tell me about Connor? Any gossip or stories you may have over-heard? Things said in passing that might help us with this search?"

And just like that they were back to business. Why did she expect anything else? From the beginning, she never understood Ryan's ability to compartmentalize his life, his feelings. She was a runner, but he was a light switch. On and off in a snap.

She shook her head with a sigh. "No. In fact, it's just the opposite. The Abenaki act as if he never existed, especially around me. Not that I've given them much chance over the last five years. When you and I ran into him and that Russian vampire at the hotel in Boston, it was the first time he crossed my mind, let alone my path, in almost four years. I may have beat myself up about Connor and his life choices for the first year, but my life was no piece of cake, either. I was just as shunned and just as alone, yet I didn't fall apart and drown in my own self-pity."

"Some people like being the victim. Then again, sometimes it becomes such a downward spiral you can't pull yourself out even when you know you're drowning. Add addiction into the mix and it becomes a lose-lose situation."

"What about you? Did Rémy tell you anything else about the Russian?"

Cars whizzed by, but Ryan kept their pace leisurely. "Rémy told me about the battles that happened between Russian explorers looking to further their holdings, and the indigenous tribes along the Alaskan coast. He said history books didn't paint the massacres the way they actually happened.

"Some of the Tlingit warriors took hostages, and though the Russians bargained for their release, it was too late for Jenya. She escaped, but somehow got lost in the wilderness. It was there she was taken by a rogue vampire. He abused her, bled her, and used her to satisfy every depraved desire. She was made to sleep with the carcasses of the dead animals he slaughtered, until she found her strength to fight back."

Emily shifted around completely in the passenger seat to face Ryan. The story held her both mesmerized and repulsed. "Fight back? Against a rogue vampire? There was no way she could win. They're too strong. What was she thinking?"

"She wasn't." Ryan looked at her. "It was complete instinct. Kill or be killed. But you're right, it ended badly."

"Obviously, she was turned, but how? What happened? Did Rémy say?"

Ryan reached behind his seat for something in a purple satin draw-string bag. "Jenya found this." He handed Emily the shiny sack.

With two fingers she gently pried open the strings. Inside she found a curved tusk, or more specifically, a broken half of a curved tusk.

Emily held the artifact in her palm. "What is this?"

"A walrus tusk."

She ran her hand over the smooth ivory, letting the tips of her fingers brush the jagged break on the end. "Are you telling me she used this to kill her torturer?"

"From what Rémy said, Jenya is extremely resourceful. The vampire had been feeding from her, and raping her over and over again, but also healing her at the same time. Every time Jenya would come close to death, he would bring her back from the brink with his own blood. It would heal her all right, but it also made her crazy addicted. Addicted and strong. She ripped the tusk right out of the Walrus carcass and hid it until the right moment presented itself."

"And?"

"And nothing. She waited until he was lost in his own lust, and then she stabbed him through the heart. According to Rémy, the vampire backed off her, his unspent member still purple and bobbing up and down. Jenya attacked, using all her newly acquired strength to tear out his heart and rip his head from his shoulders.

"The rage she unleashed was the product of years of abuse that started with the first skirmish along the coast. The war was actually a series of battles that lasted on and off for about two years until the final one in 1804. The rogue vampire held Jenya prisoner all that time. After she killed him, her transformation finished its completed course. She was a full youngblood, with no compunction and no maker to help keep her thirst at bay."

Emily looked at him, confused. "Why did Rémy say historians got it wrong? Skirmishes can be bad, but what you describe doesn't sound like the carnage he's relating."

"Wait. It gets worse. The Battle of Sitka was the last and final battle of this convoluted war. In 1804 native warriors were unsuccessful in their final attempt to repel the Russians, but rather than be taken prisoner and made slaves, they sang their swan song and tried to disappear into the forest. The Tlingit Survival March. The history books say the warriors assumed the Russians would track them by the cries of the infants in their midst, so they put them all to death."

Emily gasped. "Please tell me that's not true."

"No. the men didn't massacre the tribe's children. Jenya did."

Emily sat quietly for quite a while. She couldn't wrap her head around the kind of depraved evil that would do something like that just to satisfy their own thirst. When she finally turned to Ryan, not only was her mouth dry, but a hollow feeling had settled in her chest.

Ryan didn't say a word, just reached over and took her hand.

"This is the monster we're going up against? You said Rémy was attached to this... this creature. How? He seems as though he has human compassion left in him."

"The rogue that changed Jenya was Rémy's brother. Rémy had

been tracking him to no avail, and when he finally located his lair, all that was left were traces of Jenya and what had happened. It was enough for him to continue his search. He tracked her down to the area where the Russians settled along the California coast. When he found her, it didn't take long for him to become besotted, both with her and the idea of saving her from herself. It backfired, though."

"Clearly."

"She's the one responsible for the damage to his face. I'm not exactly sure how, because he didn't get into it, but her cruelty extended even more so to those of her kind. She set a trap for Rémy. The extent of the fire she set evident on his face. By the time he woke from his injuries, she was gone. He followed the trail of bodies until he found her again. Even injured beyond what his supernatural powers could heal, he was the one who brought Jenya back from the consuming darkness, but she ran from him."

Ran. Emily cringed at the word.

"I guess she and I have a lot in common. No wonder Connor was attracted."

Ryan squeezed her hand but kept his eyes on the road. "Rémy feels responsible because he let her go. He gave up when perhaps she needed him most. I guess I have a lot in common with him, too."

# CHAPTER
# SEVEN

GPS gave them the choice of either a straight route on Highway 101 or a scenic drive over Highway 12 toward the coast. Considering the historical tidbits Rémy had shared, they both agreed they needed time to wrap their heads around it all.

Miles of farmland and little hick towns you might miss if you blinked, gave way to breathtaking coastal vistas. The shoreline loomed large as they made their way into Bodega Bay.

"Wasn't this the town from Hitchcock's, *The Birds*?" Ryan asked, as they wound their way toward the North Coast Highway.

Emily nodded. "One and the same. Although it's not at all the way he portrayed it."

"You got that right. No creepy birds and pod-people."

"Pod-people?"

He kept his eyes on the winding road, the rocky Sonoma coast and sand beaches opening in front of him. "Yeah, whenever I watch that movie it strikes me how the people are as creepy as the birds looming on the wires and in the sky. Even the dialogue is clipped and weird. It's as if Hitchcock wanted the viewers to know the whole town was somehow— I don't know. Off."

"That's Hitchcock. All his movies are that way."

The houses along the shoreline highway were nothing special and far and few between. There wasn't much of a village, either, but along the rural stretch they passed a ramshackle place with a deli sign posted near the road.

"Finally, a bit of civilization. Do you want to stop and grab something to eat?" Ryan asked.

Emily's stomach had been growling for an hour. She had already helped herself to a banana and two of the carrot muffins Ryan had brought with him.

"That obvious?" She laughed.

"I've been listening to your stomach for the past sixty miles. I would say yeah, it's obvious."

She shifted in her seat, cracking the window open even more and taking off her jacket. "It's warmer than I thought it would be, considering we're heading north. Plus, it's always a little chillier by the water."

As she peeled off her jacket, her back arched giving Ryan a bird's eye view of just how full her breasts had become. Emily was always tall and thin. Her body that of a lean swimmer, but now she was curvier in all the right places.

He pulled into the parking lot outside the deli. "Do you want to come in with me, or should I just grab a couple of sandwiches?"

"I think I'm going to walk to the bluff and stretch my legs. I'll take a turkey and Swiss, with lettuce and tomato on a roll if they have it. If not, whatever bread they have."

Ryan headed into the deli and Emily walked across the street toward the scrub and tall grass. Someone had put a bench between two trees and trimmed back the brush, allowing for a beautiful view of the ocean. She sat, knowing Ryan would be right behind her with the food.

As if on cue, he showed up a few minutes later with a paper sack filled with sandwiches and snacks. He rummaged inside and handed her a large hump wrapped in white butcher paper.

"Turkey and Swiss, as requested. The people at the deli couldn't have been nicer. Guess Hitchcock and his birds are flapping in the wrong wind on that one."

Emily grinned and took the sandwich from his hand. She opened the waxy paper and picked up the first half, taking a huge bite. "Mmmm," the only sound she made as she chewed.

"I'm glad your appetite has improved. I hated the way you used to eat like a bird, barely picking at your food. Maybe it was me, and now that we're not together you can relax and enjoy yourself."

She shook her head, stuffing a stray piece of lettuce into her mouth. "That's not it."

He chuckled, watching her stuff her mouth. "No? Well, whatever the reason the end result looks good on you. I like the new curves."

"Curves?" She wiped her mouth on a napkin, sticking it under her leg against the wind off the water. "Are you saying I'm getting fat?"

He choked, and his eyes went wide with his hand flying to his mouth to catch spewing water. "No!" He coughed. "That's not what I meant at all."

She burst out laughing and handed him a wad of napkins from the paper bag.

He mopped up the front of his shirt, wiping his hands and face while trying to look apologetic and sincere. "Don't take it that way, Em. I just meant whatever is lending itself to your newfound appetite, it's working for you."

Eyeing him, she took another bite of her sandwich and then looked out at the water as she chewed. "Yeah, well. There is a reason for it, but it's probably not what you think."

She looked back at him, hoping to find interest in his eyes.

"What's the reason then?"

Putting her sandwich down, she shifted herself on the bench to look at him. "Well, it's simple really—"

"Hey, you two! You can't sit there. It's private property!"

Emily and Ryan both turned to see a young man approaching from across the road. He looked to be in his early twenties, and he was dressed like a surfer.

Ryan stood and Emily immediately sensed his guard go up.

"Sorry, dude. We didn't know," Ryan replied as the guy stepped through the sandy brush towards them. "We were just having lunch admiring the view. We'll move our stuff over to the picnic tables. No harm, no foul."

The guy stopped short, his eyes taking in Ryan and then shifting to Emily and back again. His demeanor changed, and his eyes narrowed. "No harm, no foul you say. Your kind isn't welcome here, so just pack up and get back in your car and go."

Emily saw Ryan visibly stiffen, and in a blink of an eye he was no longer just Ryan. He was Detective Ryan Martinez, no bullshit homicide detective from New York. "Dude, whatever prejudices you have against Hispanics, it's not appreciated. So I suggest you be the one to back off."

The surfer's face hardened, and in that instant Emily blinked, not quite believing what she saw. The man had reflecting plates in his eyes, and for a moment they flashed, glowing like a cat's eyes except there was nothing feline about the man. The high, tanned cheekbones of his face seemed to superimpose smoother, flatter planes, and she caught the distinct impression of an elongated snout above a bulky, muscular neck.

Realization dawned, and her eyes flashed to the trees and stones leading the trimmed path toward the sea. The markings were clear, as were the ritual carvings and the strategically placed shells.

She swept up what was left of their lunch and stuffed it back into the bag. "We beg your apologies. We had no idea this was an established stronghold or that you held claim to this stretch of beach. We ask your pardon."

Ryan stepped in front of Emily, clearly trying to understand why her speech had gone so formal while at the same time keeping the belligerent surfer in his line of sight.

"Emily, I don't know what the hell just happened, but stay behind me." With one arm he tried to sweep her behind his hip, but she held him off.

"Ryan, please. Just take the bags and wait for me by the car."

Frowning, he glared at her. "Get a grip. There's no way I'm leaving you alone here with Surfer Sam."

She looked at him hoping he would read between the supernatural lines and not make things worse.

"I would listen to her, young man, because right now the only thing protecting you is your willingness to protect her. I promise no harm will come to your mate. I cannot say the same for you, though."

At the word mate, Ryan's eyes narrowed, and he looked at Emily. She nodded once, her shoulders relaxing that he finally understood enough to do as she asked.

He raised one eyebrow, and she knew with that one gesture he expected an explanation without prevarication, and for once she didn't balk.

Turning his attention toward the man, Ryan pushed his jacket back flashing his badge and his sidearm. "I'll do as you ask, but for the record, my eyes and my gun will be trained on you the entire time. I'm a quick shot and my aim is impeccable. I can and will drop you like a bad habit if you so much as reach out to shake her hand." He tilted his head looking for confirmation that his meaning was heard and understood. "Got it, amigo?"

A single nod was all Ryan needed. He leaned over and kissed Emily's cheek, and in this instance she didn't mind his possessive show. He left the lunch on the bench, and walked across the street, the weight of his eyes and his intense unease making it palpable how difficult this was for him. She knew this went against his grain, and her heart skipped a beat at the faith he placed in her.

"He's quite unusual for a big cat."

Emily's eyes narrowed at the creature standing in the human guise of a twenty year old surfer. His sun bleached hair and tanned skin the perfect camouflage

"I always thought selkies were social creatures. The ones I've encountered are friendly and gregarious and welcome company, so it naturally begs my suspicion to find such hostility aimed our way. Especially when I recognize you not only as a supernatural, but also an elder."

His returned gaze was appreciative. "You're very quick for a wolf. Even so, things are different here than in the Bay Area."

Emily snorted. "Clearly. However, that doesn't explain your uncommonly rude behavior to my friend. I'm sure you realize he's a half-blood. He doesn't know very much about our world, but he's learning. If anyone is to blame for our trespass on your traditional mating territory, it's me. It's no excuse, but I was a bit... distracted."

The selkie chuckled. "Well, that's understandable. Pregnant women of any species tend to have distractible natures."

Emily's gaze jerked to meet his sea green eyes. The whole power and beauty of the ocean and its depths showed for a moment, and Emily knew compassion and kindness were at the core of this elder being, and that something was at the root of his uncharacteristic hostility.

"How did you know? No one else has sensed it yet."

The surfer's eyes shot to Ryan and back again. Emily shook her head. "No, not even him. He is the baby's father, but as I said, he's unfamiliar with our world so he doesn't understand the signs."

He nodded. "Consistent, yet sad. I only know because I heard your little one's heartbeat." He tapped his ear. "Underwater sonar. I heard the reverberation in your amniotic fluid." He glanced at Ryan's scowling face again. "Are you planning to tell him?"

"I was just about to when you charged over."

His tanned face bloomed pink and he shuffled his feet in the rocky sand. "Now it's my turn for apologies. This place—" he said, sweeping his arm toward the water, "is quite appropriate for such a conversation. Many of my kind have come here to find their mates and carry on their way of life. We call this the birthing corridor."

They were quiet for a moment, and Ryan beeped the horn waving her back toward the car.

"My friend's patience is growing thin. Can you tell me what happened to make you so apprehensive of us? Is it because I'm a wolf and he a big cat? Interspecies is not very common, although where I come from that old way of thinking is changing."

The selkie shook his head. "Not at all. Normally we would have welcomed you with a gathering, but times have changed, especially of late. Years ago we would have reacted much the same way as I did today, especially with your friend's kind. The big cats would come down from the mountains and hunt among us, steal our woman, and force them to mate. It stopped about twenty-five or thirty years ago, and we were able to slip back into a time of peace and welcome. For some reason your friend carries the scent of one who raided our community."

Emily knew immediately the selkie meant Edward Parr. Lily and Sean had filled her in about everything, including Ryan and Lily's deceased friend Terri, and their unfortunate connection to that evil sociopath.

"That connection was never known until recently, nor was it ever fostered. It doesn't matter, though, because the one responsible for bringing your people such pain is dead." She paused, her eyes meeting the selkie's dead on. "What happened recently to make you so guarded? My friend and I are heading toward the forest and mountains just beyond Fort Ross. We are searching for a missing woman. A human. Unfortunately, a shifter was involved in her disappearance. A wolf. Is there anything you can tell me that might be of help to us?"

The man's eyes grew introspective, and he considered Emily for what seemed like a long time. "We've had a few attacks in recent weeks. Not here, but in Santa Rosa. According to those that survived, their attacker was a woman, but she certainly wasn't human. She was vampire, and they also reported she traveled with a wolf. Unfortunately, no one mentioned anything about a human."

Emily nodded. "Thank you. That at least tells us we're on the right track. Again, I am sorry for our trespass."

He nodded, half turning toward the path leading toward the beach.

He glanced back, a thoughtful expression on his face. "You have the look of the unifier about you. I had the pleasure of meeting him once when he spoke to the sea shifters of his dream to bring all the species together. Are you related to him?"

Emily smiled. She had heard the nickname *unifier* before but never in such a familiar way, and her heart swelled with pride. "Yes, Sean Leighton is my brother."

A smile broke across the selkies face, and he stepped back in a deferential bow. "You and your cougar are welcome here always. If you pass this way again, please grace my table. I would appreciate any information you can spare about what is happening in our area."

"We will."

Emily felt his eyes on her as she gathered up what was left of their lunch. The selkie was probably making sure she didn't leave any trash behind, not that she would ever disrespect him or their land. When she turned to nod her goodbye, he opened his mouth as if he wanted to say something else. He hesitated, but then took a step forward, his hand out.

"I don't know if this is germane to your search or not, but there have been rumors that might interest you as well. I've shillyshallied to say, simply because it is just gossip."

Emily put the lunch bags down and walked back to where he stood on the top of the slope leading down toward the sand. "We'd appreciate anything you can tell us. In our world, gossip always holds a kernel of truth at its core."

He laughed. "Truer words never said." The man's face sobered and his eyes took on the faraway look of someone remembering. "The gossip surrounds the evil that hunted my kind decades ago. The ones that preyed on supernatural beings and humans alike. The stirrings concern the cougars, that they harbor one who claims she carries the heir to that same great evil. She has found sanctuary among the big cats, and the wolf that travels with the vampire is her minion. They both serve her."

Emily tried to keep her face passive, but she knew doubt crept into her eyes. The last thing she wanted to do was disrespect the elder selkie, especially when all he wanted was to help.

"Vampires are at the heart of our search party. The human woman is connected to them in some way. The female vampire who kidnapped her is also sought. I know a little about her history and she serves no one but herself. I can't imagine she would ally herself to a power crazed shifter. Not when vampires in general think themselves the pinnacle of existence. I appreciate your warning, sir, and I promise we will be mindful of it, but in this instance I believe the chatter is just that. Chatter."

He nodded once, but his eyes were sad as if he knew more but couldn't share. "As you wish, my dear. Godspeed you in your search."

CHAPTER

# EIGHT

"L et's get moving," Emily said as she walked toward Ryan, but as he opened his mouth she put up her hand. "I'll fill you in once we're on our way. There's more here than just an over-bearing supernatural with a hard-on for trespassers on his territory."

Ryan took the bags from her hand and slid into the driver's seat, putting the food on the backseat.

"The fort is thirty minutes from here as the crow flies. We should be there with plenty of time to hike into the woods and set up a basecamp."

"Dealing with that old one has me even more starved than before. Can you hand me the rest of my sandwich?' she said, getting in and closing the passenger side door.

Reaching back around, he handed her the paper bag and then started the car. "Old one?"

He pulled out onto the road, his eyes glancing toward the now empty bench his stomach still in a knot. He gave her a moment to unwrap the rest of her lunch and take a few bites, but he wasn't going to wait much longer.

"Oh, for chrissake already, Emily, what the hell was all that back there? I can't believe you are sitting here eating as if nothing weird just happened. You said old one, yet he looked like some asshole kid. What gives?"

Emily swallowed her third mouthful and took a swig from her water bottle. "That was no kid. That was a selkie, and an elder to boot."

Ryan gaped, his forehead puckering to the point of looking painful. "A selkie. As in, *The Secret of Roan Inish*, selkie?"

"Yes and no. That was a movie, but the premise is correct. Selkies aren't just seals, though. They can be sea lions, walrus, etc., but THAT," she paused for effect. "That was a full grown male elephant seal. You may have missed the whole superimposed 3D spectacle complete with long snout or trunk or whatever the hell they call it, but I didn't. He was frigging huge, and every NatGeo tidbit about adult males and their aggression? Completely true! He was prepared to kill you. It's only after he picked up on the fact that I'm—" She stopped, catching herself cold.

"Picked up on the fact you were *what?*" he asked, her little gaffe piquing his detective senses.

Emily shook her head, busying herself with rewrapping her sandwich. "Nothing. He figured out I was Sean's sister. The selkie met him a while back and I guess we really do have a strong family resemblance. He called Sean the unifier. Anyway, that's not the point."

She stopped to take a deep breath. "The selkie said the reason for his belligerence was because his kind had been attacked recently. The assaults were in Santa Rosa. Based on his description, it was Jenya. Connor was with her."

RYAN'S forehead relaxed into his normal detective scowl, and she breathed a silent sigh of relief he hadn't learned how to pick up the scent of evasion. She would tell him about the baby and would have done so already if they hadn't run into the surfing selkie dude.

Blurting it out mid-recap as in, oh by the way, was not the way she envisioned.

"Did he say anything else?" Ryan asked, still talking about the selkie.

She nodded, filling him in on the rest. By the time she finished they pulled into the parking lot of the historic fort only to find it closed.

"What do we do now?" Slumping back in her seat, Emily let out a frustrated breath. "The site is only open on weekends and holidays, and then only until four-thirty p.m. Not to mention the campground is closed because of cutbacks."

Ryan put the car in reverse and turned around. "What do we do? We do what any self-respecting detective would do. We plan a stake out." He pulled onto the service road and drove back toward the highway. "In the meantime, we take stock of what we already know. The questions that we need to ask, and we find a place to stay where we can plan. With three state parks a stone's throw from each other, there's bound to be something close by."

"The Fort Ross Lodge!" Emily reached for her phone. "I don't know why I didn't think of it earlier. It's straight up the coast from here, and it butts up against the woods. It's perfect. We can register as hotel guests and leave the car in the lot. That way it frees us up to head into the forest and start tracking from a home base."

They followed navigation up the coast road about five minutes, parked the car, and then grabbed the bags to head into the lobby.

"Well that's convenient." Ryan said, taking in the quaint bungalow style accommodations. "Not the Ritz, but it'll do."

Walking into the lobby, Emily took the bags and slid into one of the chairs facing the lobby entrance. Scooting around, she eyed Ryan at the front desk checking if there were rooms available for the week.

"Very good, Mr. Martinez, unfortunately we don't have any Queen rooms left, but we do have a King room that overlooks the backwoods. I can give that to you for the same price. May I put any incidentals on the same credit card?"

"Fine."

"And how many keys will you need."

"Two, please."

The girl at the front desk seemed nice enough, but for some reason the hairs on Emily's neck tingled. She scanned the registration area and honed in on two members of the cleaning staff standing beside a wet floor cone. An older woman held a mop in hand while staring at Ryan, her expression unsure. The other was young and striking, with short dark hair and dark eyes and a smirk on her face as she eyed Ryan's assets.

Jealousy prickled along Emily's skin causing sweat to break out between her breasts. Chest tight, it was hard to breathe. She shook her head to snap of it. Ryan was a free agent, regardless of what might happen when she told him about the baby. It was her own fault the final scene of this drama wasn't a happy ever after. She buried any hope of that months ago.

She watched Ryan pocket his credit card and sign the desk slip before taking the keys from the woman's hand. When he turned he made full eye contact with both women, and Emily's heart nearly stopped. He inclined his head, inquisitiveness playing in his eyes at the intensity of the housekeeper's stare.

Without as much as a backwards glance, Emily watched him walk toward the women.

"Oh God, not in front of me. I know I deserve it, but not now. At least wait until I'm not in the room, or I'm asleep, or dead." She focused on her inner wolf, bringing the animal to just beneath the surface. If she looked in the mirror her eyes would be yellow instead of blue, and her legs would be hairier than any crunchy granola hippie.

With her shifter senses focused, she honed in on the frequency and tenor of Ryan's voice. Thank God for a wolf's keen sense of hearing.

"Excuse me, but do I know you?" he asked the older woman flashing a gorgeous smile.

The woman didn't answer, but she didn't look away, either. Finally she looked at the yellow caution cone and asked, "Are you from around these parts?"

"Nope," he replied. "I'm visiting from New York, although I was born and raised in the Bay Area."

"Oh," she answered, looking up as if to memorize his face. "I didn't mean to stare. It's just you remind me of someone I used to know."

The younger one piped up, her gaze more than appreciative. "Well I would surely remember if I saw you before, handsome. Are you here for business or pleasure? I'd be happy to help with either."

A growl formed at the back of Emily's throat, and she nearly lost the tenuous control she had on her wolf. The muscles in her feet and legs bunched and spasmed, her toes aching to reshape inside her boots.

She sucked in a breath, letting it out slowly to send her inner wolf back to her inner depths. The young housekeeper would never know how close her offer to *help* brought her to having her throat ripped out.

Ryan looked over his shoulder and sniffed the air, his gaze narrowing as his eyes settled on Emily. A sharp breath brought his attention around to the older woman. Her eyes fell on Emily as well, and her hand flew to her mouth.

"What's the matter, Kai? You look as though someone walked on your grave," the younger one chirped.

The older woman didn't say a word. She just crossed herself and grabbed her mop and bucket and turned for a door marked employees only.

"Huh." The younger woman angled her head but kept her gaze on Ryan. "That's weird, but then again Kai's always seeing and hearing stuff that ain't there. Anyway, how about you buy me a drink later and I can tell you all about it?"

Ryan shook his head. "Thanks for the offer, but I'd have to clear it with my girl, and she's not the sharing type," he said pointing toward Emily sitting in the far lobby.

The housekeeper made a face, pursing her lips in annoyance. "Well, better luck next time, huh."

Ryan laughed watching the woman sashay her way toward the

employee door. He walked back toward Emily, but his face changed the minute he saw her expression.

"What?"

"Don't let me put a cramp in your style, Ry. If you want to take the happy housekeeper for a spin, be my guest."

He laughed out loud, causing a few heads to turn in their direction.

"Will you keep your voice down? You've embarrassed me enough already. Let's just go to the room, and then you're free to go catting around all you like."

"Hey, I'm single now. Remember? So I don't know what you're all hot and bothered about. For your information, I told that girl the only help I needed this week was coming from *my* girl. She just assumed it was you, when I looked over my shoulder."

"Fine. Whatever. Let's just get settled. I'm exhausted."

*Hmmm.* "Well, it's no wonder you're tired. Bringing yourself to almost full animal, and then tamping it down has got to be draining." He burst out laughing again. "Oh, Em. That's priceless. I'm not exactly shifter 101, anymore. I may not have phased yet, but I've gotten pretty damn close, so I know what it feels like to get to the brink and then get shut down. It's sort of like a case of blue balls."

Emily snapped her mouth shut and jammed her finger into the elevator button. "What floor are we?"

"Fourth. Room 402."

~

"WE CAN SET up a base camp not too far from here and take perimeter walks to see if we pick up anything," Ryan said sliding the keycard through the electronic eye on the door.

The lock snicked open, and Emily pushed the door wide.

"Sorry it's not a suite this time around, but I'm sure there are washcloths in the bathroom. The last time you we very creative with the Terricloth..." He let the innuendo about the last time they shared a hotel room drift off, but not before he caught the high color staining her throat and cheeks.

She shot him a dirty look. "A king bed, Ryan? How predictable." She dragged the tips of her fingers along the bedspread.

"We didn't have a reservation, so I took what they had available." He shrugged. "If you don't believe me you can call down to the front desk and ask. You can always get your own room, you know."

At the mix of anger and hurt pride on her face he felt like a cad. "Look, I'm sorry. This being friends thing is harder than I expected. Why don't we just focus on the task at hand, and be done with it, okay? Once this is over, the only time you'll be stuck with my presence is when we cross paths with Lily and Sean."

Emily sat on the end of the bed and ran a hand through her long blond hair. "I don't know how to be with you this way. It's either we're together and fighting, or together and in bed, or not together at all. There was never any middle ground."

He sat beside her, the bed slumping with his weight. "Maybe that was our problem."

"Maybe. Look, I'm tired, and I want to take a shower. Maybe catch a nap before we plan our next move. Those sandwiches are probably bad by now, but neither of us got much of a chance to eat. Why don't you toss them, and order in some room service? I'll be done in a jiffy." She took her travel toiletry bag from her suitcase and headed into the bathroom.

Ryan picked up the black leather bound amenities book and flipped to the in-room dining page. He kicked off his shoes and lay down on the bed. Emily's sweater was next to the pillow. He picked it up and pressed the knit fabric to his face and inhaled.

His cock hardened and he groaned into the soft material, his mind imagining the swell of her fuller breasts pressed against him. He tossed the garment onto the desk chair, and then slumped against the pillow. He had it bad, and he knew it. One week, one bed, and three days alone with her until Lily and Sean arrived. God help me.

# NINE

The spray from the shower jets was a fine mist, and Emily fidgeted with the shower head until coarse jets pummeled her chest, back, and shoulders. She desperately needed a massage, but there was no way she would ask Ryan to rub the knots out of her shoulders. It would lead one place, and that was not on the agenda.

Eyes closed she shampooed her hair. The small circular motion rubbing away the dull ache forming at the back of her skull. She finished washing and rinsed off, shutting the water before pulling back the shower curtain.

Thick white Terri towels were stacked on the wooden shelf beneath the granite vanity. Stepping onto the bathmat, she reached for one and patted her face dry before opening it full length. Steam gathered across the ceiling, sending droplets of condensation down the top of the mirror's fogged edge. Emily stood in front of her reflection, her hands molding the swell of her breasts, slipping further down to trace the slight swell of her lower belly.

If Ryan saw her now, could he tell? Her body ready to ripen as the weeks passed. Dismissing the thought, she wrapped the towel under her armpits and secured it in front of her chest before grabbing another towel dry her hair. Finishing up, she put her toiletries away and then opened the door.

"Food should be here soon," he said. "I ordered you a turkey burger, but I substituted a side of fresh fruit and guacamole instead of waffle fries. With you being carsick, I didn't think fried was a good idea."

"Thanks, that sounds great."

From her suitcase she took out clean undergarments, a pair of yoga pants and a long sleeved tee, but then stopped to glance at Ryan. "shifter you planning for us to do a perimeter check tonight?"

He shrugged. "I planned to go pace it. You know, see how long it takes to get from here to the thicker tree line. From there I wanted to see if I sensed anything." He paused. "If you're wiped out, you don't have to come with me."

She put the yoga pants away and took out a pair of jeans and then grabbed a pink plaid flannel shirt. "No, I'm good. The shower really perked me up. Once we have something to eat we should go before it gets too late." She held up the flannel and the long sleeved tee. "Layers. It gets pretty chilly here at night."

She headed back into the bathroom to get dressed. Inspecting herself in the mirror, she checked her minimal makeup and ran a brush through her damp hair. Good enough.

The food arrived, and she sat cross-legged on the bed to eat. She knew it was just her condition, but everything tasted amazing. She'd heard horror stories of woman dropping pounds and being hospitalized for dehydration because of nausea and vomiting in their first trimesters. She was lucky. Except for the fatigue and the occasional queasiness, she felt great.

"Are you going to eat your pickle?" she asked, already halfway reaching for Ryan's plate.

"Since when do you like pickles?" he asked, handing her the dill spear.

She froze. "I don't know. Why?"

He shrugged. "Nothing, it's just whenever we went out for burgers before, you never ate them. You said they were too sour or something."

"Ryan, I need to talk to you about something." She took a sip of iced tea, and then wiped her mouth, tossing her napkin onto her plate.

His gaze followed as she got up to move closer to where he sat on the bed, wariness already forming in his eyes.

"We haven't seen each other really in what, eight weeks or so?"

He nodded slowly, his expression trying to work out where she was headed.

"That last time we were together. I said some things I didn't mean. Awful things, and I want to apologize."

"What do you mean you didn't mean them?" he asked, his eyes holding her gaze.

"It doesn't really matter now, does it? What's done is done, and I don't want to rehash it. I just want you to know I'm sorry for the way I treated you. It was wrong. I was wrong."

Ryan pressed his lips together. "Let me see if I've got this straight. You're not going to give me an explanation for why you did what you did and said what you said. Just an apology for the way you went about it."

Her eyes flashed wide, and she shook her head. "No. That's not what I'm doing at all. I don't want to dredge it all up again. I mean, what's the point? So we can both feel shitty again? I don't want to do that. I just want us to move on."

He didn't respond. He just sat back and stared at her for a moment. "I thought we already did that. Move on, I mean."

She inhaled through her nose, letting her breath out the same way. "We did, and then again we didn't."

He eyed her circumspectly; the tilt of his head telling her he was considering her words. "There's something else isn't there?"

"I..."

Her cellphone rang.

Ryan picked up his fork and flung it onto the room service table.

"God Damn it! Every time we really start to talk, something gets in the way. Let it go to voicemail."

"I can't. It's Sean." Mouthing, I'm sorry, she picked the phone up and pressed answer. "Hello?"

"Yeah. No. The drive was fine. Very informative, in fact. What? No. He didn't call us. Let me put you on speaker so Ryan can hear you, too." Emily pressed speaker and then propped her cell against the lamp on the night table.

"Can you hear me?" Sean's voice was tinny and far away.

"Yeah, dude, we can hear you. Where are you calling from, you sound like you're in a tunnel."

"We're still in San Francisco. Reception's bad because you're out in the sticks. Anyway, Rémy called. There's been a sighting in Mendocino. That's about an hour and half inland from where you are on the coast. The body was brought to the county morgue in Santa Rosa. Eyewitness reports speak of a woman leaving the scene that fits our vampire's description. The undead have their own scouts looking as well. According to Rémy, the victim put up a fight and slashed Jenya across the chest."

Ryan and Emily exchanged looks.

"So what is it you want us to do? Should we contact the Santa Rosa vampires?" Emily asked. "Is there a council that should know we're here?"

"No. It's best if you stay put. I'm giving you this information as a heads up. Pay attention to the local papers, and anything that might have made the news. We aren't sure if Connor was with Jenya at the time of the attack, but he might be the easiest way for us to find her now that we have a scent trail to the vampire."

"Okay. Keep us posted," Emily said.

"What did you find out on the drive? You said it was informative."

"We stopped for something to eat in Bodega Bay and happened to run into a supernatural elder. A local dude. We didn't catch his name, but Emily poured on the charm, so he filled us in on what local gossip says is happening with the cougars. It involves Jenya and Connor, and some woman taking refuge with the pride, but it's not the woman we're looking for. Some other chick. Someone who claims to carry the heir to the whole Kit and Kaboodle."

"I did not pour on the charm," Emily interjected. "The elder just happened to be a selkie, and he wasn't happy about us being in the area. Once he realized we were on the same side, he volunteered the info." She finished filling Sean in, and there was a long silent pause on the other end of the phone.

"Sean?"

"Yeah, I'm here. I was just thinking. Jenya is damaged goods, according to Rémy's assessment. She was never properly assimilated into vampire culture, and I agree she's no one's pawn. She's in the mountains for a reason. Maybe it has something to do with the cougars, I don't know. Her returning there isn't because she's nostalgic. Nobody returns to a place of torture, unless they had revenge planned, or needed to exorcise a few demons.

"My guess is she's toying with this self-proclaimed cougar queen. Connor, on the other hand, will do Jenya's bidding as long as she continues to provide his fix. What we don't know is how this Melissa fits into the picture. Is she a plaything for Jenya, or perhaps she's a hostage. Since she's not attached to either Rémy or Sébastien, my gut says is she was an innocent in the wrong place at the wrong time."

"I agree," Ryan said, scribbling notes and questions onto a piece of hotel stationery.

"Okay then. Lily and I will see you the day after tomorrow. If you hear anything else, call."

"Will do, and vice versa."

Emily pressed end and tossed the phone onto the bed.

Ryan got up and paced in front of the sliding glass doors. "I hate this," he mumbled.

"Hate what?"

He threw his hands in the air, exhaled hard. "This." With a sweep of his arm, he gestured to the room and everything in it.

"I'm not following, Ryan."

He pulled the curtains back and pointed to the woods. "Everything we're looking for is out there. I'm not the sit and wait type, Em. You know that. Patience is not exactly my strong suit. On the job, I was never a fan of stake outs, but at least they served a purpose. Sitting here in this room serves nothing. It's a waste of time."

With a disgusted grunt, he unbuckled his belt and slipped his hip holster into place, attaching his sidearm. He grabbed his jacket and the car keys, checking for his wallet in the front pocket and then stalked toward the door.

"Where are you going?" she asked, pushing herself off the bed.

"The morgue in Santa Rosa."

"And what do you plan to do when you get there? Ring the night bell and ask to see the latest vampire attack?"

He stopped with his hand on the door handle, his eyes skimming past his shoulder to where she stood next to the bed. "I can't just sit here and do nothing."

"I get that." Emily picked up the dirty plates, and then stacked them on the room service trolley before pushing it away from the bed. "But don't go off half-cocked. It's a waste of energy and gets you nowhere. Trust me."

Ryan turned around. His arms lightly crossed in front of his chest. "You forget you're the queen of half-cocked."

"That's exactly my point. Why do you think I said, trust me? It's because I've learned the hard way to think before I act."

His expression was conflicted. He probably wondered if she meant past reckless acts, like going back to a hotel with a complete stranger like she did with him the night they met, or if it was a broader censure.

"Okay. So what do you suggest?"

"There's a plastic Ziploc bag in my pack with a shirt I got from Connor's mother. She wants him found no matter what he's done. It's what mother's do for their kids. Unconditional love."

"I'm not following."

"It's not that difficult, Ryan. Connor's scent is still on the shirt, regardless of how much time has passed. Since then he's been drinking vampire blood, so his own natural scent will be tainted. The only way we'll be able to track him is if we mix his natural scent with vampire essence. I spoke with Dr. Volkmann before we left the Compound, and he said a few drops of vampire blood rubbed into the shirt's fabric will do the trick."

Unconvinced, he made a face. "Vampire blood. I'm not trying to be difficult or obtuse, but I'm going to the morgue to check out a victim. Not hunt down a vampire like a blood bank looking for a donation."

She gave him an emphatic nod. "Exactly. A victim. Jenya's victim. One who just happened to slash her in the process."

"I'm listening."

"If we drive to the morgue in Santa Rosa, perhaps we can get a sample of Jenya's blood from the victim's fingernails or clothing. Of course, that's provided they let us through the door."

Ryan lifted the side of his sweater, and the bronze of his badge glinted in the lamp light. "They'll let us though. Professional courtesy. After all, I was instrumental in solving a case just like this in New York, and if their coroner ruled out animal attack, they may have a copycat killer on their hands." He paused. "There's just one problem."

Emily braced herself. "What?"

"There is no WE in this. I'm going. You're staying."

Emily waved her hands in front of her. "No way. You are not leaving me behind."

"You're not a cop, Em. You have no clue what to do or how to act."

"Lily goes everywhere with Sean, and she was with you in New York. She's not a cop."

"Oh, please. This is not a game of tit for tat. Lily is psychic, plus she's an NYPD Profiler. She knows what she's doing, not to mention she can handle a weapon, and is very good with weird. You aren't."

"I'm coming with you, or I'm going home. It's as simple as that. Take your pick."

"Emily, be reasonable."

She folded her arms in front of her chest. "Nope."

"You know you sound like a teenage brat, right? Okay, but I'm only letting you come with me because I don't trust you not to go off on your own."

She knew the smirk she wore wasn't the smartest way to go, and the look on Ryan's face confirmed it. "Sorry. I'm just glad you saw things my way."

He growled something unintelligible, and then pointed directly at her. "There are ground rules, Emily, and I'm not kidding. You let me do the talking. You don't touch anything unless I say, and if I say move you move. Got it?"

"Whatever you say, Detective."

An exasperated sigh left his mouth. "I have a feeling this is going to be a long night."

CHAPTER

# TEN

Rémy sat facing the fire, toying with his cellphone, turning it over and over in his hand as if willing it to ring.

"Still brooding, brother?"

The vampire didn't turn, didn't acknowledge the voice addressing him. He sat with his long legs crossed at the ankles and stretched out before him. In the firelight, his dark blond hair glinted gold, and his head inclined as he stared at the dancing flames.

Sébastien moved to the side of the heavy oak chair, resting his hand on the red and gold brocade tuft over the Queen Anne back.

"There is nothing you can do for her. She was lost to you. Lost to us, years ago my friend."

Rémy said nothing.

"If the rumors are found to be true, then she must be destroyed. You know this."

Rémy lifted his eyes to the council supreme. "I know."

"And you must be the one to do it."

Rémy didn't answer. He turned his eyes back to the hearth, and the shadows dancing along the floor. Their motion in time with the crackle and sputter of the wood in the grate.

"Rémy. I do not give this order lightly. I know what she meant to you."

The vampire lifted his chin, but he didn't turn his head. "Meant? I think you use the wrong tense brother. Jenya means everything to me."

The elder shook his head, taking measured steps to move in front of the fire and confront Rémy. "After all this time? After she disfigured you? I don't understand how you can carry such guilt for a girl who was not your progeny. Not you responsibility."

Rémy's eyes closed, and he clasped his fingers to the bridge of his nose. Sleep evaded him, though the sun burned in the sky. His rest robbed from him for weeks since Jenya had resurfaced.

"No, brother, you don't understand and never have. For that, perhaps I am at fault."

"Rémy, we have known each other for centuries. We share the same sire once removed. I have respected your privacy in this matter as a brother and council elder, but I am the council supreme and this situation has affected not only Carlos and his coven, but the peace of our territory. Not to mention you involved the shifters."

Rémy's eyes jerked upward, and his gaze tightened. "I did so with your consent."

Sébastien's face softened as emotions warred on his friend's face, his obvious unease making his hard appearance stark. "I gave my consent, but only because Jenya has a shifter in tow. He is party to her actions, and thus makes them obligated to help."

"Dražen brought this." Rémy lifted a plain manila envelope from the side table and held it out to Sébastien.

The master took the folder supplied by their scout, but he didn't open it. He slid the contents into the folds of his robe, gesturing for Rémy to speak.

"Jenya did not abduct Julian's pet human. Melissa went willingly."

Sébastien sank into his chair near the fire. "Then all this was for naught. Unnecessary, not to mention the cost."

Rémy frowned in agreement. "According to Dražen, Jenya favored the less savory alleys of our city, frequenting the blood slave markets.

She was spotted at the one located below Mott Street in Chinatown, at the time Melissa disappeared."

Slamming his hand down, Sébastien stood, his robe swirling a little too close to the fire and sending sparks onto the hearthstone. "Why wasn't this reported sooner? All this mess could have been avoided."

"The dragon coven is even less forthcoming than their human gang counterparts when it comes to questions regarding their activities. Perhaps it is time for us to speak with them."

Sébastien exhaled, his expression grim. "I suppose we must, but I loathe the thought. War is so tiring and wasteful. Almost as wasteful as this endeavor has proven to be."

"There's more."

At Sébastien's raised eyebrow, Rémy sat up, resting his elbows on the arms of his chair, his fingers clasped in front of him. "Melissa left Carlos's protection, as we were told. Some petty argument between her and Julian. She wore his mark, but it had faded to the point where she was ripe for the taking. Carlos assures me every human in his shadow house was warned of the consequences should they choose to leave."

Guttural disgust left Sébastien's mouth. "His first mistake was agreeing to release them. *Bah*. I blame his new mate. What young-bloods do for the sake of love confounds me."

Rémy's lips twitched. Only Sébastien would have cheek enough to refer to him as a youngblood. "May I remind you I am not that much younger than you, and what the heart demands has nothing to do with age. But we digress. The dragons took her for their blood auction. Jenya must have taken a liking to her, though I can't fathom why."

He paused, exhaustion edging into his voice. "Dražen obtained records that show she bought Melissa, but my gut tells me her actions aren't for the proclivities associated with this sort of underground bartering. Her reasons for all of the above are a mystery. One I intend to solve."

With a wave of his hand, Sébastien turned to leave. "Her reasons are immaterial. The girl was a free agent, warned of the consequences of her actions. Whether Jenya bought her as a chess partner, or a bed partner, is of no consequence. The only thing we have to worry about now is that she was sold in an unsanctioned brothel. Get her back, Rémy. I leave this to you." He swirled toward the steel door separating the inner council chambers from the rest of their lair.

"What about Jenya?"

Sébastien stopped, considering his blood brother. "I leave the choice to you. Either end her or save her, though I cannot understand why you would willingly yoke this millstone around your neck." Without another word, he swept from the room.

Rémy stared at the fire, and Jenya's heart shaped face and dark eyes looked back at him through the flames. "Because I owe her. That's why," he murmured.

# CHAPTER
# ELEVEN

There was no one on the road, and Emily and Ryan made Santa Rosa in less than an hour. As expected, the parking area to the back of the Sonoma County Coroner's Unit was deserted but for a single patrol car, and what Ryan assumed to be the Medical Examiner's vehicle.

On the surface, the building was a small stucco structure in a heavily shrubbed back lot, but according to record, it had seen its fair share of foul play.

Anticipating the late hour, Ryan called ahead to say they were on their way, and as promised the deputy medical examiner was waiting for them inside. A uniformed officer was also in attendance with one of the detectives assigned to the case.

Ryan rang the night bell and he and Emily were buzzed inside.

A burly man standing off to the left came forward. "You must be Martinez," he said, holding out his hand.

With a single nod, Ryan took the man's proffered greeting. "Detective Ryan Martinez. Homicide, NYPD."

"I'm Detective Sergeant Weil Davis. This is Sheriff Mike Lewis, and of course our assistant medical examiner, Dr. Ted Connelly." He gestured to the two men standing behind him.

"Pleasure. Although I do wish it was under better circumstances." Ryan gestured toward Emily standing just behind him. "This is Emily Leighton."

The detective shook Emily's hand as well. "Pleased, ma'am."

The Santa Rosa's coroner's office was no different from any other Ryan had seen. Desks with uncomfortable looking chairs were piled with stacks of case files, and a set of double doors separated the office from the autopsy suite and the morgue's refrigerated storage units.

The whole office was a dull brown color, including the leather couch and stiff backed chairs in the waiting room, and he wondered if the somber décor was by design.

Detective Davis cleared his throat, pushing his hands back on his hips, giving everyone a full view of his shoulder holster and badge. "I have to say Detective this is highly irregular, but curiosity got the better of me. What is it you're thinking to do here?"

Ryan eyed the man. His ruddy cheeks and soft jowls added years to his face, even more so than his slightly receding hairline. He was a big man, over six foot and a good two hundred sixty pounds if he was an ounce. Experience had left its mark, and this kind of attack on his watch was unacceptable. Otherwise he would never have agreed to meet, professional courtesy or not.

"I understand where you're coming from Detective Davis, believe me. This would be highly irregular in New York as well, and on a personal note, I don't know if I would appreciate another detective from a jurisdiction three thousand miles away poking his nose into my case files, either. I have to admit, I had my own misgivings while driving from our hotel. This was not the way I expected to spend the first night of our vacation, but after hearing about the attack I was compelled to do so."

"Idle curiosity?"

Ryan smirked at the man's dig. "Not in the least. I get enough of this on the job to ever want more during my hard earned R&R. No, it was the manner of the attack. I'm not sure if it made the national news out here, but I just helped solve a case involving a serial killer with a similar M.O. It was a heartbreaker, if you know what I mean. Bloody and confusing as hell. I thought I might be able to offer my help, considering."

"We're not incompetent here, Detective. I'm sure we'll be just fine."

Ryan nodded trying to keep his cool regardless of the muscle in his jaw working overtime. If this guy sent them packing, it was all over. He looked at the man, reassessing him. Experience yes, but there was doubt in his eyes despite his bravado. This required professional finesse.

"I don't doubt that for one second, Detective Davis. I just remember how it felt to look into the eyes of the family members, and have nothing of value to tell them except, I'm sorry for your loss. I hate that. In my opinion it's the worst part of the job."

The man nodded. "I hear you on that."

A spark of interest had replaced the man's proprietary wariness, and Ryan knew whatever he said next would either win the ball game or send them to the showers.

"Unfortunately, in my neck of the woods it happens far too often. On the flip side, the best part of the job aside from the camaraderie is nailing the sick son-of-a-bitches who get off committing this kind of crime. That never gets old."

The man stuck a toothpick in the corner of his teeth and considered Ryan. His eyes flicked to Emily who sat in the waiting room, flipping through an ancient copy of Good Housekeeping.

"I do remember reading something about those murders in New York a couple of months ago. The press called them the Bloodbath Murders, right?"

Ryan nodded. "Yes, I was part of the squad that broke the case. My superior was Detective Sergeant Michael Shaw."

Davis's eyes didn't give an inch. He barely blinked, and it was clear his poker-face was practiced to perfection. "Okay, Martinez. I'll let you take a look a look at the case files if you want, but there really isn't much there. I'll grab the file, but in the meantime you can go ahead in with the doc. I'm sure I don't have to tell you not to disturb the evidence."

Ryan glanced at Emily who was accepting a cup of coffee from the uniformed officer. He caught her attention and motioned towards the double doors. Her answering wave told him she understood it was now or never.

The autopsy suite was tiny compared to the one at Bellevue Hospital in New York, but it had the same sterile, stainless steel stations with slicers and dicers, scales, hoses, and overhead surgical lights.

"The autopsy isn't quite completed, Detective. What Davis said about this being highly irregular is an understatement. I'm afraid the man is as confounded by this as I am. Pathology hasn't come back yet, but so far nothing makes sense. Not the enormous lack of blood, nor the radius and force of the bite."

"Neck wounds, I presume?" Ryan asked as the M.E. pulled open the square refrigerated unit.

"No. The victim's wounds were to the femoral artery. She had been sexually assaulted first and then, well, you can see for yourself."

He reached down to grip the gurney's handle and slid the drawer completely out. The doctor pulled the sheet away, dragging it toward the victim's knees.

The body was of a young woman. Except for her blue pallor she was attractive, even beautiful, petite with long dark hair. Ryan sucked in a breath, steadying himself at how much the woman reminded him of Lily.

The woman was bruised and torn between her legs as if something had ripped her to shreds after intercourse. Her inner thighs had huge chunks of flesh missing, and there was nothing left of the arteries in either leg.

The doctor laid his hand on Ryan's arm, giving him a gentle squeeze. "It's okay, son. It's hard to take."

One side of the double doors opened, and the uniformed officer poked his head in. "Doc. Your wife is on the phone. Do you want me to tell her you'll call her back or do you want me to transfer the call in here?"

"No, Mike, I'll take it over there." The doctor pointed to a wall mounted phone next to one of the long prep counters. "Excuse me a moment, my wife probably wants to know when I'll be home. I'll just be a second."

Ryan smiled. "Take your time."

The doctor walked toward the counter and the phone rang. When he picked it up, he turned his back, and that's when Ryan moved. The girl's personal effects were in a plastic bag directly beneath the gurney. Quietly, he opened the top, rolling back the plastic, grateful it was thin and flexible instead of crunchy like cellophane.

The blouse inside was saturated with blood. The smell had vomit rising at the back of his throat, but Ryan swallowed hard keeping his focus on the task at hand. From his inside pocket he took the swatch Emily had cut from Connor's shirt and stuffed it in the bag, making sure it took on as much of the blood as it could in the seconds he had.

Pulling it out, he placed it in the Ziploc baggy Emily gave him from her toiletries, and then stuck it back in his pocket. He rolled the plastic bag closed again and wiped any residual blood from his hands on a washcloth he took from the hotel.

"I'm sorry about that," the doctor said, walking back toward the gurney. "I love her to death, but that woman could talk the hind leg off a dog."

Ryan gave the man a requisite chuckle, hoping it hid the fact he just committed a felony.

"Have you been married long?"

The man laughed. "Too long. What about you?" He raised an eyebrow and gestured toward the double doors.

Ryan shook his head. "Nah. Just friends."

"Too bad. She a pretty girl. I'd keep my eyes on her if I were you. She might disappear when you're not looking." He eyed Ryan, and for a moment almost seemed to be handing him a warning.

Ryan didn't reply, but silently wished Lily was here to take a walk through the man's head. She could tell him if the doctor's creepy comment was just a byproduct of hanging out with the dead, or if there was something behind it.

He shook off the disturbing feeling and focused on the blue horizontal body. "You can tell Detective Davis the only similarities to the murders in New York are the lack of blood and the age of the victim. In our cases, all the bite marks were on the throat and chest. Mutilations involving the heart. None of our victims were sexually assaulted. I'm sorry I couldn't be of more help, but at the same time, I'm glad it's not a copycat. Whoever did this is sick, but definitely unique."

The doctor wrote Ryan's observations down on his clipboard, assuring him he would enter it into the final report. He recovered the body, and then pushed the unit back into the storage container before escorting Ryan out.

Emily stood. "How'd it go? shifter you able to help?"

The doctor shook his head. "Unfortunately, the cases are different, but it was still nice to meet you both."

Detective Davis was in the back office with the sheriff. He poked his head out. "All done?"

Ryan nodded. "Yes, thanks. The victims share a few similarities, but not enough for me to take up anymore of your time. At this point there's no need to show me the case file. My observations are all in the doc's report. I only wish I could have helped."

Davis shrugged, putting down his coffee cup and walking over to shake Ryan's hand again. "Hey, at least you tried. You're okay in my book."

Ryan took the man's hand. "You, too."

The doctor placed his hand on top of theirs and squeezed. "It's all about teamwork." With a chuckle, the man walked back through the double doors.

Ryan let go, but he didn't say a word. The burly man cleared his throat, shooting the back office a dirty look at the sound of Mike's laughter through the door.

"You gotta cut the doc a little slack. He doesn't get out much."

Ryan raised an eyebrow before signaling to Emily he was ready to leave. "I hear that. Anyway, thanks again for the professional courtesy."

"No problem, dude. Enjoy the rest of your vacation."

Ryan took Emily by the elbow and steered her through the doors, knowing full well Detective Davis was watching them as they left.

She went to open her mouth, but he shook his head. Not a word until they were in the car and well on their way back to the hotel.

They were in the hotel room less than ten minutes when Ryan peeled the mess from inside the Ziploc bag. "Is the t-shirt ready?"

The rest of the shirt minus one sleeve was flat on a towel on the bed. Ryan took the blood coated swatch and spread it level with the remaining cotton before rolling it up in a tight cylinder. Unrolling it, he turned it ninety degrees and repeated the motion.

"It's kind of like tie-dye, don'tcha think?"

A disgusted sound left Ryan's mouth as he looked at the old blood staining his hands. "Not in the least. If you want to wrap this mess in rubber bands to ensure a saturated scent, go right ahead."

She shook her head. "No thanks. Besides, the only thing I have to use are hair ties and I don't want my scent that close to anything that might bring Jenya out of the woodwork."

"I can't say as I blame you there. You should have seen what she did to that poor girl, although I gotta say I don't think she acted alone. I think Connor was in wolf form and the two attacked together, like some depraved form of sexual after play. The girl was raped all right, and based on the amount of bruising it wasn't at the hands of a human."

Emily shuddered. "I'm glad I didn't see it. I don't know how Lily handles it. Except for that creepy detective, everyone seemed nice enough."

"He wasn't creepy. He was just doing his job albeit a little heavy on the proprietary," Ryan called over the sound of the tap as he washed his hands.

He walked out, drying each finger on a hand towel. "It was the doc who was the creeper. He said something that sounded off, almost a warning."

"What did he say?"

Ryan shook his head. "It doesn't matter. We need to remember to have each other's backs in this. After what I saw in the morgue tonight, anything can happen."

"I'm going to get some sleep. We should hang the towel and the t-shirt over the shower rod in the bathroom, so the blood dries overnight. We can get our supernatural on in the morning and see what scents we pick up."

"Get our supernatural on?"

She yawned, crawling into bed. "You know what I mean." She took off her flannel shirt and wiggled her jeans off under the covers, tossing them both onto the chair in front of the desk. "Who else is going to use Connor's vampirized scent to help track their whereabouts? The chick from housekeeping?"

"Now who's being funny? Maybe we should ask Sean to come earlier. He's the head honcho when it comes to training the hunters, he'd be the best choice for this getting done right."

She yawned again. "Maybe. I'll call him in the morning. He'll want to know operation blood trail was a success."

Ryan kicked off his shoes and lay down on top of the comforter next to Emily. Her blond hair was spread against the pillow, and he had to squeeze his fingers into his palms to stop from running his fingers through the pale mass.

"Goodnight, Em," he whispered, but all he heard was the soft sound of her snoring.

Reaching for the remote, he clicked on the television and searched for the local news. If there was anything else on the attack, he wanted to hear about it tonight. Not wait for Sean to fill him in long distance tomorrow morning.

He flipped through the channels, but nothing new made the eleven o'clock news. He settled in to watch a movie and found his eyes starting to droop.

Emily had curled onto her side, her knees up and her fists turned inward under her chin. In all the time they were together, the days and nights they actually spent in each other's company could be counted on two hands. It was the curse of a long distance relationship. He wanted more, and he let her know. Maybe that's the reason she withdrew from him. He pushed too hard, too fast.

There was still no one like her, and he had a sinking feeling there never would be again. Even when the moon had played tricks with his libido, and he thought he was falling for Lily, Emily was still there. Just pushed to the back. His feelings buried.

All it took was seeing her once for all those emotions to come to the surface, only this time he was trying not to let his anger get the best of him. Lily had called him on it in New York. She said he was a control freak, reminding him sometimes things were beyond what he could manage. She said he needed to learn to let them be in order to find himself. To accept and let go.

Of course, she referred to him letting go of his skepticism, and accepting there was a supernatural subculture living side by side with humans, and he was part of it. Like it or not. If she were here now, she'd probably tell him to let go and accept for entirely different reasons.

Meant to be. He'd heard that phrase a thousand times over the years. Perhaps it was true. He glanced down at Emily and this time he didn't stop himself. He rested the palm of his hand on her cheek, brushing her hair back from her face. Leaning down he kissed the side of her mouth and her cheek and the hollow beneath her ear.

"Come back to me, baby, "he whispered, and kissed her again.

She sighed in her sleep, and he froze, worried for a moment he woke her, and he didn't have the strength for another fight.

She sighed again and rolled over. His hand sliding across her hair, finally landing on the pillow behind her head. With a sigh of his own, he undressed, slipping under the covers on his side of the wide bed in just a t-shirt and his boxer briefs.

Reaching over he snapped off the light and then shut off the television. He slumped against the pillows, his arms behind his head. Emily rolled over again, this time flinging her arm across his chest.

Ryan dropped his chin to his shoulder looking at her close proximity and the unbelievable warmth coming off her body.

This was going to be a long night.

# TWELVE

*Knock, knock, knock.*

Ryan bolted up in bed. He peered through the darkness at the clock on the nightstand. 2:17 a.m. Who the hell would be knocking at this hour?

He threw his legs over the side of the bed, putting his finger to his lips for Emily to stay down and stay quiet before reaching for his gun in the drawer beside him.

Another series of knocks echoed in the darkened interior. A tiny swath of light from the bathroom provided enough illumination for his eyes to adjust. In a crouch, he moved quietly toward the door and peeked through the peephole.

The older housekeeper he'd spoken to when they arrived stood outside the door. It looked as though she was alone, but he wasn't taking any chances. Most of his interactions with the locals had triggered his weird-o-meter, and this just raised the bar another notch.

Leaving the latch in place, he opened the door a crack. "Is it just us or is it hotel policy to wake guests in the middle of the night?"

She wrung her hands, her eyes darting over her shoulder. "I'm sorry, Mr. Martinez, but I had to warn you. They know you're here. You need to leave before it's too late."

Ryan studied the woman's face, her pupils, and the set of her jaw. The tiny beads of sweat on her forehead. She was scared.

"What are you talking about?"

She crossed herself. "The woman and the dark one that serves her."

He opened the door and let her in.

"Explain," he demanded, closing the door, and throwing the deadbolt. He snapped on the light and stood with his gun poised at his side.

Emily was up and dressing, tossing personal items into their bags, no care for what belonged to whom.

The woman glanced furtively from the gun in Ryan's hand to Emily and then finally, Ryan. "I am risking myself warning you, but someone needs to stop them. I know you're here about the girl. I can help."

Ryan exchanged glances with Emily.

"What girl?'

The housekeeper's eyes flashed with impatience. "The one the dark woman took. I've seen her." She glanced down, wiping her hand across her forehead. She drew in a deep breath and when she lifted her eyes, her gaze locked with his. "I know you don't trust me, and I understand. Unfortunately, your lives are in danger, so you have no choice."

Ryan kept his finger on the trigger of his gun, but he reset the safety. This woman was not a threat. Not yet anyway.

He took a single step forward, moving slowly, his tone that of a hostage negotiator. "I can see how upset you are, but you still haven't answered my question. What is it you want, and what makes you think either of us is involved in any of this?"

She exhaled, her shoulders dropping in resignation. "My people..." Her eyes found his, and when she hesitated, his answering nod was all she needed to continue. She sucked in a quick breath and the rest flowed out in a single stream.

"My father was a *yee naldlooshi*. The word is Navajo, but the meaning translates to goes on all fours. What she is..." The woman gestured to Emily. "...and what you and I inherited through our half-blood makes us the same. We are dual natured. Some people call us shape shifters."

The housekeeper licked her lips, trying to keep from fidgeting in her nervousness. She spared a glance for the clock on the night table and exhaled again. "We really don't have much time. For reasons I can't explain right now, you are a threat to them and they're coming. I promise you'll be safe, and you can call whoever you need from where we are headed."

"And where is that?" Emily finally piped up, moving to stand beside Ryan.

"Las Ramblas."

Emily threw her hand up. "This is crazy. We don't even know her name, let alone if she's telling the truth." Apprehension raised her voice an octave.

Ryan lifted one hand, the motion a demand for calm. "That's a very good point." He addressed Emily, but his eyes were on the older woman.

"Please..." the woman implored.

"Ma'am, you can't expect us to skulk off into the night without a good enough reason. The ball is in your court. Either you give us the story straight or leave us in peace."

The woman clasped her hands together and drew in a deep breath. "My name is Kai Sutter. I've lived here for most of my life. I'm forty-seven years old, and I was friends with your mother."

Emily balked. "My mother?"

The housekeeper shook her head. "No, darlin'." She lifted her hand to rest the tips of her fingers on Ryan's cheek. "His mother."

Ryan's eyes widened, his lips parting as if to say something but nothing came.

"Ryan you don't actually believe—"

He waved Emily off. His eyes searching the older woman's face.

Her answering smile was sad. "You have her eyes and the set of her mouth, but it was the tiny mole on your upper lip that settled it when I saw you in the lobby, earlier."

He sank onto the end of the bed. He didn't speak, just stared at nothing.

Kai took a step toward him, but he held up his hand. She stopped short, mumbling an apology but he dismissed her.

"I know it's hard to believe. Teresa was my best friend in the pride. Cougar women weren't accepting of the humans brought in as mates. The fact Teresa was beautiful didn't make things any easier for her, either. We gravitated toward each other, and eventually became each other's strength through the difficult days. Then there was your father..."

Ryan held up his hand again. "There's no need for you to rehash who he was or what he was like. I know all about him and can only imagine how he treated her."

Now it was her turn to shake her head. "You don't understand. He loved her."

The skepticism in Ryan's eyes was dagger sharp. "Now I know you're lying. I met the man. Edward Parr was certifiable. You may not know what he did after he left the pride, but I do. He ruined lives and caused countless deaths. He was a sociopath, completely incapable of love."

At his angry words Kai reached out her hand only to pull it back just as quickly. "It's true. He was driven and maybe a little crazy."

"Maybe?" Emily snorted.

Kai's eyes darted to Emily but even with the odds against her, she continued, her voice soft. "We're not as isolated as you think. I know what he did, and in my heart I know it was because of the woman. She fed his obsession, escalating it. As for his inability to love..." She shrugged. "...perhaps that was the end result of his insanity. I know it wasn't always the case. He loved your mother. She was the key to his plan, so in his eyes that elevated her above all women. A queen to his king. No one dared get in Edward's way. Even pride elders were afraid of his plans to master our race."

Doubt fixed itself to the set of Emily's jaw. "I can see why you chose to become besties with Teresa. Nice move on your part considering the way the power play worked out."

Kai made a face. "That wasn't the case. Regardless of how the council viewed Teresa, she was alone. So was I. She was the one who took pity on me, not vice versa. Unlike her, my father sold me to the hunting circle passing through our territory.

"Sold. As in human trafficking?" Ryan asked, aghast.

She shrugged. "It was commonplace then. Half the women at the snow mountain camp were abducted, the other half were sold by their own families. The practice wasn't advertised, and not all shifters participated or condoned the goings-on. Those extremes are taboo now, or at least they were until the woman showed up." Her eyes found the top of Ryan's bent head. "That's why I came tonight."

"Which woman?" he asked. "The vampire or the human she kidnapped?"

Kai lifted both hands and let them drop. "It's complicated. Your father tried to play God and your mother paid the price. Now there's someone who wants to finish his work. The raids for suitable mates have started again, only this time the hunting circles scout populated areas, watching. The woman gave exact specifications for them to look for, and when a woman is found that meets the criteria, she's taken. The female vampire is there for security. Anyone who manages to escape—"

"They become dinner." Emily finished Kai's sentence.

The older woman nodded.

"They know you're here for the human girl. She has nothing to do with what is going on in the pride. She was a plaything for the vampire and her wolf. Someone they took at random."

"Was?" Ryan questioned.

Kai nodded. "When the vampire brought her to the mountains, the human was presented to the emancipator. That's what the woman is calling herself. The girl fit the pride's mating criteria, so the vampire sold her to the highest male bidder."

Drained, the older woman let out a tired breath. "Now my burden of proof is yours." She lifted her chin and met Ryan's eyes. "Enough?"

He stayed quiet but nodded his acquiescence.

She smoothed her palms against her coat and then took a step back, giving Ryan and Emily a little more room. "Good. Then we should get going. I'll meet you downstairs in the back parking lot. You can follow me with your Jeep."

Emily picked up her camping duffle, handing Ryan his backpack. "Kai, what is Las Ramblas?"

She pointed toward the woods and the mountains beyond. "It means the ravines. It's one of our safe houses."

The ride to Las Ramblas took two hours over terrain best suited to a bighorn sheep. The safe house was a log cabin nestled at the bottom of a narrow valley. Partially hidden by trees, it provided for a quick escape with a stream running behind the property that expanded into thick woods.

The living room where they waited was rustic in beauty. From its carved wood furniture to the Native American tapestry gracing the wall behind a camel backed sofa. Gorgeous geometric patterns in rich earth tones were plaited together and balanced by a set of crisscrossed arrows tied with hemp and hung across the top. A beautiful hoop strung with chords, raw wool and eagle feathers adorned the wall above the fireplace, and a woven hearth mat sat between two high-backed rocking chairs.

Ryan threw another log on the fire, glancing over his shoulder as Emily hung up the phone.

"So?"

She sat in the rocking chair near the hearth, kicking her feet out to stretch. The curtains were closed, but through the hanging rings she saw it was still pitch black outside. "They'll be here in the morning. Sean wants Kai to meet them at the hotel so they can follow her inland."

"That dreamcatcher above the mantel is gorgeous. Did you make it yourself?" Emily asked, getting up to help Kai with the coffee pot and mugs she carried in from the kitchen.

"No, my grandmother made it. She was kind to me growing up, which is more than I can say for the rest of my father's people. She died not long before my father made his deal with the hunting circle."

Her words were too matter of fact, and Emily exchanged looks with Ryan when Kai went back into the kitchen to grab the milk and sugar from the table. When she came back she settled herself on the floor in front of the fire and kicked off her shoes, crisscrossing her legs pretzel style.

"Did you know your mother kept a diary?" The question was posed more like a statement than an inquiry.

The firelight danced along the floor and walls, casting a myriad of shimmering shadows into the room. Ryan's expression was half hidden by those same shadows. He shook his head, but more than just idle curiosity sparked in his eyes.

"I don't suppose you'd still have it after all these years."

Kai smiled, and in that moment she seemed genuinely happy. Unfolding her legs, she pushed herself up and walked to an oak trunk on the far side of the room. She moved the woven throw blanket from the top and lifted the lid. Under pictures and collected memories, she drew out a plain composition notebook. She dusted the cover, her fingers gently brushing the surface almost as if saying goodbye.

She closed the lid on the trunk and then replaced the blanket before turning with the book. "I don't know why I kept it all this time. When your mother went missing, your father returned from the search party carrying her bloody clothes in his hand. Her scent trail had gone cold, and everyone thought the worst."

Handing the book to him, her fingers brushed his in the process. "In my gut I knew she didn't die in the woods. I would have felt it, felt something inside me snap. That feeling found me much later. It was then I knew she died giving you life. I prayed you survived, and that happiness would find you."

The older woman's eyes were wet with unshed tears, and she

wiped them with the back of her hand. She touched his hand again, this time waiting for his eyes to meet hers. "Ryan, whatever you told yourself in the past, I want to know you were very wanted and much loved. From the minute Teresa knew she carried life within her, all she thought about was getting away so she could give her child a chance at a happy life."

Ryan's eyes closed, and his fingers gripped the yellowed composition notebook. Every muscle in his arms, back and chest contracted, and his lungs squeezed. He couldn't breathe. A torrent of emotion beat against the protective wall he built around himself and the force threatened to pull him under.

He shuddered, his arms wrapping around his stomach with the book pressed against his heart. Emily got up from the rocking chair and put her arms around Ryan's shoulders as they shook with silent sobs. He leaned into her embrace, tears flowing unashamed. Tears for his mother, his sister, and himself and the life they missed.

# THIRTEEN

D awn broke, sending shafts of pink light in through the curtain tops. Emily's eyes opened and she blinked. She lifted her head off the arm of the couch and looked across the floor at Ryan still in the rocking chair. He sat in the dark, tossing broken pieces of kindling into the dying flames.

"Did you sleep at all?" she asked, pushing herself up onto her elbow.

He shook his head, getting up to add a few more logs onto the fire. "Too much to think about."

Shivering in the early morning chill, she dragged a colorful quilt with her while scooting back into a sitting position. Kai must have covered her after she fell asleep.

She watched Ryan slump back in the rocker, his feet pushing the chair into a light, rhythmic back and forth. He closed his eyes, his fingers coming up to pinch the bridge of his nose.

The clock on the mantel chimed, and she squinted to read the time. 6:00 a.m. Sean and Lily wouldn't be here for at least six more hours.

"Where's Kai?"

He opened his eyes, releasing the finger pressure on his nose.

"She's in the kitchen." He let his hand fall to the arm of the rocking chair, his fingers curling around its smooth curved edge.

The scent of fresh coffee and cinnamon drifted in from the open doorway and he inhaled the delicious aroma. "I thought police officers ranked at the top of the list when it came to cups of joe, but Kai wins hands down. She's making breakfast, but that has got to be the third pot of coffee since we got here."

Emily smiled. "Maybe it doesn't count once the sun comes up." Despite his tired eyes, he was good spirits. Perhaps he and Kai had a chance to talk after she conked out. "You sound like the two of you hit it off."

With a not so cheerless sigh he shrugged. "I guess." He glanced toward Emily on the sofa, his face thoughtful. "You remember how nuts Lily was when she figured out I was Terri's twin?"

Emily nodded through a yawn.

A small smirk pushed at the corner of his mouth, and he chuckled low. "I never really got how she could attach such familiarity to me when we barely knew each other. Now I understand how she feels. I don't have my mother. My father was a psycho, and my twin sister dies just months before I would have had the chance to meet her..."

He paused. "You know, Lily once told me I was the closest thing to Terri she had, and I'm not ashamed to admit her intensity freaked me out. But now I get it, and I feel the same way about Kai. She's the closest thing I'll ever have to my mother. Just like Lily is the closest thing I'll ever have to my sister. My life is suddenly all turned around and confusing, but in my gut I know it's all good."

Emily swung her legs over the end of the couch and stretched. "You don't have to explain. It's what you feel, and feelings are never right or wrong. They just are. If you don't deal with them, you end up like me."

She stood and finished stretching, her eyes dropping to the floor under the heavy weight of Ryan's gaze.

"Anyone hungry?" Kai asked, carrying a large tray filled with cinnamon buns, buttermilk biscuits, butter, fresh fruit, a fresh pot of coffee and what looked to be homemade jam.

Ryan jumped up to help, and they set everything on the coffee table.

"Help yourself." She swept her hand across the spread before sitting down to pour herself a cup of coffee with cream.

Emily picked up a cinnamon bun, licking the creamy icing from the side of her thumb as she brought it to her mouth. "*Mmmm,* these are delicious," she said, and reached to put another one on her plate before the first was finished.

"Hey, bottomless pit. Leave some for the rest of us."

Emily threw a crumb at Ryan, a grin breaking out across her face when he caught it open mouthed.

"You two been together long?" Kai asked, amusement filling her eyes as she watched them banter.

Emily stopped chewing. Her mouth full as her eyes flicked toward Ryan. She swallowed hard, forcing the food down and trying not to choke.

Taking a paper napkin, Ryan wiped his hands not quite making eye contact with either woman. "That's kind of a complicated question, and one I think best tabled for now. We've got bigger fish to fry."

Em noticed he averted Kai's questioning look, busying himself instead with the contents on his plate. Without lifting his eyes, he gestured toward the older woman with a forkful of cut strawberries.

"While you were in the kitchen, I skimmed through my mother's diary, and in more than one entry she talks about how you would spend hours telling Navajo legends to take her mind off things." He wore a cajoling smile. "I'd love to hear one."

Emily used a napkin to hide her smirk at how deftly Ryan circumvented the topic of their thorny relationship. He was right, of course. Newfound mother figure or not, now was not the time to get into it.

Kai's grin spread from ear to ear, and her eyes told them she knew exactly what he was up to. "Why not? We've got a little time before I have to meet your friends."

She dusted bits of crumbs from her hands and took a sip of coffee, thinking. "I know which one to tell you. The story isn't Navajo. Its origin comes from the native tribes here in California. Teresa loved it. It always made her laugh." Settling herself against the foot of the couch, she began...

*Cougar was walking in the forest, and he jumped onto a fallen log to look around. From inside the log came a tiny voice.*

*"Get off the roof of my lodge!" ...and out from the rotten end of the log came a tiny cricket. "You are standing on the roof of my lodge, Cougar," said the little insect. "You must step off now, or the roof-pole will break, and my lodge will fall in."*

*"Who are you to tell me what to do?" asked Cougar sternly, although he did step off the log. He lowered his head until his nose was very close to Cricket. "In this forest, I am the chief of the animals!"*

*"Chief or no chief," said Cricket bravely, "I have a cousin who is mightier than you, and he would avenge me."*

*I don't believe you, little insect," snarled Cougar. "Believe me or believe me not," said Cricket. "It is so."*

*"Let your cousin come to this place tomorrow, when the sun is high, and we will see who is the mightier," said Cougar. "If your cousin does not prove himself to me, I will crush you and your entire lodge with my paw!" Cougar turned and bounded off through the forest.*

*The next day, when the sun was high, Cougar came back along the same trail. He stopped over the log and called to Cricket. "Cricket, come out! Let me meet your mighty cousin!"*

*Just then, a tiny mosquito flew up from the log and buzzed into the big cat's ear.*

*"What is this?" cried the cougar, which had never seen or heard a mosquito before. The mosquito began to bite the soft inner ear of the cougar and drank from his blood. "Ahrr! Ahrr!" cried the cougar in pain, "Get out of my ear!" The cougar pawed at his ear and ran around in a circle shaking his head. The mosquito bit him again and again.*

*Cricket came out of the log and called up to the cougar. "Are you ready to leave my lodge alone?"*

*Cougar said he would, so Mosquito came out of Cougar's ear and went into the log lodge with Cricket. Cougar ran off down the trail, and never went that way again.*

Kai inclined her head at the end of the story, and both Ryan and Emily clapped.

"That's great. I bet Teresa loved the idea of something so small and insignificant getting the better of a cougar."

Kai smiled, and in true maternal proxy form, she ruffled Ryan's hair as if he were still a boy. "You bet she did. In fact, she'd turn to me and mouth, *get off my lodge*, whenever your father or anyone from the pride got a little too big for their britches. We'd crack up and they wouldn't have a clue."

Emily made a face. "What is up with the whole arrogant cougar thing anyway? There are so many species of shifter, not to mention the other varieties of supernaturals in this world. I thought vampires held the monopoly on the whole master race ideology, but I suppose oligarchy is not an exclusive concept."

Kai reached for another biscuit, slathering it with butter and apricot jam. She took a bite and while she chewed, she held the remaining portion out toward Emily, bouncing her hand up and down in small tight movements while she finished her mouthful.

"There's a lot about dual natured cougars that you don't understand. First off, they aren't really that different from their animal counterpart. Even in the wild, cougars are called ghost spirits or ghost walkers because of their secretive habitats and the stealth way in which they hunt.

"According to totem lore, the cougar contains the energy of leadership and balances intention. They embody grace, strength, and responsibility. Tribes say if you listen to the cougar you learn to become the kind of leader people follow by choice, not by force. This was something your father used to say over and over again. It was almost a mantra—that cougars have the wisdom to lead through bond and not through fear."

"Yeah, right." Emily snorted.

"Oh, it goes on from there. Cougar people must ignore those who balk at their assertion to lead, and never allow others to keep us from our natural path. Especially those who have grown complacent with the status quo," Kai continued.

"Wow. That sounds an awful lot like indoctrination."

The older woman plopped the rest of her biscuit in her mouth. "Yup. Kool-Aid in every flavor. Crafted by our council of elders and poured down the throat of everyone who stepped foot on pride ground. The snow mountain pride was very widespread. They took in a lot of territory, covering many states. It didn't start out that way. It was Edward's doing. The start of what he called The Rebirthing.

"It's why this woman is so dangerous, now. The cougars are following her the same way they followed him." She looked at Emily. "Your brother got in Edward's way with his unification plan and the experiment you call the Compound. Edward had to stop it. That's why he went east. It was to infiltrate and take it down. His biological warfare was all part of it, but you know that already. Your family shut him down, and the emancipator won't let that happen again."

The clock above the mantel chimed and Kai glanced up. With an exhale she pushed herself up from the floor, dusting any remaining crumbs from her pants. "I've gotta go or I won't be there when your friends arrive."

She walked toward the front door and took her jacket from the coatrack at the base of the narrow stairs. Fishing in her pockets for her keys she gestured toward the bedrooms on the second floor. "This place has two small rooms set into the eaves upstairs. One is my bedroom, and the other is the guest room. Feel free to crash in either for a couple of hours."

She slipped her arms through her jacket sleeves and shrugged the denim and sheepskin the rest of the way onto her shoulders. "I should be back by twelve. I plan to make a quick stop at the store before I meet up with your friends. Do you need anything in particular?"

Ryan got up and took a handful of cash from his front pants pocket and walked it over to where Kai stood with her hand on the door.

"Take this, please. You shouldn't have to feed the army of shifters hiding in your home. It's the least we can do."

Not shy about it at all, she took the money from his hand and pressed a kiss to his cheek in exchange. "Thanks," she replied. "This will help a lot." She folded the bills and stuck them in her front pocket.

Standing in awkward silence, she looked at the two finally opening the door. "My house is your house, but whatever you do, do not answer the phone, or go outside. This house is safe, but the forest surrounding it is still cougar territory. Cougars are amazing trackers, and relentless once they catch the scent of what they are pursuing." She dropped her chin and eyed them both.

Emily nodded in reply. "Don't worry. We'll behave."

With a wink, she chuckled. "I'm not worried about that, just don't do it out in the open or the scent will bring the cats for sure!"

# CHAPTER
# FOURTEEN

R yan peeked through the vertical blinds. "Jesus, the forest is so dense it's still dark out back."

Emily walked behind him and peered out across his shoulder into the thick trees. "What did you expect? We're at the bottom of a ravine at the edge of a deep, dark wood. All this place needs is seven little people whistling out of the gloom with picks and shovels singing a twenty-first century version of *hi ho, hi ho.*"

He grinned over his shoulder at her. "And I suppose that makes you Snow White?"

Grabbing an apple from the bowl of fruit on the table she tossed it up and then caught it before taking a bite. "Well, if the apple fits," she teased, chewing.

The kitchenette was a small L shape, with barely enough room for them to maneuver around the two person café set doubling as a dinner table and work surface. A narrow galley housed Kai's refrigerator and stove on one side, with a yard's width of hardwood separating the sink and kitchen cabinets on the other. A short Formica counter jutted out from the side of the sink but was only long enough to hold the toaster and of course, the coffee pot.

Ryan let go of the blinds and leaned against the edge of the counter, one leg crossed over the other. "So if you're Snow White, does that make me the prince?"

Emily took another bite of her apple. "Ribbet."

"Ha. I think you've got your fairytales mixed up."

"Maybe," she said wrapping the rest of her apple in a napkin and putting it on the counter next to the toaster. "Then again I wasn't much of a fairytale fan growing up."

With two quick steps Ryan was toe to toe with Emily. Placing his hands on her shoulders. He walked her backward until her butt was pressed against the stove, and he was pressed against her. He slid his arm around her waist and pulled her even closer. "Perhaps you need the right kiss to wake up that part of you."

His lips found hers and she stiffened again. This time he wasn't going to let her pull away. He was hungry for her and had been since the minute he clapped eyes on her again. As if his body was starved for the feel of her skin, his fingers glided over her arm, caressing the silky curve of her neck before burrowing into her thick blond hair. He fisted the pale gold mass, tilting her head up so he could relish the taste of her mouth even more.

She moaned into the kiss, her breath sweet with the taste of apple and her arms snaked around his waist. He broke their kiss and pulled back to look at her face. Inhaling, he caught the scent of her arousal, and Emily glanced away as if hiding from her body's betrayal. He wasn't having it.

He turned her chin back, so she had to face him, rubbing his thumb along her bottom lip. Leaning in he kissed her again, his tongue dancing with hers, deeper more intense. In that moment, she gave in, and her acquiescence rumbled at the back of her throat, the vibrations sending a shockwave straight to his cock.

His crotch tightened, and he dropped his hand to the nape of her neck, drawing it down the sexy line of her backbone. With both his hands splayed across the flat of her back, he slipped his fingers beneath the waistband of her jeans, urging her hips further into his own.

"Can't you feel how much I want you," he whispered into another kiss. "I know you feel the same way, and this time I'm not letting go."

Her fingers gripped the fabric of his shirt, twisting it in her fists urging him closer, grinding herself even more against him. She moaned, her breath coming in short rasps as she tore her lips from his.

"Ryan..."

Eyes on hers, he shook his head. "You're not running again." Breath ragged, he reached for the top button of her pants, but she rested a staying hand on his chest, and he froze waiting for her to pull away.

"I got this," she murmured.

Her blue eyes were dark with need as she unbuttoned her flannel shirt, tossing it to the floor along with her camisole. She stood naked from the waist up, cupping her full breasts, her thumb and forefinger pinching her hardened nipples teasing him.

He growled, and the sound was feral and possessive. Grasping both her hands by the wrists, he drew them above her head and locked them in one of his hands while the other trailed down across her throat and décolleté, his thumb grazing one taut peak.

His mouth found the other and he worked them both with his tongue and fingers until Emily arched back, urging his mouth for more. His fingers tightened on her wrists, and she whimpered, the sound a complete mix of pleasure and pain.

He released her, sliding the other hand down to work her breasts. Heat flooded Ryan's body, his cock hard and throbbing inside his jeans. Freeing one hand he unbuttoned the top of his fly, pushing his pants down enough to free his swollen flesh.

Emily's hands found his hips, and she slid her fingers over the muscular V leading to his hardened member. She wrapped her fingers around the thick, corded mass, sliding her thumb from the base to just below his moist tip. She moved slowly, applying pressure from the pad of her thumb to the large vein along the entire length of his cock.

A sharp hiss sounded through Ryan's teeth, and he grunted,

moving his hands to Emily's shoulders, pushing her to her knees. He fisted one hand in her hair while the other circled his cock, rubbing the bulging head along the seam of her bottom lip.

"Come on, Snow White, take a bite." His voice was more growl than murmur, but Emily's eyes burned as she looked up at him, her tongue darting out to flick the underside of his head with a quick, suggestive lick.

He urged her forward, pressing his cock to her lips and she opened her mouth sucking in the full length of him. A visceral groan left his throat, and he froze letting the pressure of her tongue and lips pulse shockwaves through his body.

His legs tensed, and the muscles in his stomach shook from holding back. With a guttural moan he pumped his hips, driving his cock further and deeper into her hot, wet mouth until he exploded, his climax ripping through his body as she sucked him dry.

Slumping forward, he hugged her to his thighs, not caring she wiped her mouth on his jeans.

"That was incredible." His voice ragged and tense as his muscles twitched and pulsed. He kissed the top of her head, helping her up from her knees.

Cupping her face, he kissed her mouth, his lips claiming hers until she sighed against him, taking his hand and drawing it down to the juncture between her legs. "My turn," she whispered.

This went against everything she had promised herself, everything she swore she wouldn't do, yet here she was, her traitorous body singing with need. This was wrong. She was being dishonest, but as heat sluiced through her body a warm slash of hope followed in its wake. If they could bridge this gap then perhaps...

He was right, she wanted him as badly as he wanted her even if it went nowhere from this moment on. At least she would have today. She pushed all her worry and doubt to the back of her mind. She would deal with the fallout later.

She held his wrist out and stepped around him. The kitchen was suddenly claustrophobic, and she needed fresh air, craved it as much as she craved his hands. With one hand she flipped the latch on the sliding glass doors that lead to the back of the house. Taking a dish towel with her, she moved to stand in front of the redwood table sitting on the grassy area off the narrow slate threshold. Kai had said for them to play indoors, but the picnic area was only five feet from the kitchen door so technically it wasn't out in the open.

With two fingers she unbuttoned the top button of her jeans and guided the zipper down. Leaning forward, she slid her fingers into the open waistband and pushed her pants down but kept her thong in place. Stepping out of her jeans she kicked them through the sliding door into the kitchen near her shirt and camisole. Barefoot, she beckoned him, her index finger trailing the thin scrap of lace standing between him and her still swollen clit.

His cock was hard again, and his pupils had dilated to dark pools. He was ready and one sniff told her this time he didn't want her mouth. She slipped her fingers beneath the delicate fabric and stroked herself, her eyes glued to his. "You want this, Ryan?"

An answering growl was all the response she needed. She withdrew her hand, instead pushing the thin material aside letting him have a glimpse of her swollen nub and slick, flushed sex.

"You can have it, but you're going to have to work for it this time." Her fingers teased between the wet folds, her thumb rubbing her clit in a slow circular motion. She closed her eyes and spread her legs wider, moaning as her other hand came up to cup her breast.

She opened her eyes and looked at him. He licked his lips as she removed her fingers from between her legs and opened her mouth to suck them. "Think you can take it from here?" she teased.

With one long stride he took her by the waist, his mouth on her throat as he inhaled deeply. "This is what I remember," he murmured against the side of her neck. "You, fearless and flushed. Passionate and wonton in your demands."

He lifted the dishtowel from the picnic table. "It's not a washcloth, but I think I could make it work." Rolling the cloths rough quilted edge, he dragged the seam across her clit and she gasped but shook her head just the same.

"No props this time. Just you." She turned to spread the checkered rectangle over the edge of the redwood table and then leaned back onto the material.

With a smirk, he stepped in and nuzzled her neck until she pushed his head down with both hands and he went to his knees just as she did, his hands trailing every inch of her chest and stomach as he sank down to the moist earth.

Ryan pushed the lace aside, his fingers deliberately rough and she hissed through her teeth yanking his hair. With a low chuckle he tongued her nub, flicking and sucking as her fingers dug further into his hair.

He slid two fingers into her slick entrance and worked her while he bit and licked, and when her juices dripped down his chin he slipped a third finger inside. Her hips ground against his mouth and Emily shuddered, her body tensing as he caught her nub between his teeth and pulled.

"You taste so good, Em...even better than I remembered. Sweet and salty..." he moaned, stroking the soft skin between her folds with a sweep of his tongue.

With one quick motion he lifted her onto the table and drove his cock into her swollen sex. Emily wrapped her legs around his waist as he thrust harder and faster until she screamed, her climax shuddering through her body. With a guttural yell, Ryan's cock pulsed his release as aftershocks took her body, milking every last drop from him.

With her legs still wrapped around his waist, he lifted her off the table and carried her through the door, sliding it closed with his foot.

"What about our clothes? Kai will be back soon," she whispered, as he carried her through the living room and up the stairs to the guest bedroom.

"Kai won't be back for hours yet." With one hand he drew back the coverlet and placed Emily on the bed. "We both need rest and I want to feel your warmth beside me."

"Ryan..."

"Emily," he mimicked, but the look on her face won out and he went back downstairs to retrieve their clothes.

"Better?" he asked laying them across a rung-backed chair in the corner.

She nodded, holding her arms out to him and he slipped beneath covers alongside her.

# FIFTEEN

"Ryan!" her voice was a harsh whisper. "Someone's outside."

He sat up, and it was déjà vu from the hotel room all over again. Like before he put his finger over his lips but motioned for her to get dressed.

He slipped on his pants and shirt and padded barefoot down the stairs, wishing he had taken his bag upstairs along with their clothes. His gun was in the duffle bag still against the side of the couch in the living room. He would have to cross the short hallway and the front door to reach it, and whoever was outside was already on the porch.

Making a dive for it from the bottom step, he rolled into the living room landing in a crouch beside the bag. Unzipping the top, he grabbed his 9mm SIG and stuffed an extra magazine into his back pocket.

The door smashed open and two of the largest mountain lions he'd ever seen this side of the Discovery Channel charged in, teeth bared. One ran straight up the stairs and the other wheeled around, it's thick muscled shoulders and heavy forelegs bunched and ready to pounce.

Ryan got of two shots, the sound muffled by the high-pitched screech that tore at his eardrums before the large animal pinned him to the ground, its teeth seizing his head and part of his neck.

Emily's scream reached his bloodied ears, but Ryan couldn't move under the weight of the cat. His eyesight narrowed and when the cat shook him, everything went dark.

"Leave him, Cole. The emancipator wants them both alive." The words came from a tall, muscular man with a full beard and long wild hair curling around his ears as he stepped over the shattered door.

The big cat let go of Ryan's head and his limp body fell to the floor. He spat out part of Ryan's shirt collar and then proceeded to lick the wounds he inflicted. In a snap of bone and muscle spasm the big cat phased to its human form. He looked down at the unconscious man and spat again. "Fucking half-blood."

Another man walked down the stairs with Emily thrown over his shoulder.

"She faint or did you hurt her like this idiot?" The tall burly man asked gesturing toward Cole.

The man on the stairs glanced at his partner as he shook his head. "No, Sam. All I did was run into the room and chuff, like you said. She screamed and then her eyes rolled back in her head. It was lights out after that. Too bad really, because she smells like the half-blood just fucked the shit out of her."

Sam grinned. "Enough of that, Liam. Let's load'em up and get the hell out of here. Kai's not around so there's no telling who she's got joining this rebellion of hers."

Cole grunted. "You should have let me take care of that old bitch when I had the chance."

Sam backhanded him across the jaw, sending the big cat flying into the rocking chair shattering the spindles. "She's Catori's mother and besides, James would never allow it."

With a curse, Cole got to his feet, brushing broken pieces of wood from his skin. "Dude! That fucking hurt! Now I've got splinters in my chest! Who cares what James thinks? He's too fucking old school with his vision quests and the rest of his shaman bullshit. As for Catori, you've gone gaga over her ever since the emancipator promised her to you."

Sam growled low in his throat, shooting Liam a dirty look for nodding. "I should kill you for that right now, but you keep wagging your tongue and Jenya's going to do it for me."

The two men visibly blanched at the mention of the vampire's name. Sam's eyes narrowed and he chuckled low in his throat. "That's right, shit for brains. You better watch what you say, or the emancipator will let her shove a giant splinter up your asses and then laugh while you bleed. Now pick up this half-blood and let's get out of here."

KAI DROVE through the rough terrain, she and Lily making small talk. Their words were white noise in the background as Sean mulled over all the older woman said about recent events surrounding the Snow Mountain pride, but as far as he was concerned their issues were no longer his worry.

He and Lily were here for one reason, and that was to pull Emily and Ryan out before the situation escalated. As Alpha of the Brethren Sean already called the vampire council informing Rémy there would be no further involvement on his part.

As far as Sean was concerned, the shifters had fulfilled their end of the bargain and located the human girl and the female vampire. Now it was up to the vampires to send in their own to collect. He also alerted Rémy of Connor's formal abnegation from any and all packs within Compound jurisdiction.

The Jeep jostled back and forth, and Sean stretched his legs in front of him, closing his eyes. Rémy reluctantly accepted Sean's stance, assuring he would bring Sébastien up to date before heading to the mountains to finish the job himself. Sean figured it would take that long because most of the Rémy's reinforcements were not yet old enough in undead years to tolerate prolonged daylight.

The vampire was resolute, and Sean tried not to think of what lay ahead for Connor at the hands of the undead, but the boy had made his choices and would have to pay his part.

Kai's off roader bumped over uneven road, gears grinding along the unpaved path muddied from overnight rain. The trip was taking too long. Sean's gut churned with dread. Alarm sizzled across Sean's skin the deeper they headed into the woods. He spared a glance for Lily.

*"The air doesn't feel right to me. I've got a weird, panicked feeling I can't explain floating on the periphery of my mind. Can you sense anything off?"*

Kai caught the tail end of the mental exchange and her eyes flashed around to Lily. She slammed on the breaks, jerking the Jeep to the side of the dirt road. "Stop! Are you trying to invite trouble? The cougars are waiting for you to do something stupid! Don't you know the minute you home in on them, they home in on you?"

Lily immediately closed a wall on her senses. She looked from Sean to Kai, her expression doubtful. "Give me a little credit, will you? I didn't use the common shifter path, so there's no way they could sense my reach."

The older woman shook her head, her expression less than courteous. "I have no time for citified self-importance. You can either listen to me or suffer the consequences. There is a real danger here. You think to grab your people and go. That our provincial problems don't affect you. Well, I'm here to tell you you're wrong.

"What's happening here is a cancer, and it's fast growing because it feeds on want and resentment. The cougars have kept themselves isolated for a very long time, but in recent years some migrated to the city. Trouble started the minute they returned to the mountains. They want what everyone else has, but never once thought about how to provide for that want. The cougars aren't educated thinkers; for the most part they're followers."

"Kai what are you talking about? What has this got to do with us?" Sean asked.

"You don't get it. You are the Alpha of the Brethren. You represent all they have been told they can't have. The emancipator has blamed you for their lot in life. She's told them you lie, and the concept of the unification for all shifters is self-serving propaganda."

"Me? Does this emancipator as she calls herself even know me?"

Kai nodded. "She says she knows you well. Telling people she lived at your Compound, and that you are a false prophet."

Lily snorted. "Prophet? Whoever this chick is she's slipped a cog. Sean isn't a prophet, he's the Alpha. The elected Alpha, I might add."

Kai's eyebrows went up and she cocked her head. "Ah, well. Therein lays the rub. Elected by whom?"

Lily and Sean exchanged looks, but Kai's only response was a resigned sigh as she shifted gears, pulling back onto to the road. "The cougars had no say in your election. So it's easy for them to swallow what the emancipator feeds them. It all ties back to Edward Parr, and what he fed them about taking their place in the hierarchy of shifters."

A guttural noise left the back of Sean's mouth. "That's ridiculous. I reached out to every shifter group in the country. I did so by region and held town meetings to cover more ground. In fact, I made such an impression on the selkies of Bodega Bay they were able to pinpoint Emily as my sister without her saying a word. This is bullshit. I was here, Kai, and I specifically sent the invitation to the Snow Mountain shaman. A man by the name of..."

"James." Kai said, finishing his sentence.

Sean nodded. "Yes, that's the one. He agreed to meet with me, but he never showed."

Kai's eyes softened, but pain edged her gaze as she stared ahead at the dirt road. "James suffered a stroke right before he was to meet with you. He was so excited to hear what you had to say; confident what you offered was the answer we prayed for to bring the pride into the modern world. Edward was gone at this point.

He left for the east coast to try and dissuade the idea of unification. He told the council he had a plan, but when he didn't come back, James finally found the moment he'd been waiting for to turn things around for the better. The council elders took his stroke as a bad sign. A sign you were a stranger not to be trusted and that Edward was right.

"Of course, James could barely move and couldn't speak at all. He had no way to argue with them. They let the meeting fall to the wayside, and when you didn't reach out again, it only reinforced their suspicions."

Sean rubbed his face and sat back against the passenger seat. "That's when the shifters at the Compound started falling ill. It was devastation, Kai. A virus that turned even the best of us into base creatures. A virus created by Edward Parr. I put all my plans for expansion on the back burner in order to deal with the chaos. I'm sorry."

She lifted one delicate shoulder and let it fall. "What happened is not your fault. We we lucky. We heard about the virus, but we were spared in our isolation. As to the council and what they've done or refused to do, it's what happens when people have been held back for so many decades. They become secretive and suspicious, and they turn on each other, too. Then the woman showed up telling them she had the answer to all their problems."

"Do you know this woman's name?"

Kai shook her head. "She won't tell us. Saying her name is of no consequence. She claims she is not the one who will lead us, but simply the vessel carrying the one who will."

"She's pregnant?" Lily asked.

Kai nodded again.

Sean glanced at the backseat, watching Lily stare out the window as she chewed on her bottom lip. He knew that look well. She was weighing and discarding everyone they crossed paths with over the past six months. The woman was someone who knew them, but that didn't mean they knew her.

Could it be someone attached to a visitor who came to the Compound, like Angus Flanders, the shifter from Indiantown Florida who accused Lily of murder? Or was it someone closer to home? Sean's head swam with the percentages.

So many people had suffered. It could be anyone, but at the same time it would have to be someone with a connection to the cougars and the only people he knew who did, were dead.

Lily turned her gaze from the window, and their eyes locked and in that moment he knew who it was.

# SIXTEEN

Emily lifted her head and winced, her hand reaching for the side of her head. With her eyes squeezed shut, her fingers probed the tender area surrounding the large knot above left ear.

"Damn it," she hissed, slumping onto what she thought was Kai's guest room pillow, but the cloud of dust particles that puffed out made it clear she was nobody's guest.

Ignoring the pounding ache and ringing in her ear, she sat up, panic clearing any remaining cobwebs from her memory. She fainted when the cat charged into the room at full lope. That much she remembered.

The tawny animal bounded up the stairs toward her with its teeth bared. The thought of its high pitched scream raising gooseflesh on her arms.

She sneezed, rubbing her nose with the side of her hand.

"Gesundheit," a feminine voice said from the door.

Emily squinted, her eyes trying to adjust to the dim light criss-crossed by narrow swaths of daylight stripping in through the slats in the side wall. She was on a narrow cot set against a wall on the opposite side of the room. A TV tray holding a plastic picnic pitcher and two matching cups sat near the head of the cot, with a thin camp-style blanket folded beside it neatly.

"You're welcome," she added, clearly amused.

Emily didn't need a mirror to know her face was a mixture of pain and confusion. "Where am I?" She focused on the woman standing in the half-light. She was big. With straw-like blond hair hanging in dirty clumps from her scalp.

The woman's wide shoulders shook along with her ample bosom, but her amusement was mirthless. "You are the guest of the emancipator. Just like your unconscious friend over there."

Bales of freshly stacked hay blocked Emily's line of sight and squinting from the pain chewing its way across her head didn't help.

She narrowed her eyes and focused her gaze on what she could see. Shit. Ryan's black boots poked out from behind one of the sweet smelling blocks.

Emily stood up and a wave of dizziness and nausea took her. She listed sideways, grabbing onto the trough-like base of a wheelbarrow propped against the wall. Steadying herself she sucked in air, trying to quell the whirly feeling.

"I would worry about you, sweetheart. Your friend will be lucky if he makes it through until tomorrow. If Cole's bite doesn't kill him, bets are the emancipator will." She tossed a white metal box with a large red cross on the lid onto the shorter of the haystacks. "Try this. Not that it'll help."

Emily glared at her. "Get out."

The woman grinned, her dirty fingernails reaching for the door. "It's too bad about your friend, though." Her covetous gaze oily as it slid toward Ryan's still form. "We don't get lookers like him very often."

She glanced back, her narrow gaze tight as she gave Emily a once over. "Half-blood males never last. You though. You're exactly what we need. You're full-blooded and ripe as a berry." With a wheezy cackle she grabbed herself by the crotch. "My guess is she'll have you mated within the month." With a wink and a click of cheek, she left.

Dust swirled in the woman's wake, tiny particles sparkling in the thin shafts of sunlight. White knuckled, Emily gripped the curved edge of the wheelbarrow, her mind reeling.

She needed to check on Ryan, but she also needed to figure out where the hell they were and how to get out of here. She closed her eyes and concentrated on her brother, her mind focusing on the mental pathway they used as kids. Ironic really. She hadn't sought this thread in over a decade, but there it was covered in cobwebs and dust bunnies.

Despite the channel's unpracticed and awkward feel, she whispered Sean's name hoping the urgency in her tone spoke volumes so she wouldn't have to. Without warning, white hot pain exploded behind her temples, and she clutched the sides of her head.

Scalding, sharp spikes pierced her mind, blurring her vision and she screamed stumbling backwards while struggling to slam a wall down on the open pathway.

Vertigo hit and she doubled over, vomiting onto the dirt floor. Dry heaves eventually replaced the wet retching and her nausea receded along with the pain in her head.

She slumped back onto the cot, clammy perspiration trickling between her breasts and under her arms. With shaking hands she poured a glass of water from the plastic pitcher, gulping it down.

Lily told her Sean blocked her psychic abilities with something akin to static when she first came to the Compound, but there was never pain involved. Edward Parr had been the one to develop that little trick, testing his experiment when Jack took Lily hostage.

Now both fuckers were dead, but that was courtesy of Lily and Sean, and of course, Ryan. She was snug as a bug in San Francisco learning about it second hand.

She glanced at Ryan's motionless boots still peeking out from behind the hay bale. Swallowing another mouthful of water, she wiped her hand across her mouth. Fat tears formed and she rubbed them away. "That's right, Em. Sit and cry like a baby." Her voice broke in the quiet despite herself, and she scuffed her boot over the packed dirt in frustration.

*Designer boots aren't going to help you if you don't know how to throw a decent kick, Emily.* Lily's words came back with a vengeance. *"If you can't think, you can't plan, and if you can't plan how are you going to save your life?"*

Like a spark to a flame Emily knew what her sister-in-law would say now. Take inventory of the situation, and then weigh the options and the odds.

With a sniff, she eyed the first aid kit still sitting on top of the stacked pile of hay. "First things first," she murmured, and got to her feet from the cot. She grabbed the first aid kit and turned it around, flipping open the lid to look inside at its contents. Band-Aids, antibacterial ointment, burn cream, gauze. Standard stuff.

Chewing the inside of her cheek she rummaged further in and found a small bottle of rubbing alcohol, a pair of scissors, two ace bandages and medical tape. She picked up the scissors and touched her index finger to the sharp point and smiled. *Possibilities.*

All she needed was a lighter or book of matches and for Ryan to wake up so they could start a firewall with all this hay and maybe even something explosive with the alcohol. Too stupid to live was not the way she would go out. Lily would go down fighting, and so would she.

Steeling herself, Emily closed the lid and tucked the metal box under her arm. She moved past the bales of hay and walked around Ryan's feet. From the awkward lay of his body it was obvious he had been tossed here, not placed.

She swore under her breath and knelt in the dirt beside him. His t-shirt was ripped down the front and soaked with blood. There were deep lacerations across his chest and throat, and when she turned his chin she gasped. Puncture wounds penetrated his scalp above his right temple and through the soft tissue beneath his jaw. It was clear Ryan had been mauled, and the majority of the blood on his shirt had come from the wounds on his head and neck.

Emily sat back on her heels. She opened the first aid box and took out a large sterile gauze pack, ripping the paper with her teeth. Grabbing the bottle of alcohol, she unscrewed the top but then stopped, cap in hand. Ryan's wounds needed to be cleaned well, and a tiny bottle of isopropyl alcohol wasn't going to cut it. She placed the gauze in its paper wrapper and recapped the bottle. For this she would need the water pitcher.

Using the first aid scissor, Emily carefully cut the rest of Ryan's tee-shirt down the middle, exposing his wounds. Four parallel slash marks scored his shoulder and chest, the deep lines puckered and raw.

He should have healed somewhat by now, but the injuries were so severe he'd need at least a week to recuperate, and from the angry red forming along the edge of his torn flesh, he'd probably need a course of antibiotics, as well. Neither of which he was getting anytime soon.

Dogs barked somewhere outside, and Emily heard voices not far off. Dry mouthed, she swallowed back her fear and self-doubt, pressing her lips together. Now was not the time for indecision. If the situation was reversed, Ryan would move heaven and earth to help her, and she knew it.

She filled one of the plastic cups halfway and dipped the clean gauze into the water, saturating the square. Using gentle strokes, she cleaned away the dried blood, his body twitching involuntarily with each pass. The cool bath seemed to help, though, and on the second go she added a squeeze of alcohol to the water and the wounds seemed to lose their angry red appearance.

Perhaps there was something in the cat's claws or saliva that prevented healing and washing the component away was key. She'd never heard of such a thing, but then again maybe it was another of Edward's advancements the cougars had acquired like the mind block death grip.

The bite wounds on Ryan's temple and neck were another story. The ruptures were profound and there was no way to ascertain how deep the damage went beneath the surface.

She pulled her makeshift triage kit around and knelt behind his head, her knees pressed against the top of his shoulders. With another piece of gauze she prepared a sterile area, unfolding the large square and laying it across her thighs before lifting his head carefully onto her lap.

Hands poised over his head wound Emily's fingers curled in uncertainty. There was so much dried blood in his hair and on his throat. What if the puncture near his temple perforated his brain? Didn't she just read an article on how jaguars kill their prey by biting through their skulls? Could Ryan be brain dead?

He was still unconscious but breathing on his own. His chest rose and fell beneath her hands as she cleaned his wounds, and even jerked in response to the alcohol and water.

The injury on his throat was more ragged, but at least there was a definite entry and exit point where the cat's canine penetrated the soft tissue under his jaw and exited through his cheek. The rupture was a perfect hole, almost as if hit with a leather punch and then released.

How the strike missed Ryan's carotid was a miracle, and considering big cats kill by suffocation and shaking their prey, it was a wonder he still had a face.

She cleaned both wound sites the best she could, washing the blood and dirt from his hair and neck. Exhausted, she sat back, rolling the stiffness from her shoulders. There was nothing else to do now but wait. Or was there?

A scrap of memory hit, and Emily's brows knotted together as she tried to remember. Jerard had been fighting in the playground at school. The bite mark on his arm from the other child was small, yet deep enough to require stitches. Emily sat up straighter.

She remembered going with her mother and father to the infirmary. Jerard was only eight years old, but the image of him sitting on their mother's lap and her rocking him back and forth with her lace handkerchief tied around his wound was as clear as day. The same lace handkerchief she watched her mother spit into.

Why didn't she think of it before? Her grandmother had told her about the healing quality to their saliva. To anyone else it would seem unsanitary, even dangerous and irresponsible, but plenty of human mothers lick their own thumbs to clean their children's faces, right?

She chewed on the inside of her cheek. Should she try it? What if she made things worse and gave Ryan an infection? After all, he wasn't a wolf. For the first time in a long time she wished she had paid more attention as a child.

There was one square of gauze left in the first aid kit. The marks on Ryan's chest had healed enough for a fine layer of new skin to form along the abrasion lines. It was shiny and would eventually scar, but at least there was no threat of infection.

Throwing caution to the wind, Emily ripped open the last package of gauze and snipped it in three pieces. Lifting the pitcher, she let a trickle of water fall into her mouth to moisten her tongue and soft palate. Gathering the sterile fabric she squeezed a generous dollop of antibacterial ointment into the center of each square.

Once done she poured alcohol over her index finger to sterilize the tip and then spit onto each of the gauze pieces, swirling everything together into a paste. "Here goes nothing," she breathed, and then smeared each puncture wound with the mixture, sealing the ruptures with the lubricated gauze like a protective plug.

This was a long shot, and she knew it, but Ryan wasn't moving, and his body had taken on the scent of death. Leaning sideways against the wall she closed her eyes, squeezing against the tears threatening. Now for real, there was nothing else to do but wait.

EMILY WOKE WITH A START. Her eyes flew open, and she jerked forward.

"Hey, take it easy up there."

Emily's looked down. Her breath locked in her throat. "Ryan?" she croaked.

He nodded, wincing in the process. "In once piece, although I don't know how."

She squealed, wrapping her arms around his shoulders. At his prolonged hiss of pain, she immediately let go. "I'm sorry. Did I hurt you? Oh God, I'm so stupid!"

He chuckled, grimacing with the effort. "It's okay. I'm just glad I'm still here for you to abuse."

She frowned. "Don't joke like that."

He lifted one hand and touched the rolled up gauze protruding from his throat, his fingers moving up to do the same to the one in his cheek. "What's this? Was I leaking?"

"Something like that.

"So your answer is a shifter version of the little Dutch boy?"

She frowned. "Don't you remember what happened?"

He winced, trying to move. "Sort of. It's all a little jumbled, but I remember feeling like my head was in a vice." He slumped back but then his eyes flew open, and he looked at her, his throat working to swallow back against the clear flood of memory.

Emily nodded. "Your head was in a vice, but I used an unorthodox home remedy to help you heal, and seeing how well you look and sound, I think it worked."

"Don't tell me, there's one of these in my head too?"

She nodded. "Yes, but I think it's safe for me to take them out."

He held up one hand. "Help me up first."

"Are you nuts? You can't stand up. I just got you to the point where you stopped looking like a chew toy."

He shook his head, moving a little as possible. "I don't mean that. Just prop me up against this wall of straw. I want to see if I can tolerate the movement or if it's going to wipe me out."

Emily lifted his head, holding the gauze from her lap to his shoulders as she shifted enough to lay the square on the ground beneath his head. She walked around to the front and straddled his legs, one knee on both sides of his.

"Ready?" she asked holding her arms out.

With a smirk he nodded, and she slipped her arms under his and slowly pulled him up.

"You know, this is one of my favorite positions," he murmured next to her ear.

She kissed his cheek, her throat tight. "Mine too." Not giving him a chance to talk more, she rolled back onto her heels and stood, dragging him as best she could against the hay bale.

"You okay?" she asked, still holding on. "I can lay you down if this is too much."

"I'm good, you can lean me back."

She rested him as gently as she could and then let go. He slumped back against the straw, wincing a bit. "Is there anything to drink?"

She nodded. "I have some water left, and there's a blanket if you're cold."

"Thanks."

Emily poured him the last of the water and helped him with his ruined shirt before draping the blanket around his shoulders. She balled the bloody garment in her hands and threw it against the wall.

"I should never have let you come with me," he said in a low rasp, his voice harsh and rough from the trauma to his throat.

She looked at him. "It's not your fault, Ryan. None of this is. And besides, I wouldn't have taken no for an answer."

He didn't answer.

Emily bent to pick up what was left of the first aid kit, taking the alcohol bottle from the bottom of the bin, and grabbing the scissor to snip off a medium strip from one of the Ace bandages.

"I need to take the gauze plugs out and clean the wounds one more time." She eyed him holding the alcohol in her hand. "It may sting a bit. Are you up for it?"

He laughed out loud. "I've survive a mauling and you're asking if I'm up for a little alcohol burn?"

She smirked, pouring the antiseptic on the flesh colored cloth. "Here goes nothing." She gently pulled the gauze from his head wound and swiped the scrap of bandage over the wound.

Ryan hissed, jerking his head away. "Ouch!"

"Come on, Ryan, it's not like I have a lot of options here. I need to use the alcohol full strength. I gave you the last of the water to drink."

He made a face and tilted his head in her direction. "Just finish it and be quick."

She made fast work of the rest, and Ryan didn't move or make a sound, but the protruded exhale when she finished let her know his level of discomfort.

"There's antibiotic ointment in here with pain relief. I put some on you before, but I think you need more." Without waiting for him to reply, she slathered the ointment onto his neck and cheek and then into the puncture wound above his temple making his hair shiny and slick on that side of his head. She reached to do the same on his chest but hesitated, holding the tube out to him instead. "Do you want to do the honors since you're awake?"

He smiled. "Nope. You've got it down to a science."

She did as requested her fingers massaging the slick cream into the shiny scarred flesh. "I think this will help a lot."

He wrapped his hand around her wrist and brought her fingers to his lips. "Thank you, Emily. Whatever you did, you saved my life."

He let go of her and she slid the palm of her hand onto his uninjured cheek. "I would do it again in a heartbeat, but let's stack the odds in our favor against that, okay? You need to get your strength back so we can get out of here."

With a ragged breath, he glanced around their prison for the first time since regaining consciousness.

"This looks like a storage shed or makeshift barn. Any idea where we are?"

She shook her head. "Not a clue. My guess is we are somewhere in the Snow Mountain Wilderness in the middle of your father's pride."

Emily filled him in on what the woman said, even letting him know they were taking bets he didn't survive the attack.

The little muscle in Ryan's good cheek worked overtime as he processed what Emily said. Clearly they were still in a lot of danger. When he finally made eye contact with her, he shook his head lightly.

"I'm the reason you're in danger. I'm injured and who knows how long it'll be before I get enough strength back to move let alone run. You have to go, Em. Sean and Lily are probably tracking us now. Maybe you can reach him through that hoodoo that Lily does."

Emily balked. "I'm not leaving you here alone! Ryan, whoever this emancipator is she wants to kill you, or so the filthy, fat woman said when she practically kicked dirt in your face laying there. No way. There's something really weird about this whole situation."

He snorted. "You think?"

She shook her head, making a face. "I mean besides the weirdness we know about. I tried to reach Sean through our sibling path..." At his confused look, she explained. "It's like the hoodoo you just mentioned. Certain shifters can do it too, especially if you share an intimate link like a family member or a lover."

He raised an eyebrow.

"Nice try, but you haven't phased yet. Once you do, who knows?" She explained about the pain that almost incapacitated her, and the expectant look on his face melted into a scowl.

"I see."

She paced, kicking up small dust clouds in her path. "Well I'm glad you do, cos I don't. We've been in here for God knows how long, and no one has even checked to see if we're dead or alive."

He looked at her considering. "Maybe that's a good thing. If they think we're incapacitated, there's no way they'll think us capable of escape. We need recon."

"Recon?"

He nodded.

"And how do you suppose we do that from in here?"

"Exactly."

She threw her hands up. "Ryan, I think the puncture wound in your head has affected your brain. We're locked in, and except for the little slats in the wall there's no way to see out."

"Are you sure they've locked us in?"

She stopped, her eyes moving between him and the door. "I just assumed..." She sputtered, walking toward the door and wrapping her fingers around the handle.

"Well?"

She lifted the barn latch, and a three inch swath of fresh air and sunlight permeated the dark, dusty interior. Closing the door again she turned toward Ryan, watching a slow grin spread across his face.

"Well, I'll be damned."

He shook his head. "Not on my watch."

# CHAPTER
# SEVENTEEN

"Where are they?" Sean stood in Kai's foyer, his breathing slow and methodical as his hands clenched and unclenched. With a rough growl, he picked Kai up by the throat and threw her across the room.

"Sean!" Lily cried, her hand darting out to grab his arm.

"Lily, let go of me. I don't want to hurt you." His shoulders bunched, hard muscles coiled and ready under his skin.

"No! This is not the way to handle this."

He turned, and for the first time since they first met she saw the predator in the animal simmering beneath the surface, ready to kill.

Even when he attacked Ryan that day in New York outside the morgue, he still held a modicum of control. This was pure lethal. His eyes were yellow, and his canines dripped. "Let go," he growled, his voice like gravel and slurred through his elongated teeth.

Her fingers pressed into his flesh, and he snarled. Heat slicked across her skin and her chest tightened. A low rumble of her own rolled from the back of her throat, and as if answering her plea, his yellow eyes flashed blue for a moment.

"If Kai knows anything, she'll tell us. I'll make sure of it." Her chin dropped an inch, and she eyed him, knowing he'd understand her meaning.

She'd tap dance all over the woman's mind, and Kai would help them find Ryan and Emily whether she wanted to or not. "Besides, if you kill her who will show us where the pride is hiding?"

"I will." A deep accented voice answered from the shadows.

Lily's eyes jerked from Sean, peering into the darkened kitchen. "Show yourself!" she demanded, easing the pressure on Sean's arm in case he needed to vault and phase on the fly.

"Easy, my little witch. Your disquiet is making me thirst, and that is never a good thing."

"Rémy! What are you doing here?"

"I came to finish what the wolves began, but it's obvious the game has changed, no?" He inclined his head toward Sean and his advanced state of rage.

The vampire inhaled. "I've never experienced a shifter on the verge of phasing. Their scent leaves a tang of bloodlust in the air." His eyes flashed over red, and he took a step forward.

Lily let go of Sean, and in seconds his clothes shred amid a snap of bone and muscle, and a gigantic black wolf stood between them, saliva dripping over bared teeth.

Rémy bowed his head and took a step back. "My apologies." He breathed. "I have yet to replenish myself from the exertion of my journey west. I will leave you now to remedy myself."

He turned to exit out the back, but stopped, and when he spoke it was with his back to them. "Please do not leave until I return. This will not happen again. You have my oath."

Without another word, he vaulted through the open glass door and took to the sky. Sean skidded after him to the tree line, snarling and snapping.

Lily watched from the kitchen doorway, leaning back to peer into the living room for any movement from Kai. When the older woman finally sat up, her hand went to the back of her head, and she winced.

After watching her try and shake it off, Lily rummaged in the top kitchen drawers for a clean dish towel and wet it, carrying the damp cloth into the living room.

"Here, press this to the back of your head. You're not bleeding, but you're going to have quite an egg back there."

Kai took the wet towel from Lily. "There's ice in the freezer."

Lily nodded and walked into the kitchen just as Sean stepped back through the door. He was human and naked, but at least he was calm.

"Kai's conscious. I'm getting her some ice for her head."

He didn't respond.

"You know, she may have a slight concussion."

He pressed his lips together.

"Sean, you could have let her talk before you went ape shit. She looked as shocked as we when we walked in and guessed what happened. I know Emily is your sister, but Jesus. Now is not the time for you to lose your equilibrium."

"She set us up." His words were clipped tight.

Lily closed the freezer door with her hip, wrapping the ice in another dish towel. "I highly doubt that, and I already told you I would find out for sure." She brushed past him and his crossed arm stance.

"Ryan's bag is in the hall. I'll give Kai the icepack and then see if there's anything in his duffel to fit your big bad wolf butt."

"Not nice."

She held the ice out in his direction. "Neither was throwing a middle-aged woman across the room before you gave her the chance to speak." Lily exhaled, wiping the loose end of the dishtowel across her forehead. "Look, this was the last thing both of us expected, and we're losing time arguing. If you hadn't lost your cool we would be in the woods tracking Emily and Ryan by now. Rémy will be back faster than you think, so I suggest we get it together and form a plan."

She turned to leave, but Sean held out his hand. "Lily, wait."

With an expectant look, she turned halfway.

He ran a hand through his hair and then let it drop to his bare hip. "You're right. I lost it, and I'm sorry. We both know what's happening here and who's behind it. That means nothing is off limits. Find out what you can, and then let's get moving. I want to find my sister before nightfall. Rémy should have reinforcements by then."

Lily nodded. "Having Rémy here will help, but I'm not sure about his backup. The timing doesn't work. His early arrival shocked me enough. In fact, he must be older than I thought because he flew through prime daylight to get here."

"Not as old as I'm getting standing here freezing."

At her raised eyebrow, he gestured toward the doorway with his chin. "Unless you want Kai to faint when she sees me..." He flicked an eye toward his rather endowed nether regions and a snort left Lily's mouth, despite the playful smirk on his face.

"Yeah, right." Unfolding the dishtowel she plopped the ice into her palm and tossed the damp rag at Sean's chest. "Here's a loin cloth, Tarzan. Jane's a little busy right now. Ryan's bag is the orange canvas duffle in the hallway. Knock yourself out."

Rémy returned not long afterward. He surveyed the damage, along with Sean, stacking broken pieces of Kai's furniture to one side of the room. The carpet in the entry was beyond repair. It was soaked with Ryan's blood.

"Sir, if the scent is too strong for you we can sit outside. Perhaps that would be best." Kai inclined her head and winced.

"I'll get you some more ice, Kai. Try not to move around so quickly, okay?" Lily got up from the couch and went into the kitchen, her hand trailing a light pat on Rémy's sleeve as she passed.

"Our little witch hasn't lost her fire, no?" He chuckled, and Kai swallowed at the glint of fang showing through his small grin.

At her look, he sobered. "You have nothing to fear, my dear. From me or my... appearance." His hand swept upward grazing the burned side of his face.

Kai blanched and shifted in her chair. Lily walked back in and at the older woman's pallid expression, her gaze trailed from one man to the other. "Okay, let's get this straight now. We are a team. Kai has already shown me inside and out that she only wanted to keep Emily and Ryan safe. Sean and I figured who is behind this mess, and I don't mean Kai's cottage. I think it's time to share what we know."

Rémy raised his arm and let it drop. "It matters not who instigated this attack. They will meet their end soon enough. Let's be done with this and go. I have tracked Ryan's scent to a small city surrounding the big lake."

"Clearlake," Kai nodded. "It's on the eastern shore not far from Lakeport and Soda Bay."

The vampire nodded. "Aptly named, for what I smelled there was certainly as sweet as any fizzy, twenty-first century drink."

Kai coughed, and Lily slapped her hand down on her thigh. "See, this is what I'm talking about. Kai isn't used to you Rémy, and it's not because of your injuries. It's because you're a VAMPIRE." She whirled on her heel to look at Sean. "And I don't have to tell you why she won't even make eye contact with you."

She exhaled, hard. Glaring at both men. "Enough. If this search and rescue mission is going to be a success, and that's exactly what this is, search AND rescue, then stop intimidating the infantry!"

Rémy opened his mouth to speak, but Lily shushed him. The vampire raised an eyebrow, but his eyes sparkled with affection.

"I know it was unintended, Rémy, but that's not the point. Until Kai is comfortable with your brand vampires-gone–wild sense of humor, put a lid on it in front of her, okay."

Kai laughed, but the sound was more nervous twitter than giggle. "I guess I have been isolated out here in the woods."

Even Rémy cracked a smile. "Please do not take this the wrong way, my dear, but I can sense the blood pooling around the contusion at the back of your head. I could help you. One drop of my blood would cure your pain and speed your healing. I promise there will be no ill effects. In fact, the benefits would be most enjoyable."

She looked at him and blinked, but this time the color didn't drain from her face. "Maybe later, if my headache worsens."

Lily winked Rémy's way, and the big vampire lifted one shoulder and let it fall. At least he was dressed like a normal person, and not in his usual flamboyant eighteenth century style. Even his long golden hair was pulled back in a messy style ponytail with a side piece hanging loose over the scarred side of his face.

Sean bent over Ryan's pack, dragging Emily's alongside. "I think we should take their jackets and a spare set of clothes. It looks as though they were taken by surprise, and not given a chance to grab anything."

Lily didn't say it out loud but one look at Rémy's grim face and she knew her gut was right. They weren't given a chance at all.

They had been at Kai's for less than an hour, but it seemed forever. At least they knew Emily was still alive. Lily reached her senses to Em but found nothing but static. Sean had tried as well, and his jaw tightened at the nothingness on the other end.

When she questioned him he shook his head, and Lily knew it was the same kind of nothingness he felt when Jack had taken her hostage for Edward Parr just months before.

If Emily was dead, it would feel void. At least the nothingness they sensed was forced. That meant it was artificial and hiding something, and that something was Emily. Ryan was another story. Since he never got the chance to phase, there was no shifter path to connect. So his fate was a coin toss that left Lily's stomach in knots.

Kai was in the kitchen packing food and water when Lily interrupted. "We should take a first aid kid, and whatever pain meds you have. We don't know what we're walking into or what we'll find."

The older woman shoved the last water bottle into a side compartment of one of the two backpacks on the chair. She lifted one bag, letting it drop to the chair with a thud. "The men will have to carry these. Unfortunately, they're too heavy for both of us, but we are going to need the water."

"Pain meds?" Lily asked.

She gestured toward the cabinet above the toaster. "In there."

Lily went up on tip toe and took down a large red canvas first-aid bag and a plastic Tupperware container lined with short white pill bottle. "You have enough ibuprofen to dose a small village," she said, taking two containers from the set and putting the rest back.

"Well, we're isolated here, and the last few months there have been plenty of runaways coming through. I never know what shape they'll be in, so I like to be prepared," she answered with a shrug.

Lily slung the red medical pack over her shoulder, slipping the ibuprofen in through the side zipper. "An underground railroad for escaped shifters. Who would have thought we'd have the need in this day and age."

Kai's eyes were wet. "I help where I can, and that way I get news about my daughter. She's still on the mountain. Her father keeps her under constant watch."

"Why?'

"Because he's the Alpha, or he was until that woman showed up. She's got him so wrapped he forgets himself and his duty to his pride." Kai paused, her eyes assessing. "Do you really know who she is?"

Lily nodded. "All too well."

The four of them bundled into the Jeep, their supplies in the very back. "Are you sure you're okay to drive?" Lily asked, eyeing the older woman's head and then her eyes.

"I'm fine, darlin'. I may be a half-blood like Ryan, but I still heal like a shifter."

It took a while to get from the cottage to the main road, both Sean and Rémy riding shotgun on either side from the front and back, each watching and waiting for an attack. The cleared the off road and made it to the highway without incident but didn't get more than two hours out before Kai glanced at the gas gauge hovering near empty.

"We need to stop for gas. According to GPS, Mendocino National Forest is still a two hour drive. If we don't fill up now, we might be shit-out-of-luck later on."

Odds were even if the Jeep made it to the next town they wouldn't find an open gas station. Streets rolled up early in this neck of the woods. Clearlake was their best bet.

The town spread out on both sides as Kai pulled the car off the highway onto Lakeshore Drive, and within ten minutes they were parked at a pump.

Sean got out of the car to fill the gas tank. "Anyone need to use the restroom, now's your chance," he said, poking his head through the front passenger window, glancing between Kai in the driver's seat and Lily sitting beside Rémy in the back.

The lake that gave the town its name was only blocks away, and not far in the distance were the looming slopes of Mt. Konocti. Shadows played along the angles, creating dark and foreboding landscapes, and a chill had crept into the air.

With a population around fifteen thousand, Clearlake was considered a small city, but even so, the community wasn't that large, leaving Lily wondering where Rémy had fed, and more to the point, on whom?

Vampires for the most part were heartless in their supremacy, but Rémy had too much at stake in this to invite unwanted trouble. Especially the kind that carried a badge. She trusted him enough to believe he was divergent and discreet, at least in this situation.

Sean slid his credit card into the pump before unhooking the fuel hose. He uncapped the gas fill, inserting the metal nozzle. "I'm going to grab a cup of coffee inside, does anyone else want anything?"

"I'll go in with you," Lily said, grabbing her small backpack from the floor behind the front passenger seat.

"What about *him*?" Kai gestured to the vampire still sitting in the rear of the car.

Sean shrugged. "Rémy in a death sleep. It's what happens to his kind during the day. Though at his advanced age, he can withstand much more than a youngblood." He squinted toward the late afternoon sun. "Don't worry. He'll be up and raring to go soon enough."

Kai visibly shuddered. "I just hope wherever he went earlier was enough of a fill up to last."

"I hope so, too. Especially since humans are in short supply where we're headed." Lily gestured for Kai to follow, and the three of them headed into the gas station.

"Where are you all from?" the clerk asked handing Sean his change.

"Back east," he replied, pocketing his money. "Just out visiting friends and checking out the area."

The clerk was an older man with a receding hairline and a deeply lined face from too many hours in the sun. "Figured. Can't say you're out of luck for a summer rental. Usually everything's booked solid on the lake this time of year, but this year, not so much."

Sean shrugged. "That's the economy for you, I guess."

The man studied Sean for a moment, and then shook his head in a deliberate fashion. "I'm not one for taking local business away from my neighbors, but you've got two nice looking women with you, so I feel obligated as a Christian to warn you. We've had some problems in the area."

Lily walked over and took their bag from the counter, glancing between Sean and the clerk.

"What kind of problems?" Sean asked.

"We had a death early this morning. Local kid gone bad, if you know what I mean. Got mixed up with drugs or something and came home to mooch off his family. His poor mother just about reached the end of her rope. As it is the boy gave her ten stitches just last week, so I can't say as anyone is sorry to hear he ended up dead." He paused, his eyes darting past Sean to the door. "It's the way he died that's giving everyone the willies."

"What do you mean, the way he died?" Lily questioned, her stomach knotting.

"He was mauled. Can't tell if it was from a big cat or what, but that's not the scary part." The man licked his lips, his fingers reaching for a cigarette though the sign above his head clearly read no smoking.

He stuck the cigarette in his mouth and lit it taking a long drag and blowing the smoke out the side of his mouth. "The boy didn't have no blood in him, and what was on the ground under him weren't enough if you get my drift. It was like what killed him sucked him dry, too."

The man's hands shook as he took another drag.

"You said problems. Plural. Has this happened more than once?" Sean asked.

The clerk shook his head. "Lake County has run-ins with wildlife from time to time," he gestured toward the water and the mountains beyond. "But nothing like this." He waited, watching Kai walk toward the front counter. "You two ladies need to be careful," he nodded, pointing toward them with the cigarette wedged between his fingers, the smoke curling up toward the ceiling. "We've had two girls go missing without a trace. Both just about your age." He indicated Lily.

"How long ago," Kai asked.

"Over the past couple of months. The dead boy this morning makes three incidents, and his death just might kill this year's high season."

Sean took the bag from Lily and slipped his fingers beneath the cardboard carrier holding their coffee. "Thanks for the heads up. We appreciate the info."

"No worries, man. Take care," the clerk replied, stubbing out his cigarette on the bottom of his shoe.

Taking Sean's lead, Lily nodded once to the clerk and then turned to leave but paused looking back for a moment. "If you don't mind my asking, where did they find the boy's body?"

The clerk looked up, hesitating for a moment before dumping his cigarette butt into an empty soda can on the counter. "The parking lot at Main Street Bar and Grill." He pointed out toward the street. "Just follow Lakeshore. If you pass the turnoff for Olympic Drive you've gone too far."

"Thanks."

He watched her for a moment as she turned to leave. "Why do you want to know?"

She shrugged. "Just curious, that's all." Kai held open the door and the two walked toward the car.

"Not a word until we're on our way," Sean said, gripping the gas nozzle handle and gesturing for the women to get into the car. He squeezed the last few drops of gas from the end and then replaced the hose, taking his receipt.

Sliding into the front passenger seat, he found Kai's expectant look waiting for instruction. "Go. We have a lot to discuss. And I don't want to do it here."

"Sean, I really think we need to check out the parking lot where they found that kid's body."

"Lily, we're wasting time we don't have to waste. Plus, the last time you did this you were dizzy and nauseous for days. I need you healthy and sharp, not nursing a psychic hangover."

At his impatient tone, she gestured toward Rémy. "I'm not the only one who thinks it's a good idea. As for the side effects?" She shrugged. "If you and I stay linked I should be okay."

Rémy opened his eyes. "Our little witch is correct."

Sean's face was not happy. "What is that particular crime scene going to tell us that we don't already know?"

She tilted her head, a knowing smile crossing her lips. "Motive."

# CHAPTER
# EIGHTEEN

T he parking lot adjacent to the restaurant was empty except for a lone police car and a long stretch of yellow police tape cordoning off an area to the far left of the entrance. It wound around a copse of four tall trees and a green metallic looking fence.

"Nothing like a murder to put off business, eh?" Kai observed, but her pale cheeks spoke volumes about how freaked out she was despite her small attempt at humor.

"Stay in the car." The directive was aimed at the older woman. Lily opened her door and stepped onto the pavement. She looked around, keeping the police car in her line of sight.

Sean got out of the Jeep as well. "I'm right here if you need me," he affirmed, propping himself against the front bumper.

The vicinity was devoid of movement, and it was too quiet. Even the birds across the street at the waterfront park were noiseless, and traffic seemed non-existent.

Lily sent her senses out, but there was no sign of the duty officer or anyone else for that matter. The restaurant was shut up tight, and from vague images on the periphery she knew local detectives had finished their initial canvas.

Despite discordant variables their thoughts settled on the most convenient and logical explanation. Animal attack. The body was in transit to the county morgue for standard autopsy to try and identify the guilty species. "Yeah, good luck with that," she muttered to the transient flickers and closed the car door behind her.

Leaving a fresh crime scene unattended would never happen in Manhattan, but she wasn't there to question their luck or the competency of local law enforcement. Sean wasn't happy with her, so she needed to get out and back as quickly as possible.

The car door opened behind her, and Rémy stepped into the late afternoon sun. Lifting his hand to his eyes, he squinted, his nostrils flaring slightly.

"Rémy, it's too bright out here for you. Stay in the car with Kai. I've got this," she said, gesturing toward the Jeep.

He slid a pair of dark Ray Bans onto is face and shook his head. "I believe Kai would rather I didn't, and while I appreciate the concern for my well-being, I am nearly eight hundred years old, and the sun no longer poses a threat. I can smell Jenya from here. I want to see for myself what she is up to and why."

Sean nodded, slipping his own sunglasses onto his nose, and the three of them walked toward the line of yellow tape. Rémy rubbed the back of his neck, turning up the collar on his jacket against the sun beating on his back.

"Rémy, threat or no, there's no reason for you to make yourself uncomfortable. I can relay everything I find to Sean through our telepathic link. He can relay any impressions I find. I already know the boy's body is on its way to the morgue, and the police are satisfied with their pat conclusion. Case closed."

The vampire's definitive frown conveyed his resolute stance, despite the tiny beads of pink-tinged sweat across his forehead. Lily handed him a tissue from her pocket, and he mopped his brow streaking the soft white paper with red.

She ducked under the tape and walked toward the dried stain darkening the pavement at the center of the marked area. Squatting, she inhaled, holding her hand over whatever blood and debris remained. Most likely the bigger fragments had been collected as evidence and went with the body to the morgue for analysis. There wasn't much left on the pavement, but enough to give them the answers wanted.

A breeze lifted loose strands around Lily's face, and the various scents from the parking lot mingled, the sharpest a metallic tang of fresh blood and motor oil. Vertigo surged like a punch to her stomach, and she pitched forward.

*Sean...I need you.*

The urgency in her plea had him jumping the yellow police line with Rémy hard on his heels. Sean's fingers closed over her shoulder.

*I'm here, babe. Hold on to me.*

Gulping down air, she steadied her mind, focusing on the sound of Sean's heart and the thrum of his voice. Once centered, she reached out to the far edge of the residual patch, trailing her fingers across the circumference.

Images cascaded. A young man waited in the dark, alone. She tasted the sharp edge of his anticipation, his movements jumpy as he ran a finger under his nose. His tongue pressing repeatedly against the inside of his upper lip. He needed a fix.

Lily's head jerked around, her eyes moving to the sidewalk across the street. Rémy's gaze tracked hers, but there was no one there. She was clearly seeing something he was not.

"This isn't going to work," he announced, the tone and volume of his voice intruding on the psychic surveillance.

"Don't interrupt. You're going to make her sick," Sean replied, annoyed.

"I'm sorry, but I need to see what she sees, feel what she feels, and more importantly, smell what she smells. I need to take a few drops of her blood. That will be enough to give me a link to her thoughts."

Lily pulled her senses back. She heard Rémy as if listening to him through water, but his meaning was clear enough.

"Touch her and I will kill you deader than you already are," Sean's voice dripped with warning and menace.

"It's the only way, unless she takes my blood."

"I'm sorry, but that's not going to happen." Sean was resolute, and Liy moved to finish her mental canvas when Rémy's hand shot out and grabbed her wrist.

Sean's snarl echoed in the empty lot, and he moved like lighting yanking Rémy back. "Get your hands off my wife."

Rémy let go of Lily, putting both hands up. "I would never hurt her, Sean. That you think otherwise saddens me."

"I don't give a flying fuck, vampire. Lily is my alpha female. A shifter, and anything involving your blood is taboo."

Rémy looked from one to the other. "I understand your concerns, but secondhand impressions aren't going to do us any good. Jenya has taken my blood and I hers. We share a bond, but the link is hazy, the strand nearly dead. If I can get close enough to her essence, then I can read her emotions and perhaps even her thoughts."

Fists clenched Sean took a step forward. "Forget it. My wife is not walking around wearing anyone's mark but mine."

"I'm standing right here, or did you two Neanderthals forget?"

"Lily..."

She shook her head. "No, Sean. I don't want to walk around wearing any man's mark. I have a wedding ring that speaks to that, but so do you." She held up her left hand.

At Sean's less than happy exhale, she shifted her attention to Rémy. "If I take a drop or two of your blood, what will it do?"

Sean took a step forward, but Lily put a hand on his arm. "Let's hear him out, Sean. It might be okay. Neither of us knows the ins and outs of vampire relations. I want to know. This may help us get Emily back faster."

Sean's eyes narrowed, but he nodded once in agreement. The two of them turned toward Rémy, waiting.

"If Lily takes a little of my blood, no more than three drops, it will allow me access to the images she senses. Olfactory and visual impressions will hit us simultaneously, much like when she keeps the link open between you," the vampire said, gesturing between them.

"I don't like it." Sean said, shaking his head at Lily. "I don't like the idea of Rémy having access to your mind."

"Agreed." Lily nodded. "I don't want that either."

Rémy held up his hand. "You didn't let me finish. Three drops, no more, only allows me access to Lily's impressions, not her mind, and *only* if she permits. She will hear my call, and then she can refuse or grant me entry. I hold no sway over her, her thoughts, or her emotions. She remains in complete control. Any more than three drops and the game changes."

"If you're lying, I will kill you, and it won't be the kind of death you can rise from." Sean eyes were daggers.

"Regardless of the kind of deception you think my kind capable of, I am not foolish enough to lie to the Alpha of the Brethren. More importantly though, I would never lie to my little witch."

With a smile he lifted his index finger to one razor sharp canine, puncturing the tip. Black blood welled, and he held his finger over Lily's tongue allowing three small drops to fall.

She swallowed, and then looked up expectantly. "Well?" she asked.

"Well what?"

"I don't feel any different, should I?"

He laughed. "As I said, the amount is far too meager to alter you. You will not even carry my scent." He shifted his gaze to Sean. "Are we good?"

Sean's eyebrows inched together. "Good?" He blew out a long breath. "We'll see about that." He pressed a kiss to Lily's temple, his fingers trailing through her chestnut hair. *"Let's get this over with, okay. I've had about enough of the undead version of mastermind."*

With a smirk Lily squatted again, watching as Sean moved far enough back to let her work, yet close to keep an eye on Rémy.

She closed her eyes and inhaled, letting her fingers trail the cracked edges of the pavement.

Rémy stood to her left, and she felt him hovering at the fringe of her mind. "This one was no guiltless addict just looking to score," she said opening the channel for both Sean and Rémy.

Images swam again. Desperation licked at Lily's sympathetic nervous system kicking in her fight or flight response. Violence seeped from the boy's skin, and the stench of his addicted rage made Lily gag.

From his vantage point hidden by the trees, he tracked a lone girl to a bench overlooking the darkened beach. His body tensed at how easy it would be to take her money and whatever else he wanted from her. His crotch tightened at the thought of her struggling body, but his fingers closed over the twenty dollar bill in his pocket. Not tonight. His mother had been generous enough.

The boy spat, and Lily cringed at the memory of hard plastic hitting the middle-aged woman across the back of her skull trickled through to her senses. She squeezed her eyes against the cold satisfaction that cascaded from him standing over his mother's crumpled form while he rummaged through the woman's purse.

Lily dragged in a breath. Her head jerked up, and fear gripped her stomach. The hair on her arms rose and she sniffed the air. She was truly in his head. The boy's eyes darted to the beach, but the girl was gone. Instead Connor walked out of the shadows. Jenya behind him.

*"You looking to score, buddy?"*

The kid licked his lips, and Lily's throat tightened along with the memory. He nodded.

*"Good, so are we."*

Connor lunged. His clothes shredding as he took wolf form, his teeth sinking deep into the boy's neck.

Jenya's eyes flashed red. *"Connor, let me see him."* Her accented voice was soft and dulcet.

The wolf froze, answering her request with wet sloppy grunts.

She knelt, dragging a finger through the blood that spurt from his open veins, nothing but gurgling sounds emanating from his crushed windpipe.

*"Your blood smells like shit, you know that? My guess is you're not worth*

*my time."* She licked the blood from her finger, and her eyes flew wide. Her lips peeled back from her teeth and her nose flattened as her jaw elongated to accommodate long and dripping canines.

*"Honor thy father and mother, you piece of garbage!"*

With claw like hands she shredded his dirty jeans and most of his skin, sinking her teeth into his femoral artery. Hot blood coated Lily's throat and she dry-heaved.

Rémy groaned in her mind, his bloodlust showing red and black around his essence. Without warning Sean yanked Rémy from Lily's mind, and that instant they were gone from her head. She released the images, sinking to the rough pavement.

Sean knocked Rémy to the ground, his muscles bunched and ready to strike. Rémy's fangs receded, and his eyes cleared, but Sean kept him pinned until Lily got up and brushed off her clothes.

Shaken, she stood over both men. "Well, so much for your promise not to be a threat, Rémy. I guess the road to hell is paved with blood-lust as well as good intentions."

Rémy tried to sit up, but Sean shoved him back against the asphalt. The vampire exhaled, his eyes finding Lily's skeptical gaze. "I have no excuse. I was remiss in attempting this without feeding first. I am sorry."

Sean snorted. "You bet your ass there's no excuse. I think maybe you'd better take off on your own from here."

At the pained look on Rémy's face, Lily shook her head. "I'm in no danger, Sean. We need Rémy with us if we are going to enlist Jenya's help in freeing Emily and Ryan."

Sean's look was incredulous. "Her help? She's a fucking psycho, and you know it! Didn't you feel her crazy, or was watching her shred that kid not enough proof for you?"

Lily put her hand on Sean's arm. "Let him up, babe. There's a reason she's here, and it's not what we think or what she's led the cougars to believe."

Rémy nodded. "Lily is correct. It's a ruse. I felt it, but more importantly, I tasted it in her rage as she fed. It all makes sense now.

The Jenya I know and the Jenya we've found here. She will be an ally."

Sean let Rémy up, holding out a hand to help him from the ground. "I hope you're right, because I don't want be on the losing side and find out otherwise."

Smoothing his hair and ponytail, Rémy considered the two. "Perhaps it's time I shared a story with you..."

# NINETEEN

The door to the shed opened and a tall man with a full beard and long wild hair stepped over the threshold. "Come with me," he said eyeing Emily.

Ryan struggled to sit up, but the man waved him down. "Not you half-blood. Only the wolf."

Ryan's jaw tightened, but he was still too weak to move.

"I'll be okay. Don't worry," she said as the long haired man held the door open for her to follow.

The man smirked, a sarcastic laugh on his lips. "That's more than I can say for you," he shot back, giving Ryan a chin pop.

The door slammed leaving Ryan alone, but there was no telltale bolt shot or click of a key. A rough breath left his mouth, and he leaned back against the hay bales. Guess they really didn't think he was much of a threat. They weren't wrong. Injured, he was of no use to Emily or anyone else. Even if he still had his gun.

Now it was his turn to wait.

~

THE MAN LED Emily through a ring of cabins. From outward appearance the structures small. Not more than eight hundred square feet, or the size of a studio apartment. Each had a little porch at the front, with a low slung roof that jutted over the stoop.

A grassy square sat at the center of the ring. It seemed to be a public green of sorts, complete with a communal well. The sloping hills on either side of the property were dotted with more cottages, only these were built into the mountain's incline.

The sun was shining and the sky clear, and the air temperature chilly but not cold. Patches of snow still covered the ground in spots, and she wondered what this place was like in winter with the weather extremes typical for this elevation.

Most of the homes were modest and rustic, but a few sported satellite dishes so the cougars weren't as cut off as Kai led her and Ryan to believe. In fact, the cottages were very reminiscent of Kai's place, except these were all single story.

As the man crossed the square with her in tow, she noticed chickens and goats penned on the side of a few buildings. Children poked their heads out, sneaking a peak at her as she passed.

"They're curious about you," he said, heading between two of the larger buildings.

"Why? It's not like I have horns or three eyes."

He chuckled. "Nah. It's just besides the emancipator, you're the only other wolf we've got."

"You don't have me. You took me. There's a difference," she shot back, and he slid his eyes her way, appreciation clear in his blue eyed gaze.

"Is spunk something that's bred in wolf bitches, or did we just get lucky?"

Emily's lip curled in disgust, but she didn't respond. He snorted a laugh and took her elbow, pulling her toward a long rectangular building at the foot of the steepest slope.

"After you, princess." He gave her a blocky-toothed grin.

Emily ducked through the low threshold, surprised it was so small considering the cougars didn't appear to be that diminutive in size. The structure was set up like a Native American long house, and it was clear this was their meeting place.

A roughhewn log table sat horizontal to the length of the building, with five chairs across the back. A stack of papers and an open book were at the center in front of the largest chair. The emancipator's chair.

The man inclined his head, touching his finger to his forehead in deference and then ducked for the back door. "I trust I don't have to tell you what will happen to your friend if you bolt." His words were said as if an afterthought, but Emily knew better. It was a threat.

Split-log benches were set in tandem facing the table. Emily sat on the edge of the one closest, rubbing her arms against the chill. The floor was stone which added to the cool temperature in the room. She scraped her boot against the smooth surface, grateful she had presence of mind to shove her feet into her hikers just before the cougar charged through the guest room door at Kai's place.

A door opened and closed as she stared at her feet, and when she glanced up her mouth dropped to her boots.

"Hello, Emily."

"Delia! What are you doing here? Are you a captive? Are they collecting wolves or some crazy shit like that?" Emily stood, not sure if she should hug the woman or question her more. Her eyes dropped to the woman's hand, and how it rested on her burgeoning belly.

"You! You're behind this?"

Delia waved her hand in the air. "Who else?"

Emily sank back onto the bench. "Why?" Before Delia could answer Emily's eyes widened, and the pieces fell together. "You and Edward Parr. That's his baby you're carrying."

Delia leaned against the council table folding her hands above her belly, giving the bump a loving pat. "Good for you, Emily. You're not a stupid as the rest of them."

Throwing her hands in the air, Emily shook her head, dumbfounded. "I may not be stupid, but why here? Why the cougars? Why would you want to have your baby in this god-forsaken wilderness? Delia, you can't be that desperate for a pack."

The woman laughed. "Desperate? Emily, come on. Do I look desperate to you? I'm their queen. They do whatever I say because they know I hold their future within me. Edward's territory spread far and wide before Sean and his human bitch took him down. I admit he went a little too far when he started poisoning shifters, but he was trying to bring Sean down and purify the races at the same time."

Emily stood, staring Delia down. "My brother Jerard was not one to be purified. Our family is pureblooded wolf, descended from a line of Alphas. How does that work with Edward's purge? Rissa, too. His bio-genetic bug attacked her and her baby until my brother's human bitch, as you call her, came in and saved the day."

Delia took a step forward, rage bulging. "Your family has brought nothing but dishonor to the wolves. First you disrespect the Abenaki and refuse to marry your father's choice, and then Sean chooses a human over me as his alpha-female. Did you think you were brought here by mistake? It's all part of a plan I've been hatching since your brother humiliated me in front of everyone. Oh, the players have changed, but the end game is the same. I win. Leighton's lose."

Emily shook her head. "You're a liar."

Delia let one shoulder rise and fall. "Perhaps, but not in this. Does the name Davis ring a bell? As in the Sonoma County police department?"

Recognition dropped Emily's jaw, and her eyes narrowed. "The detective. He's a cougar?"

Delia snorted. "He wishes. No, he's human, but he provides me an invaluable service. He's my procurer. He sells me the female vagrants and illegal aliens that cross his path. Of course, he knows my specifications as to age and general health, blood type and such."

Anger shook Emily to the core, and her eyes flashed. In her condition, Delia wouldn't stand a chance if Emily phased for attack, but then again neither would Emily. In this instance they were both hindered by the same thing, and Emily wasn't about to risk losing

Ryan's baby before she even had the chance to tell him about it. As it stood now, those odds were slim at best.

"Take my advice and keep those pretty blue eyes of yours blue. If I see even a streak of yellow, you'll be sorry. I have guards posted outside. One word from me, and your boyfriend is a dead man. How you hooked up with a cougar is beyond me, but your feline preference will make it that much easier to pawn you off."

"I'm no one's pawn, Delia."

The woman chuckled. "Oh, honey. This is my chess game, and I will move you around, or knock you off the board as I see fit. Either you're an asset or a liability. It's your choice."

A knock on the door had both women turning. A girl came in holding the arm of a frail, older man.

"Ah, James. How wonderful to see you up and around! Please sit. I'm sorry to disturb your much needed rest, but I wanted you to meet an old friend of mine. This is Emily Leighton. I'm sure you remember my stories about her family. Her brother is the Alpha of the Brethren, the same man you were to meet before you're untimely illness."

Delia's tsk of unfortunate luck was so deceitfully sweet, it made Emily's teeth hurt.

"You are our beloved shaman, and as such I want to reward your service by honoring your family. I am giving Emily to your son Ethan, as his mate."

"What!"

The tense muscles in Delia's jaw belied her otherwise bored, yet polite, tone. "Another outburst, Emily and I'll have you chained. This is an honor bestowed on you. Ethan is the Alpha of this pride, so it's fitting. I haven't decided what to do about your friend, though. Perhaps, he would be a good match for Catori." She paused. looking at Emily. "Catori is Ethan's daughter, so you'll be one big happy family."

"I wouldn't be so quick to sell Ryan to the highest bidder, Delia. Then again, you were never one for thinking things through. What happens if that hybrid whelp you're carrying is a girl? You know a female can never be the Alpha. Even in the most evolved packs, it just isn't done. To entertain the likelihood, especially in a backwoods hell-hole like this is foolish at best."

Delia moved very slowly, her steps deliberate and her eyes cold, until she was a foot away from where Emily stood seething. "Why?"

Emily pressed her lips together, shaking her head. "Like you said, this is your game. You figure it out."

"Cole!"

A large man with scraggy pockmarked skin stepped through the door. "You called, ma'am?"

"Bring Connor to me."

Emily felt the blood drain from her face, and Delia's mouth spread into a grin. "You Leightons. Always thinking you know it all. However, I've got secrets of my own that will make your life hell. Connor knows you're here, and he's already thrown his hat into the ring for you. Something about unfinished business."

The man turned to leave, but hesitated. "Ma'am?"

Delia closed her eyes in disgust. "What?"

"The vampire hasn't risen yet, and you know how she gets when Connor isn't with her when she wakes up."

A long repulsed breath hissed between Delia's teeth. "I don't give a rat's ass about that fanged bitch. Bring him."

James's young helper skulked in the corner, trying to be as invisible as possible, but she was out of luck. Delia snapped her fingers and the girl jumped, actually curtseying when she came to a stop in front of Delia.

"See if the half-blood in the shed has recovered enough to be moved. I don't want him hurt, but if he can walk, I want him brought to me as well. Tell Sam to see to it."

The girl bobbed her head and then ran from the meeting room. Delia slid herself onto the council table, swinging her legs back and forth like a child. "This is so much fun. I love games of wit and parry. I only wish I could trade you for Sean and his new wife." Her mouth puckered at the word.

Emily didn't respond. Not giving an inch.

"Oh, I know all about it." She pulled an iPhone from the front pocket of her jacket. She held it up, shaking it from side to side. "My sister, the bitch that she is, was nice enough to text me pictures. I have to say your mother's dress did nothing for the human, but then what else could anyone expect?"

Emily stayed quiet. There was no way she was letting on that Sean and Lily were more than likely on their way here. Even so, they were too outnumbered, and Delia was completely batshit. The combo was not good. Their only hope was if Kai had people on the inside ready to help.

# CHAPTER
# TWENTY

E mily held her breath not knowing what to expect next. When
the door to the longhouse opened again, she braced herself. It
was only another young girl carrying a tray with food and a
pitcher of water. She put it down on the table, and then left without a
word.

Delia uncovered a plate of fruit and sliced cheese next to a basket of
fresh rolls. She plopped a strawberry in her mouth and chewed self-
ishly. When she finally swallowed, she paused while reaching for
another and then looked at James.

"Would you like me to bring you a plate, James? I know you can't
really help yourself." She shifted her eyes to Emily. "You, come make a
plate for him. He's our shaman and he's unwell. Show some respect.
You can make a plate for yourself, too." She smiled wide, gesturing for
Emily to get up.

The woman was certifiable. Manic at best. Friendly and accommo-
dating one moment and scheming, the next.

Emily pushed herself up from the bench and approached the table.
A quick nod from James gave her a little encouragement.

She filled two plates, carrying them both to where James sat quietly. Emily handed him the dish and then sat down beside him. She had no appetite, but she ate a little for appearance sake.

Delia stuffed her mouth, humming as she chewed. When done, she wiped her mouth and then pushed her plate to the side. "Being pregnant really gives you quite an appetite," she giggled to herself.

"Fucking nuts," Emily muttered, aimlessly pushing a few berries around on her plate with a wedge of cheese.

"You need to eat. If pregnancy is the reason behind her healthy appetite then you must be starved by this point." James alluded, silently to her still flat belly.

Emily's eyes widened, and she opened her mouth to reply but the old man's sharp look stopped her cold.

"Don't bother with small talk, Em. Since his stroke James can't really speak. Not that anyone listened to the old coot anyway." Delia waved them off, burping in the process.

James took Emily's hand and squeezed it. His eyes were kind, and the intensity of his gaze left her gut churning. She returned the gesture, but her heart dropped realizing the old guy probably wouldn't be able to help at all.

The far door opened, and Sam came in half carrying, half dragging Ryan beside him. "Here he is, boss. As requested." He tossed him on the ground. Ryan's body hitting the stone floor with a painful thud.

"What did I say about hurting him?"

"I didn't. He fell a few of times on the way over."

The corners of Delia's mouth pulled down as she raked her eyes over the dirty haired man. "Yeah, like prisoners fall down flights of stairs on their way to holding. Get out before I decide to escort you over a cliff!"

Sam actually bobbed his head, muttering an apology as he turned to leave, but not before he shot Emily a dirty look.

"Don't even think about it, dirtbag. She's not for you," Delia snapped.

Sam's head jerked around, and he glared at Delia. "I don't want her. You promised me Catori."

Delia slid down from the table and then walked to where Ryan groaned on the floor. "Help him up. I want him seated, not groveling. He's still a cougar, regardless of his parentage."

James coughed, clearing his voice. "His parentage may prove to be of interest to you, my dear."

Delia whirled on her heel. "When did you regain your speech?"

"Does it really matter? These days I don't have much to say. As you so eloquently put, who listens to the old coot, anyway."

At least Delia had the shame to blush, and she ducked her head for a moment before meeting the old man's eyes. "I was only joking, James. As our holy man, I hope you can forgive me."

The man blinked at her. "See to the young man, Sam. You heard Delia. Get him a chair and some water."

Sam didn't move at first, but when Delia snapped her fingers he walked around the side of the council table and dragged one of the heavy chairs forward. He hooked his arms under Ryan's and then hefted him onto the seat.

Delia waved Sam off, and when he left, she turned closer attention to Ryan, studying his face. The bite wound on his head was bleeding again from the impact on the floor. She walked to the tray and took a wad of napkins, shoving them at Emily. "Clean him up as best you can. I'll get Catori. She can help with medicinal herbs."

She left, and Emily dabbed at the wound which was luckily only bleeding from the surface. "Are you okay," she whispered.

"I hope so." He winced. "To wake me up the big guy decided to practice clogging on my back and chest. I think he broke a rib."

James stood, leaning on a knotty pine cane. "Allow me," he offered, extending a hand toward Ryan's chest.

Emily grabbed the old man's wrist, nearly knocking him over. She steadied him, easing up on her hold but didn't let go.

"I don't think I want you touching him. You already proved your allegiance when you dangled the little tidbit about Ryan's parentage to Delia. She's going to find out Edward Parr is Ryan's father, and when she does she'll have him killed."

James shook his head. "Not necessarily. You played your cards well, sowing doubt in her mind about the reality of her child becoming the Alpha. She's been asking me to divine the sex of her baby for months. It's a girl, but I haven't told her."

Ryan's eyes shifted to the old man standing lopsided in front of him. "If the baby is female, she won't have a leg to stand on politically. Her hard sell rhetoric won't be worth the breath she wasted spewing it. Why haven't you said anything?"

The old man shrugged, taking a seat again, but moving closer to Ryan. "Because I saw you coming. You're going to save us. It won't be easy for either of you. You will both be tested."

Emily crossed her arms in front of her chest and looked up at the low beamed ceiling. She exhaled, letting her gaze drift to the old man. "I feel for you and your people, James, but it's too dangerous. We're outnumbered. We don't know the lay of the land. We have no weapons, and Ryan is injured. I'll do whatever I have to do to stall Delia's crazy plans, but as soon as Ryan gets his strength back, we're out of here."

James shook his head, but the motion was deliberate, weighty.

"What aren't you telling us?"

"I can help you heal right now. You'll be full strength in a matter of hours."

Ryan exchanged looks with Emily before he turned his eyes to James's hopeful face. "How?"

The old man pulled a small vial from his coat pocket and held it out in his palm. "A gift. It's what helped me regain my strength."

Emily took the ampule from his hand and held it to the light. "Is this what I think it is?" she accused. Not sure they should trust him.

The shaman nodded. "Yes. I know it's taboo, but I added herbs and a special tincture to ensure there are no foul side effects." He patted

Ryan's hand. "It's up to you, but if you want a fighting chance you are going to have to trust me." He paused, lifting Ryan's chin to search his eyes. "So like your mother."

Ryan wrapped his hand around the older man's wrist, his grip soft but at the same time demanding. "You knew her?"

The old shaman nodded. A sadness edging his eyes. "Yes, my son. I knew her. I was the one who helped her escape."

Ryan's fingers tightened, slightly. "Son? Are you my father?"

The old man shrugged. "It's a possibility. Did your sister survive as well?"

The nod Ryan gave was sharp. "Yes. Though I never got to meet her. She died about six months ago. Edward's biological weapon back-fired, and the wolves he infected turned vicious. One escaped and killed her. She was best friends with Emily's sister-in-law."

The man sat. His face pained. "So much death. So much sorrow. I tried my best to keep Teresa safe. She was such a loving woman. So full of life and laughter. Your green eyes hold the same kind of depth. In my vision quests, I saw her blessed with two children. A girl and a boy. The girl was from one branch, the boy another.

"I'm not sure of the meaning inherent in my trance. It could've meant you were destined for different paths, or it could've meant you had different fathers. From the moment your mother understood Edward's plans she begged me for help."

The old man exhaled, running a hand over his forehead. "It doesn't matter anymore. You need to fulfill your destiny here, but the only way to do so is to become an accepted member of the pride. You have to embrace your parentage and allow the council to initiate a phasing ritual. Delia will never allow this unless she believes you are Edward's true son. Until you phase, your options are tenuous at best."

Emily handed Ryan the vial. "Drink it. I think we're going to need every bit of help we can get."

Ryan glanced at the vial in his palm. James covered Ryan's hand with his and whispered a chant. When the old man lifted his hand,

Ryan pulled the cork and swallowed the vial's contents. Coughing and sputtering, he handed the empty vessel back to James.

"Now we wait."

"WHERE IS SHE?" The door slammed open making everyone jump.

Delia looked up from the typography maps on Ethan's desk. "Connor, how nice of you to finally show up. I asked for you come to the meeting house, but that was hours ago."

"Don't play with me, Delia. Where is Emily?"

Delia folded the map and tossed it to the side with the others. "She's with Catori. I've promised her to Ethan, so she is preparing. The mating ritual is set for tomorrow night. Emily is in seclusion until then. No one sees her without my express permission."

The vamp-addicted wolf snarled. His eyes flashing to a blackish yellow before fading back to a rheumy blue.

Delia laughed. "You're pathetic, Connor. Your body is so polluted I doubt you could even phase. Your eyes can't even shift color. I wouldn't give Emily to you if you were the last wolf alive. I may hate her family, but even I wouldn't do that to one of my own regardless of my threats."

She stood, resting her fingertips on the desk. "Have Jenya come see me. I have a job for her."

Connor's eyes narrowed. "What kind of a job?"

A cold smile spread across her mouth. "I need her nose. She will be the one to verify certain claims made by our shaman."

"You mean the half-blood? I heard you were planning to mate him yourself. You do know he's been fucking Emily, right?" Connor sneered. "That mongrel cat's scent dripped from her cunt when they took her."

"Pfft. That was then, but Emily has graciously renounced all prior claims on Ryan, and acknowledges he belongs with me. After all, if James's claims are true, then the connection binding us is too strong to ignore. Who better to step in and raise my child than Edward's first born son." Delia leaned forward, pressing her swollen breasts together in a deliberate tease "After Jenya is through with him, all that remains is a phasing ritual. It's been arranged for tonight."

"I thought Ethan was the one in charge of all things cougar."

A deadly stillness came over Delia, and she turned her narrowed gaze on Connor. "Ryan is the rightful Alpha, and I will be his alpha-female. Anyone who gets in my way will be very sorry."

# TWENTY-ONE

T he road broke winding northward as they began their ascent into the mountains. An air of nervous anticipation settled on the group, but Rémy remained quietly staring out the window. His thoughts trying to make sense of everything Lily pulled from the crime scene.

"You're very quiet," Lily prompted. Though Rémy made the initial offer, no one pushed him about his history with Jenya.

The vampire nodded but kept his gaze on the dusky landscape. "I apologize. It is not my intention to be rude. Memories I thought dead and buried have resurfaced. Though I persuaded myself I could endure their weight, I confess I am no longer sure."

"Does this mean you've decided not to help us?" Sean asked from the driver's seat.

Kai curled up on the front passenger seat while they were still at the parking lot. The greenhouse effect of the sun through the car windows and her own lack of sleep had been too much for her and she fell asleep. No one had the heart to wake her when they got back to the car, so Sean took over driving.

"On the contrary. I will do everything in my power to help. If

Melissa lives, I have every intention of returning to New York with her intact. I will fulfill my duty to the Vampire Council, but I am not ashamed to admit I am apprehensive about seeing Jenya again."

"How long has it been since you last saw her?" Lily asked.

"Almost a century." The vampire cracked a smile at Lily's surprised expression.

"Don't look so taken aback, little witch. A century to the undead is a blink in time."

"Was that when you were injured? Ryan had mentioned something —" Her words clipped short, and she glanced down at the car's floor. "I'm sorry, I didn't mean to pry."

The vampire took her hand and lifted it to his lips. He inhaled her sweet scent, and the truth of her concern and interest washed over him like a cleansing breath.

He released Lily's hand and then turned in his seat to better address both her and Sean. "I said I would share our story, and it's time to pull myself from my musings and get on with it."

"Good, cos the suspense was killing me." Lily admonished with a wink.

Rémy cracked a smile. He shifted his gaze toward the darkening sky, and after a moment he closed his eyes. Memories flooded back unhindered, as rich, and alive in his mind's eye as if they happened only days ago.

"I was turned in the fifteenth century. The date and the exact year are immaterial. It was the time when the middle ages overlapped the age of rebirth, or what you know as the dawn of the renaissance. It was a time of great excess. Of exploration and invention, and in that time, the arts flourished. Including the art of war and political intrigue. It was the time of Michelangelo and Machiavelli, of the Medici and the Borgias.

"France had suffered years of war and plague. Mostly because the king sought to acquire the two wealthiest realms of the time. The Duchy of Milan and the Kingdom of Naples. It was during the midst of this plague that my twin brother, Claude, met his dark end. He was turned as he fled Naples, a deserter from the French armies besieged by the disease infested city.

"His maker thought it a grand gesture. A jibe at the universe to leave his victims with a single spark of life. Not enough to prolong their human existence, but just enough to tease ingress into immortal darkness."

Rémy opened his eyes at that point, a glum smile on his lips. "I know I sound melodramatic, but I need to impress upon you how bewildering it is to be left with an unquenchable thirst you don't comprehend. To have your eyes and ears assailed by sights and sounds the like no human has ever encountered, and of course, no one to warn against the painful sun."

Lily put her hand on the vampire's arm. "There's no judgement here, Rémy. If more of us shared our stories, then perhaps we'd see we're more alike than not."

"Your strength never ceases to astound me, little witch. Especially in one so small." He patted her hand, and then looked out the window again. "Claude stumbled through his new existence. How he survived his way back to France is still somewhat of a mystery. My guess is there was so much death and destruction, no one noticed a few more bodies along the way. He fed where he could and made it to the coast, stowing away in the belly of a ship, subsisting on rats."

"Rats?" Distaste clear in Lily's voice.

Amused, Rémy slid his eyes to her again. "What was it you used to say? Any port in a storm?"

"Lily hasn't been a supernatural long enough to grasp what the words *beyond nature* truly mean." Sean chuckled. "I can't wait for her to get down and dirty in wolf form. She's not quite there yet."

A lopsided smile formed on the vampire's lips. "So you decided to race the moon after all. Brava, little witch. Watching you phase will be one of the highlights of this trip. The moon may no longer be full, but I think at this elevation its draw will be strong enough."

"Not this trip, Rémy." Sean interrupted. "Phasing will be hard for Lily at this point because she is not a blood shifter. It takes way too much energy, and it can be dangerous. Eventually, she'll be able to phase as seamlessly as I do, but until then I don't want her to risk it."

Lily pulled a bottle of water from the side of her backpack and cracked the top. "I think I've been doing pretty well, considering."

"No doubts there, love." Sean blew a kiss into the rearview mirror. "While practice does make perfect, it's still out of the question. Not here, not now, and definitely not for Rémy's entertainment."

The vampire's laugh was thick and throaty. "Relax, my furry friend. My little witch is much more than just a means of entertainment. I cherish her dearly and would gladly rip out the heart of anyone who tried to harm her."

"Glad to hear it. I may need you to live up to that promise once we get where we're headed."

Lily exhaled an impatient sigh. "Okay, you two. I'd like to hear the rest of the story if you're done."

"Me too," Kai said, sitting up and stretching. "Rémy's voice is like a drug. So deep and musical. I kept my eyes closed while you spoke, and my head buzzed with my own recollections. It was like listening to the legends of my tribe as a child in Arizona. All that was missing was the crackle and pop of a bonfire."

Lily passed the older woman a bottle of water and a small bag of trail mix, and then nodded for Rémy to continue.

"Well then, miladies." The vampire chuckled at the two women. "Where did I leave off?"

"Rats," Kai replied, making a face "And for the record. I have been phasing since the day I turned sixteen, and I have never eaten a rat or any other animal while in bobcat form. That's just gross."

"Amen, sister." Lily held up her hand for a high five.

"You've got a strong aura, Kai. I would have sworn you were a bigger cat," Sean added.

Rémy coughed. "Do you wish me to finish my story, or are we back to discussing the pros and cons of feasting in the raw?"

"No, no." Kai laughed out loud. "By all means, finish the story."

"Good. Like I stated, my brother survived on rats and whatever else he found in the ship's hold, including one or two of the crew. He made it to the port of Marseilles and then found his way home to Avignon. As you can imagine Claude was much altered. He stumbled through the city's ramparts and found our home, but when our father saw him he turned him away in revulsion. Much like your reaction when I mentioned the rats.

"Claude cried out for my father, but the man refused him. He was always a cruel man. He was a merchant, dealing in imports from the east and had grown rich. As his wealth grew, so did his cruelty. Especially to our mother who he blamed for hindering his social climb.

"She was a dear woman of simple stock, but he broke her heart and eventually she died of neglect. My brother and I never forgave the man. So when I heard Claude crying in the alley beneath my window, I ignored my father's edict and opened the door to welcome him home.

"He was so changed, it frightened me. Father was enraged when found Claude huddled by our kitchen fire. He struck Claude with one of the fire irons. I tried to stop him, and in our struggle my father was cut. Blood flowed, and Claude couldn't contain himself. He attacked the man, ripping his throat out.

"In a blood-infused rage, Claude swept through the house killing everyone. Our stepmother, the servants, even the dog. I ran from the house in horror, but when I returned he was seated in front of the cold hearth with the dog on his lap, weeping.

"He looked up and with blood tears asked if I still loved him. When I answered yes, he ran from me. It was two years before I saw him again. Claude returned, lonely and longing for comfort and love. I foolishly agreed to take his blood, thinking we would be together and continue the life of adventure we dreamed when we were boys. In my naiveté I had no idea what my decision meant until it was too late. Claude changed me, but it was my choice."

Hmmm. "I thought you and Sebastién had the same sire." Lily raised an eyebrow at the new information.

"We shared the same sire once removed," Rémy clarified. "The vampire who sired Claude also sired Sebastién. He was an old one, like

Carlos's sire, Dominic. When a vampiric blood line is that ancient, it can imbue strength, but with that strength comes the risk of madness. Claude and Jenya suffered the latter. I was lucky."

"Is that why you are so different from the other vampires? Or is it because you gave your consent?" Kai asked, her tone mesmerized by the story.

Rémy shrugged, making the innocuous gesture seem regal. "I suppose both are key. Claude suffered at the hands of his maker through neglect, and in turn made Jenya suffer. I was different than Claude. I knew he loved me, but there was a growing malice within him. We left Avignon and traveled, but the farther afield we went the more he seemed to enjoy the kill. He lived for the cruelty he could inflict. I tried to speak to him of it, but he would only laugh and call me weak."

Rémy ran a hand over his forehead and asked for water. Lily handed him her bottle and he took a sip. Kai's eyes widening as he did.

"Don't look so shocked, my dear. Vampires can often tolerate certain human foods. Water is the easiest, as it is one of the main components of blood."

"Go on, Rémy. You were saying..."

# CHAPTER
# TWENTY-TWO

Remy took another draught from Lily's water bottle. He wiped each corner of his mouth with his knuckle and then continued the story. "Afterward, Claude and I found ourselves in Paris. Even then the city was glittering, despite the crowds and the filth.

"The parties and the court were filled with perversions that delighted Claude. I found myself growing more and more disgusted, so I immersed myself in books. I mentioned Machiavelli earlier. His work *The Prince* fascinated me to no end, as did his treatise on war and politics. Then the unthinkable happened.

"Claude attacked a member of the royal family. Her nickname was La belle Rouhet. Louise de La Béraudière, mistress to the king. Though the woman lived, the scandal was too much. So much so even the French covens wanted nothing to do with Claude. He was exiled."

"Exiled?" Lily remarked. "How does one exile a vampire?"

Rémy shrugged. "The King's court didn't exile Claude. The Parisian Council of Vampires did. They sent him to the new world. To New France. What we know today as Montreal and Quebec. I was forbidden to follow. Claude was bound in silver and placed in a box for the overseas journey, with council minions there to release him once he arrived.

"At that time, Montreal was a place of disease and death, so Claude fled west to the wilderness. He subsisted on the blood of native peoples and large predatory animals. Through our blood link, I sensed my brother's descent into madness.

"I broke ties with the Parisian council and tried to find Claude, hunting him the same way one would track an animal. He was already dead when I found him in the cabin outside Sitka, Alaska."

Rémy told them about Jenya's arrival with her family as part of the Russian exploration into the maritime fur trade in Alaska. He recalled Claude's degeneration and the torture and indignities she suffered at his brother's hand.

"I saw her through my brother's eyes as I tracked him. She was beautiful. Fine boned, with a heart-shaped face, long ebony curls, and eyes so dark they seemed fathomless. As if they held the secrets of the universe. Despite his treatment, she managed to find happiness for a while in the beauty of the forest, but eventually he broke that in her as well."

"You fell in love with a girl you never set eyes on." Kai's words were a validation, not a question.

Rémy nodded, and a tired sigh left his mouth. "Every scream. Every time he bled her, I saw her pain. Watched her die a little more on the inside each day. Claude's apathy leeched into my skin, and as he reveled in inflicting pain, I suffered. The ice of it sluiced through my veins, and my own skin felt as if being flayed from my body. I tried to influence him through his dreams to release her, but he was beyond reach. My heart broke for Jenya each day I couldn't be there to stop the monster Claude had become. When I finally reached them, it was too late."

Rémy pulled the walrus tusk from his inside pocket. "I pulled this from my brother's chest, watching my own reflection flake to dirty ash before my eyes. On the outside we were identical in every way, but polar opposites in nature. I left the cabin knowing there would be nothing to bury, and anyone who found the location would think it a deserted poacher's lair."

"Have you been carrying that with you all this time?" Kai asked.

Rémy turned the broken tusk over in his hand, his fingers brushing the smooth ivory. "No. I gave this to Ryan when he agreed to help me the night of Lily and Sean's wedding. I found it in his bag at your house." He gestured to Kai with the pointed tip.

"How did Jenya have enough strength and presence of mind to best Claude? A sane vampire is a force incarnate, but an insane one has got to have the same power and then some," the older woman countered.

"Jenya grew strong on the blood he fed her, and eventually it forced a conversion, but not before she killed him." He held the tusk up for them to see. "I knew I had to find her and try to make things right. To explain the best I could and show her a different way of living." He shook his head. "Jenya ran from me in horror the minute she saw me. I had the same face as the man who tortured her for two years. She fled into the woods, running from the specter of the monster she thought she killed."

"What happened to her? I thought you said she was responsible for what happened to your face?" Lily asked.

Rémy explained about the Tlingits and their survival march. "Jenya read the minds of tribe elders, and knew they planned to club the infants and small children like seal pups. Amid the blood and the screams, something snapped inside Jenya, and she attacked, slaughtering the lot of them.

"I tracked her to the western shore, following her as she made her way south to the Russian settlement near Fort Ross. She tried to kill herself, and it was then that I found her. For six months we lived together in a secluded cabin. I nursed her as best I could. Her broken body healed almost overnight, but her broken spirit..." his voice drifted off.

"Six months is a long time. You must have made progress with her, at least enough for her to trust you," Sean commented.

"You're right. She did grow to trust me, but every day I saw how hard it was for her to look at me and not see Claude. It was a long and arduous journey, with many steps forward but just as many back. I loved her and wanted to make her happy. Not because I felt guilt over Claude. He was responsible for his actions and whatever judgment he reaped in the next life. If we had remained alone, I think Jenya's mind would have healed.

"She wanted no exchange with people, so we lived on large preda-tory animals. Until one night while out for a hunt, we came across a trapper's camp. Animal skins hung in bloody ruin from the trees, their carcasses thrown in a rotting pile, discarded. Jenya became enraged at the waste. I calmed her and we finished our hunt.

"Later that night she crept back to the camp. She heard a sound like the mewling of a cat, and as she crept closer she saw the trappers had a small child. A tribal child of about ten or eleven years old tied down. She was beaten and bruised, and blood covered her inner thighs. I found her as she lunged. In her rage for that child, her fury for her own suffering boiled over and she shredded those men in a fury that seethed hotter than the fires of hell. She ripped them piece by piece, letting every exquisite moment of agony and horror linger before she ended them.

"I wiped the child's memory and cleaned her up the best I could. Daylight was coming, and though I knew I could withstand the early rays, Jenya could not. I brought her back to our cabin, but she begged me to take the child back to her family. I couldn't refuse, but when I got back to the cabin, Jenya had bled herself to the point of extinction.

"I slit my own wrist and fed her from my own veins. My strength surged through her even as my own depleted. I lay with her in a near death sleep until I woke for the evening. Jenya was gone. I was still very weak, and I thought she'd gone to hunt.

"When she came back she didn't look right. Her eyes were wild and her hair disheveled and full of twigs and leaves. I called her name, but she didn't seem to hear. I struggled to stand and called her name again. This time she came to me, but when I put my hand on her shoulder she lashed out, ripping the side of my face. Blood dripped from the deep score marks that ran from my eye to my jaw, and my torn flesh hung loose and raw. She shrieked at the sight of me, breaking the furniture and tearing at her own hair. I shouted for her to stop but that only made her more distraught. She grabbed a straw broom and ran for the fireplace. She burned my face as I struggled to try and stop her before she burned us both into true death. She struck me with the broom's handle across the side of my head. I crumpled to my knees, and it was too late. The cabin was engulfed in flames in a matter of minutes.

"Jenya was gone, and I had to go to ground to heal for weeks. The scars so evident on my face are because of my weakened state when injured. I barely had enough blood in my body to survive. I didn't chase Jenya after that. I licked my wounds and picked up the pieces of my life."

Lily put her hand on the vampire's arm, his whole body slumped in exhaustion as if he'd relived all his anguish again through the retelling.

"You can't blame yourself, Rémy. This is not your fault. Maybe Jenya needed to find a way to deal with her pain and her guilt. You saw the same thing I did at the crime scene. She's only here to keep Connor in line. She's his keeper, but not for the reasons we thought."

Sean looked in the rearview mirror at Lily and she nodded. "It was there in the images. Jenya hunts, but she doesn't kill randomly. She pinpoints criminals who abuse women and children."

Rémy agreed. "It's why she took Melissa. I found out after I called you that Jenya rescued the girl from a Chinese blood brothel. She had been taken after she left the protection of Carlos's shadow house. Jenya saved her, and by all accounts Melissa followed her here of her own volition. It all makes sense now. Jenya has found a way to live with her hurt by being a modern day savior.

"I know Julian wants Melissa, and I have every intention of taking her to back to New York, but only so she can escape her embroiled fate. If she doesn't want to be with Julian, then I will offer her sanctuary and my protection."

"Agreed. The poor girl did not plan to go from a vampire auction block to one run by a crazed shifter." Lily squeezed his arm. "You are a good man, Rémy. Eight hundred years hasn't changed that, and I don't think any amount of time will."

Sean nodded in the mirror. "I second that but hang onto your hats people because I think we've hit the end of the road. Literally."

They had been driving on packed dirt since they turned onto Elk Mountain Road. From there Sean navigated the twists and turns up the mountain to Bear Creek and three different rural forest routes. Now there was nowhere left to drive. Sean pulled the Jeep over and the four of them got out.

Night had fallen, and the temperature had dropped significantly, and Lily pulled on a shearling lined jacket and a hat and gloves.

"It's hoofing time from here," Kai said, opening the hatch and pulling out her backpack.

Sean came around and took two of the heavier packs, sliding one over each shoulder. "Let's hit it. Maybe we can do some damage under the cover of darkness."

Closing the car's doors, the four of them headed out. Rémy with a bemused smile at choosing to walk instead of fly. Sean took up stride beside the vampire while Kai and Lily walked behind.

"Would you like me to do an aerial run and see if I can find the camp?"

Sean shook his head. "I want to press on. We're all supernatural and have no problem seeing in the dark."

"Sean, maybe it would be better if you and I phased. We could cover more ground in animal form. I can run for miles as a cat but as a human I quickly feel every one of my forty-seven years. I don't want to slow us down." The forest was alive with noise and movement, making Kai's suggestion all the more appealing.

"Lily can't phase fully yet. It's too dangerous for her to risk it," he replied, shaking his head.

"I could fly with her as I did in Central Park. I will need a few undead moments, though, to— how is it you say— fuel up?" Rémy countered with a wicked grin.

Sean shifted the pack further onto his shoulder. "What about our gear? Kai and I wouldn't be able to carry it. Would you be able to take some of it and still safely carry Lily?"

Rémy laughed launching himself to the top of one of the tall pines. "Like a bag of feathers. Just give me a chance to feed." He jumped up and down on one of the larger branches, bending it like a springboard and vaulted into the sky.

"I'll never get used him doing to that," Lily said, sliding her arm around Sean's waist.

He chuckled watching the black sky swallow Rémy's silhouette. "Me neither."

# TWENTY-THREE

"*Knock, knock.*" A softly accented voice called from the screen door.

"Who is it?" Catori called, poking her head through the kitchen doorway.

"Jenya." The voice was soft and musical.

Flipping a dishtowel over her shoulder, Catori walked to the door but didn't open the latch. "I don't know, Jen. Showing up before the sun has even set? Getting a little rebellious don'tcha think?"

The vampire's dark eyes brightened, and her pale face seemed to glow in the late afternoon sun. "People already think you're a blood donor, so what the hell." She let a hint of fang dip below her lip.

"Cute. You might want to tuck those in if you plan on getting past my front porch."

The dark haired vampire pursed her lips, a smirk teasing a corner of her mouth. "I'm just teasing, Cat. Please open the door."

Catori shook her head. "You haven't answered my question yet, so I can only assume you're not here to see me."

"Astute as always. No. I am not here to see you, however much I enjoy your company. I need to speak with the wolf."

Catori frowned at the vampire's obvious bait. "That's not going to happen, and you know it."

Jenya spread her hands on the other side of the screen door. "If the mountain won't come to Mohamed—" Her voice tinkled like bells. "If you don't let me see her, Delia will end up bringing her to me. Don't make this harder than it already is for the girl, Catori. Do I need to remind you your fate is still in the emancipator's hands. From what I hear, Sam has... what is the mountain slang? Staked his claim. He wants you badly, and like you, Liam can't say a word let alone complain."

Catori exhaled, her eyes narrow and hard, but she unlocked the door handle and pushed the screen open.

The vampire smiled wide, full fang tips in view. "Why thank you, Catori. Regrettably, I have no stomach for tea, but if you're willing to offer an alternative libation, I might be persuaded to partake."

Catori made a face, pointing the way toward the kitchen. "Sorry. I'm fresh out of O-neg. I guess water will have to do you fine."

A snort of laughter eked from the vampire's nose.

"Well, that's a first. Sort of humanizes you a bit, Jen."

An unnatural flush stained the vampire's cheeks, and her embarrassment bubbled up in a quiet laugh. She rubbed the end of her nose with the side of her index finger before taking a seat at Catori's kitchen table. Lips soft, she smoothed the yellow and orange floral tablecloth with her palm.

"Have you seen Liam today?" The casual question rolled off her lips, but Catori knew she wasn't fooling anyone. Especially not Jenya.

The two had formed a tenuous friendship, and when the vampire offered to be the go between so she could see Liam, Catori didn't hesitate. Though maybe she should have.

"Sam keeps Liam busy running the perimeter. I can get him a note if you wish, but I don't think it wise for you to try and see him tonight. Everyone is on edge. Delia specifically. She's expecting trouble, or at least guesses something is up."

Catori nodded slowly. "Okay."

"Where is the wolf?"

Catori glanced down the hall to the closed door across from the tiny bathroom. "She has a name, you know. Emily is in seclusion. Why does Delia want you to talk to her?"

"She doesn't. I want to talk to her."

An annoyed frown bit into Catori's forehead. "So why did you say she did?"

"It's a matter of semantics." Jenya shrugged. "Delia wants me to give Emily's boyfriend the sniff test. She's asked me to verify if James was telling the truth about Ryan being Edward Parr's son."

Catori exhaled again. "So? What has that got to do with her?"

Jenya rolled her eyes, her hand coming down hard on the tabletop. "Don't be thick, Catori. Delia wants to mate with the half-blood if she's satisfied he's Edward's true son. She knows it's the only way the pride will accept him, and it's the only way she can insure her place as queen bitch. Why else would she promise Emily to your dad? She needs the wolf out of the way."

Confusion shadowed Catori's face, and she sunk into a kitchen chair across from Jenya. "Is he Edward's son?"

"How would I know? I'm a vampire. Not a bloodhound."

Catori snorted. "Now there's a joke."

"Haha. Can we stay focused here?"

"If you can't puzzle out Ryan's sire, then what can you tell?"

Jenya blew out a long, sweet, scented breath. "Not much. Obviously he smells like a combination of cougar and human." She sniffed for effect. "If Edward Parr were still alive, I might be able to catch a whiff of something similar, but not from the paltry piece of clothing Delia shoved under my nose. If her baby was born I might be able to sense kinship, but that won't happen for months yet, and the man doesn't have months. He's got hours. That's why I need to see the wolf."

Catori made a face.

"*Emily.* I need to speak with Emily."

The woman hesitated, but then got up and went to knock on the bedroom door. When Emily opened it a crack, she whispered something and then turned around and walked back to the table.

"Well?"

Catori slid back into her seat. "I would've bet you could hear that a mile away."

"Wow. Stereotype much?"

Catori waited.

"Fine. I heard it, but I wanted you to tell me anyway."

Drumming her fingers on the table, Catori considered her undead friend. She was tiny, with long dark hair that curled to the small of her back. Her dark eyes mesmerizing enough to give her already mysterious lure even more appeal.

"You know your speech patterns are more snarky teenager than two hundred year old vampire."

Jenya leaned forward, her eyes closing to a sexy half-mast. *"Ya mogu vypit' tvoyu krov' za sekundu no u menya bolit zhivot iz za bol'shogo kota"* Blowing Catori a kiss, she sat back in her chair and laughed.

"Hilarious. What did you say, or don't I want to know?"

"I said I could drink you dry in seconds, but big cats give me indigestion."

"Nice. And I thought you said you were on our side?" Catori got up to open the fridge for two bottles of water.

"I am, and don't forget it." The vampire replied, taking one of the bottles and putting it down beside her.

Emily cleared her throat, standing at the entrance to the kitchen.

"Oh! Hey, Emily." Catori pushed her chair back, scraping the metal feet against the planked wood floor. "This is Jenya, but you already know that."

Emily bent her head once. "I suppose it's nice to finally meet you. I've heard a lot about you from Rémy."

The vampire licked her lips, her eyes narrowing to slits. "Rémy?"

Emily leaned on the doorjamb crossing one leg over the other. "Yes, he's friends with my brother and sister-in-law. He was the one who asked my detective friend to help find you."

She stood up. "Rémy is searching for me?"

Emily shrugged. "In a way, yes. The girl you took? Melissa? She's very important to a couple of Rémy's friends. Perhaps you know them. Carlos Salazar? Julian Trevelyan? He, and everyone else, are a little curious as to how Melissa ended up here with you."

Catori's eyes moved from one to the other, not sure what to do. "*Uhm*, maybe this wasn't such a good idea."

Emily took a step toward the young cougar, putting her hand on her arm. "It's fine. The last thing I wanted was to make you uncomfortable in your own home, especially when you've been nothing but kind since Delia sentenced me to house arrest. You said Jenya was a friend and someone we could trust. Unfortunately, that's not the story I've been told."

Jenya chewed on her lip watching the exchange.

"Okay, Em. Well, now's your chance to decide for yourself instead of relying on hearsay." With a nod to Jenya, Catori walked toward the hallway, gesturing to Jenya she'd be in the living room.

"Why did you do that?" The vampire asked, dubiously.

Emily pulled Catori's chair out from the table and sat. "Why not? I think I've just shown that I know you a little better than you know me. You obviously came here to either tell me something or ask me something. So what is it?"

Suspicion bloomed in Jenya's mind, and she sat back in her chair. "Who is Ryan? What is he to you? And why are you really here?"

"To the point. I like that. To answer your questions in order, Ryan is a half-blooded cougar whose father, as far as we know, was a sociopath bent on trying to control the supernatural world. He is my lover and my friend, and I already told you our reasons for being here."

Jenya leaned forward again. "As far as you know his father was a sociopath? I assume you're referring to Edward Parr."

Emily rested her elbows on the table linking her hand together. She nodded. "James informed us there's a possibility he might be Ryan's dear old dad as well. It seems Ryan's mother Teresa had a hard time adjusting to life as a brood mare. James was her only solace. James and her friend, Kai. Together they helped her escape."

Jenya looked down at the table. Her fingers tracing the edges of the floral pattern. "What did Rémy tell you about me?"

Emily leaned back. Her gaze sharp. "The truth as far as he knows it. If you have anything to add or rebut, I'm all ears."

The vampire's head jerked up, and she fought the urge to lash out. She dropped her gaze again before lifting her eyes to meet Emily's steady stare.

"I'm not what I was," she began, her voice small. "Rémy and I haven't set eyes on each other for over a century. He no longer knows me the way he thinks he does. I've made mistakes, but I've also learned from them."

"Does that include kidnapping innocent humans, or do we have bad intel on that, too?"

Jenya's mouth pressed to a thin, harsh line, and blood dripped from her lower lip. "Intel?" Her tongue darted, swiping the trickle of red into her mouth.

Emily pursed her lips, inhaling slowly through her nose. "That was hostile, and I apologize. I was referring to the story Ryan and I were told before we came. Is it true or are there mitigating circumstances?"

That Rémy thought her capable of plucking someone off the street like garbage threatened to shatter her composure, as well as her heart, but she'd never show weakness in front of this shifter.

"Respectfully, I'm not about to explain my past, or my demons, to you, regardless of the secrets Rémy chose to share. I am what I am, and I can't change the things I regret. However, I've learned to keep the past in the past, and not allow it to govern my future. In the years since Rémy and I parted, I have spent the last century keeping young girls safe from monsters.

"Your new friend Catori is about to be mated to someone more animal than man. I need to do what I can to stop that. Whether you want to admit it or not, you need my help as well. Ethan only wants power, and right now that power is Delia. Getting you is a consolation prize, and he's not happy about it."

"Okay, so you're a vampire human rights defender. That's impressive, but what has that got to do with Ryan?"

"Delia plans on making him her mate."

"I know."

Jenya swore a blue streak in Russian under her breath. "And you don't care?" She inhaled, and her eyes became slits. "Considering your condition?"

Getting up from the table, Emily slammed her hands flat. "Why is it everyone can tell I'm pregnant except the baby's goddamned father! I suppose you can tell by the way I smell, right? James knew because he's some kind of hoodoo visionary."

"You didn't answer my question."

Emily folded her arms at her chest. "Of course, I care. If I tell Ryan now, he'll never agree to the mating ritual. If he doesn't agree, Delia will never allow him the rite of passage to phase."

Catori poked her head through the door. "I'm sorry. You two were getting kind of loud. Did you just say Ryan can't phase unless he has some sort of rite?"

Emily nodded.

A huge smile broke across the young cougar's face. "That is pure bullshit. If it's in him to phase, all he needs is a catalyst. It will happen, regardless. The rite was only instituted to help the young ones to manage their animal. I'm not sure if it is the same with wolves, but for a young cougar there's a lot of power and strength that courses through a body during a first phase. Teens sometimes have a hard time adjusting. Ryan is a full grown male. He should be fine."

Emily nibbled at the corner of her mouth. "I suspected as much, but what do I know? Wolves have something similar. It makes sense that it's propagated bunk. What better way to keep the young ones in line, then to tell them they can't come into their own without the pack's help. I remember when Connor phased. It's risky, and not all wolves survive."

"It's the same for us cats. Maybe the risk was another reason for holding a rite of passage."

Jenya swung her gaze around to Emily again. "You know Connor?" The vampire tilted her head, and her gaze took on a thousand mile stare. When her eyes went wide she nodded. A knowing smile on her lips. "You! You're the bitch in heat we ran into at the hotel in Boston!"

Emily winced, her cheeks flushing red.

"I'm sorry." Jenya reached out to apologize. "I didn't mean for it to come out the way it did. Connor was so upset that night. He disappeared later on, and when found him he was pacing the floor outside your hotel room..." Her eyes widened even more. "You're the one who wouldn't marry him."

Emily folded her arms even tighter. "I was being forced to marry someone I didn't love. I wasn't about to shackle myself for life and be miserable."

"I'm not blaming you. Though, I can't say the same for me, *moy dorogoyov*. Connor was broken when we met. I thought I could help, but he is too consumed with his own pain. I can't reach him, so I can't help him to let go and move on. Now I keep him with me out of obligation. I only came here because we ran into Delia not long after we saw you in Boston. She coerced him to help her with her plans. Besides power, vengeance is at the heart of her actions. She wants retribution on your brother almost as much as Connor wants payback on you." The vampire winked. "See? I know things about you, too."

"So you're only here as a what? A spectator?"

The vampire shook her head. "No. I'm here to keep Connor in check."

"I don't understand." Emily paced in front of Catori's orange Formica countertop." Ryan told me about the body in the morgue in Santa Rosa. It was a woman, and the markings had your signature all over them."

Jenya nodded. "That woman was selling her own children to pedophiles. Two little girls and one little boy, ruined. I made sure she suffered before she paid for her actions. I tracked her for months because she was pregnant when I first found out what she was doing. I wouldn't hurt an unborn innocent, but once she delivered, her ass was mine. Now those children are safe with their grandmother. I wiped their memories, so hopefully they'll have a fighting chance at happiness and a normal life."

"What about Melissa?"

Jenya put her chin to her chest. "I failed with Melissa. I tried every kind of persuasion, even vampiric glamour to keep Delia from marrying her off, but the only thing I could do was stall for time."

Catori's face was a picture of disgust. "Delia organized a blood challenge. It was awful."

"One candidate was worse than the other. Except for one man. Denny. I sensed he would be kind and that Melissa would be happy with him, so stacked the odds in his favor with a little of my blood. At least this way she would be safe until I convince Connor to leave. Obviously, Denny won the challenge. He's gentle and seems to genuinely care for Melissa, and she likes the rustic life."

"Why couldn't you just take Melissa and go? Why risk it? If Connor wanted to stay because of some half-baked vendetta, then that was his choice."

Jenya lifted her eyes to both women. "Connor is my obligation. My debt. I hold myself accountable for his addiction to vampire blood. In the beginning, I hoped my blood would lift his spirits and make him feel better. Ingesting undead blood in small amounts creates a feeling of euphoria, but unfortunately it's short lived. The little I gave him wasn't enough, and he started trading himself for blood in back alleys.

"I had to do something." The vampire shrugged. "Keeping him with me was the simplest and safest choice. Do I still give him blood? Yes. But only enough to stave off withdrawal pain and keep him from hurting himself."

"The vampiric equivalent of a methadone." Emily shook her head. "Jenya, you're not helping him."

A harsh exhale left her mouth, and she nodded. "I know. I can't abandon him. There are no halfway houses for people addicted to vampire blood."

"When Sean and Lily get here, let us take him home. His family will care for him. It's not up to you anymore."

It was clear the topic of Connor was closed. "So what happened with Melissa? I haven't seen her, and no one has mentioned her either. Is she still part of the camp?"

Catori rocked her hand back and forth in a half and half gesture. "Cougars tend to be sore losers. After the challenge Denny moved with Melissa to Clearlake. They've assimilated into regular society but stayed close enough to feel connected to the pride."

"You do realize Rémy is coming here to take her back with him." Emily eyed the vampire. "When he gets here, you'll have to explain."

Dread streaked across Jenya's chest, tightening her lungs. Her knees buckled, and she fell into one of the kitchen chairs.

"Jen!" Catori rushed to her side, but the vampire held up one hand.

"I'm okay, but I can't face Rémy.

Emily's hand covered Jenya's vise grip on kitchen chair. "You can. You've proven yourself to be a proud, determined woman who refuses to be a victim. One who uses her strength and skill to stand up for those who can't stand up for themselves. Show Rémy that."

Blood tears fell in tiny red splats on Catori's wood planked floor.

"I hate to break up this love fest, but what are we going to do about Delia and her plans?" Catori asked. "We don't have much time. If Emily's brother gets here with your vampire friend, it's game over. Half the big cats will riot, and the other half will run."

With a sniff, Jenya wiped her tears into a red smear across her cheek before cleaning it with a napkin. "I have a plan, but it's a risk."

Both Catori and Emily focused on Jenya.

"Here's what we need to do..."

# TWENTY-FOUR

A shooting star streaked across the inky black, the illumination turning night into day for a single moment. Delia looked to the heavens before dropping her chin to the crowd standing in the darkened square. Smoke billowed from a carefully constructed bonfire crackling in front of the long house.

She smiled, raising her arms to quiet the hum of anticipation. Ryan stood to her right, flanked by Sam and two of his men. To the crowd, it was a place befitting a newly ranked cougar, but to Emily and Catori, the opposite was clear. Ryan was a prisoner, complete with leather bonds around his wrists.

He stood tall, with his wide shoulders back and a fierce look of resolute defiance on his face. Even from this vantage point, Emily saw his wounds had completely healed. He radiated health and strength, and her arms ached for him. If she and Ryan made it out of this alive, she'd never run from him again.

Sam eyed Catori, his eyes hungry and his mouth a nasty slash. She was free now that Delia had staked her claim on Ryan, but the emancipator had decided Emily was a better fit for Sam, after all. So much for the crazy woman's claims toward wolf solidarity.

His daggered stare found Emily, and for a moment their eyes locked. His eyes radiated cruelty, and Emily clutched the fabric of her borrowed dress closer against an invisible. A dread-filled lump forming in her throat.

Jenya's plan had so many holes, someone was bound to end up dead. At this point Emily preferred death over being held captive.

Delia called out for quiet, and Sam along with everyone else turned their attention to the emancipator.

Emily focused her attention on Ryan. Her eyes glued to his profile. She closed her own and searched inside for any thread that might spark a link. Catori said all he needed was a catalyst in order to phase. Well, she had a doozy.

*"Ryan..."*

Her voice feathered out, hoping he'd hear. She concentrated on every emotion churning through her mind and heart. Her want of him. Her love. Her fear of commitment and betrayal, and her absolute love for the child she carried.

She focused on the night they met. Their instant connection, and the heat and lust that consumed them.

*"Ryan..."* she tried again.

He turned, and their eyes caught.

*"Surprise."*

*"How?"* His thoughts whispered back, stunned at how easy the transference felt.

She shook her head ever so slightly. *"I don't know how. All I know is you were right all along and I'm a coward."*

His eyes filled with longing and need, and he took a step toward her only to have a large hand clamp down on his shoulder.

"I don't think so, lover boy. You belong to the emancipator, and she belongs to me." Sam leered, grabbing his crotch with his free hand. "And I'm going to work her good."

Ryan's eyes flashed over yellow, and a low thrummed growl rumbled in his throat.

"Nice try, Simba". Sam shoved him sideways. "Come growl at me once you earn your canines."

*"Ryan, you've gotta keep your calm. Jenya's got something up her sleeve with James. Just be ready, okay?"*

Emily's tone carried the weight of her plea. If Ryan lost it before it was time, it was game over.

*"Jenya? As in the vampire who slaughtered a tribe of children? Em, what's going on?"*

*"Yes. Jenya. Rémy's not exactly up on his facts, but we don't have time to go into specifics. Just keep your eyes on James."*

Emily issued a silent prayer. Let it be enough.

Neither she nor Ryan had been paying attention when Delia announced his name. Ryan's head jerked around, and Delia's eyes tracked to what had kept him absorbed during her speech. The woman actually hissed when her gaze landed on Emily.

Silence fell across the square as Delia's mouth mashed to a thin, bloodless line. Her nostrils flared, and with a wave of her hand the two men standing with Sam stalked toward Emily each grabbing her under her arms.

"Strap her!"

With her scream they jerked her forward toward a wide, wooden board. The horizontal plank was raised on an incline, with leather restraints drilled at the head and foot.

Ryan roared, erupting forward only to have Sam grab him around his shoulders. He tried to fight but his bonds tightened, cutting into the flesh on his wrists.

Emily screamed again as one of the men shoved her down. She fell forward, her hand catching the brunt of her fall. Seizing her wrists and ankles they strapped her down, her arms and legs spread across the width of the plank.

With a nod from Delia, the other man produced a bowie knife from the side of his boot. Snatching the front of her dress, he slit the knit fabric down the middle exposing her completely except for the lace triangle between her legs. Tears ran down her face onto her bare breasts, the wetness puckering her flesh in the chilled air.

Delia's grin was a cruel gash, and she yelled for Sam to claim his prize. He pushed Ryan forward. "Guess who's getting his and guess who gets to watch?" Sam's tongue darted licking his lips.

James pushed his way to the front of the crowd, his hand raised, and a loud rhythmic chant echoed into the crowd. The cougars fell silent, even Sam stopped short, jerking Ryan to a halt.

"Delia Monroe! Stop this!" he cautioned. "You have no right!"

Stepping down from the makeshift podium, Delia stalked the short length of the square. Raising her hand she slapped James hard, the smack echoing in the silence.

"Don't tell me I have no right! I am the emancipator! I will do as I please. Edward Parr named me his heir the moment his seed took root in my belly!"

James lifted his chin, countering her slap with defiance. "Your seed will never be our Alpha. You are no emancipator. You only look to enslave! No cougar would ever treat one of their own the way you have treated yours." His arm flung out toward Emily still lying strapped to the board.

Catori ran forward to cover Emily with her sweater, but Sam grabbed her by the hair and shoved her down beside the board. "You're next," he growled.

James let out a high pitched yell and the crowd covered their ears, fearful. They knew the call to the spirit realm, and some of them cowered, huddling together against the unknown. "Ancestors take this imposter from our midst!"

"Imposter!" Delia's veins bulged, and she shrieked enraged.

"Edward Parr's true heir is shackled by your men! You look to spill our blood, our spirit, and defile our future! She carries the true heir's child in her belly, yet you strap her like a common whore!"

James gestured wildly toward Emily, his voice gaining in power and volume. "Her child will be a strong Alpha male, and he will lead us into the future following his father's lead!"

Ryan's head jerked toward the board and Emily's tearstained face.

*"Is it true?"* His voice rough and tight across her mind.

She nodded, her breath hitching as fresh tears fell. *"I've been trying to tell you since we left San Francisco."*

An enraged leonine scream built in his belly and exploded from his mouth. Power crackled and surged through his arms and legs, coursing like live current across his flesh. His back hunched. Muscles tensed and coiled beneath his skin. Heavier. Thicker. Energy and raw strength. The leather restraints on his wrists snapped, and Ryan threw his head back and roared. He fell to all fours, his clothes shredding with the snap and tear of bones and sinew.

In Ryan's place stood a massive lion with deadly canines the length of a man's hand. A full American Lion in all its majestic glory, extinct no more.

A forbidding growl menaced from Ryan's throat, and his big head swiveled toward Sam. The crowd shrieked, and people ran in all directions. The man turned to run, but a single swipe from a massive paw stopped him cold. Sam landed face first in the dirt. His shriek of fear echoing into the trees.

"Catori!" James rushed to her side, helping her up from the ground. "Quick, darlin'! Untie Emily!" The two unstrapped her shivering form, covering her with Catori's long sweater. "We need to the longhouse. Now!"

Six inch incisors crushed Sam's skull, impaling his throat. Blood spurted everywhere, coating the lion's thick mane and tawny face in crimson. The sickening crunch left no doubt the man was dead. The lion tossed the limp form at Delia's feet, and the woman eyes bugged. Her mouth worked but no words came.

"This is what happens when you play with people's lives, Delia." Jenya walked out of the darkness, a long cape billowing behind her giving her an air of menace. "Be happy Ryan hasn't ripped your head from your shoulders. I wouldn't be so forgiving."

A piercing howl echoed from the tree line and a large rust colored wolf charged the square, his paws skidding on the damp ground. His head pivoted from side to side, and polluted foam dripped from bared teeth.

"Connor! No!" Jenya yelled.

The wolf snarled and snapped, and the vampire jumped back. Delia ran for the woods, but Jenya's attention was on Connor. He was crazed and dangerous. He loped toward James, his eyes a black streaked yellow. He skidded short, and in a single vault landed with a thud in front of Emily.

"Ryan!" she screamed running, but the wolf's his heavy paws hit square in the back, forcing the breath from her lungs. She stumbled, trying to phase but Connor was too fast.

An agonized sob ripped from Emily throat. "NO!" He pinned her beneath his snapping jaws, but he didn't go for her throat. Instead he sank his teeth into her belly.

Massive jaws ripped the wolf from Emily's body. The force crushing the wolf's chest and neck with one strike. The lion shook the wolf like rag doll, snapping every bone in Connor's body. He dropped the tainted beast to the ground. Its last whimper lost to the wind, dead.

Ryan's lion shuddered and convulsed, and another leonine scream turned into a human's anguished cry. Naked and shaking he got to his feet and ran to where Emily lay limp and bleeding.

He gathered her in his arms, rocking her back and forth. "No. No. NO! Her blood coated his naked flesh.

Jenya threw her cape from her body and shoving it under Emily's head. "Catori! Bandages! Now!"

"Can you sense the heartbeat?" James asked, hovering behind the vampire.

"Let me concentrate!"

Catori ran back with three pillowcases. ""This is the best I can do, but at least they're clean."

Taking the cloth in two hands, Jenya tore them into shreds. She wiped the surface blood away to better see the wound. Chewing on the side of her cheek, she shook her head. "I don't know if I have the strength to do this. I haven't fed in weeks."

"Jenya, please. I just got her back. I'm begging you." Ryan face was hard and full of suffering.

"Perhaps, I may be of assistance." The deep and resonant voice came from behind Ryan.

"Rémy." Jenya's voice was a mere whisper.

"Hello, my angel." He pressed a kiss to the top of her head.

Jenya opened her mouth, but no sound came.

"Dear God! Emily!" Lily fell to her knees beside Ryan. "Do something, please!" Her eyes flashing towards the woods. "Sean! We need you! Now!"

Rémy's arm reached toward Jenya. "Take my hand. If we combine our blood it should be enough to begin her healing. Emily first. Then you need to feed."

Rémy took Jenya's hand and lifted her wrist to his lips. Kissing the tender flesh, he then pierced her vein. Biting down on his own wrist, he gripped her hand, squeezing. With a nod he urged her to tighten her hold, the added pressure forcing their thick, black blood to the surface.

It ran in heavy rivulets over the wounds, saturating the tears and punctures from Connor's bite. They held their combined strength over Emily lips, gesturing for Lily to open her mouth so the blood could hit her tongue.

The wounds closed, and color returned to Emily's face, but her eyes stayed closed. Sean ran from the woods with Kai at his heels. His big black wolf whimpering and submissive, laying his head on Lily's lap close to Emily's face.

"What do we do now?" Catori asked, her breath hitching.

"We wait." James answered, running his fingers through Kai's tawny fur as she sat beside him.

Sean licked Emily's face, and then bumped Lily with his nose. His big black head swiveled toward the woods, his eyes hard and angry. A low snarl slipped past his lips. He got to all fours, and grazed Lily's arm with his muzzle.

"Are you sure you don't want me to come with you?" She slid her fingers through his fur, tugging gently.

The black wolf dropped his head, and Lily wrapped her arms around his thick neck. "Come back to me, Sean. We have a honeymoon to finish."

He licked her face, and then whimpered in Emily's ear one last time before taking to the woods.

With a whiff of ozone and electricity, Kai phased back to human, tucking her naked body under James's arm. He shrugged off his jacket and draped it over her shoulders

"Mama!" Catori slid her arms around Kai's waist. "Thank God you're safe."

"If I had been at the cottage when Delia's men came for these two, I'm not sure I would be."

Catori peered into the dark woods. "Where did the black wolf go?"

Lily's eyes found Ryan, before turning her gaze to Emily's unconscious face. "That wolf is Emily's brother and my husband. He's the Alpha of the Brethren, and he has some unfinished business to take care of in the woods."

Catori looked to her mother and James for a more concrete answer. "He's going to kill Delia, sweetheart," the Shaman replied. "It's his right as Alpha of the Brethren for crimes against her own kind.

Jenya's eyes flashed red, and she let go of Rémy's hand. A snarl in her throat.

"Jenya!' he warned.

"Delia's pregnant, Rémy! That baby is innocent!" she railed back. "The wolf can't kill her!"

Rémy took Jenya's still bleeding wrist and swiped the wound with his tongue, sealing it. He did the same with his own and then pulled her into his arms.

"Sean Leighton is a fair and just man, and a compassionate leader.

236

If there is a way to bring Delia Monroe to justice without taking the life of her baby, he will find it. On that you have my word, little bird."

He kissed the top of her head. "Now, we need to help Ryan move Emily inside and keep her warm. You and I are on vigil tonight. There is another tiny life who needs us."

# CHAPTER
# TWENTY-FIVE

Ryan sat at Emily's bedside. Her pale, cold palm pressed to his lips as he muttered half remembered prayers from his childhood. Worry creased his forehead, his exhaustion evident in the dark smudges beneath his eyes. Even his fatigue was laced with tension, his shoulders knotted and ready to strike if necessary.

At least Lily convinced him to wash the blood from his body and put on some clothes.

"Pull yourself together, Ryan. You want Emily to go into shock the minute she comes to? She's got to believe you're okay. Even if you're not. Right now she's our focus. You can fall apart later. If you're going to be a member of this family, you have to learn to stay calm and think."

He forced his face into what he hoped was a tired smile. "Stay calm and think? This from the woman who put the Vulcan death grip on me when I didn't know anything about lunar driven lust."

Lily smirked, but her curled lip was full of warmth. "Lunar driven lust, huh." She glanced at the tiny baby bump showing through the blanket covering Emily's body. "I think you know all there is to know about that."

"She didn't tell me, Lils. Or I'd never have let her come to this crazy place."

"I know, Ry." Lily rubbed her knuckles on his upper arm. "C'mon. Only positive vibes. It's going to be nice to have you as my actual brother. Terri would be so happy."

Ryan blinked at the wetness in his eyes, unashamed. "Not as proud as I am. I love you, little sister. Even if you are a pain in my ass." He yawned, placing Emily's hand on her chest. He laid his head next to her arm and closed his eyes.

"That's it, buddy. Rest." Lily covered his back and shoulders with a small woven blanket from the chair beside the bed. "It's the best thing you can do for yourself and for Em."

⁓

"CAN YOU HEAR IT?" Jenya whispered, her hand resting over Emily's still form.

Rémy nodded. "Yes. The heartbeat is strong and fast, but I think the speed is a result of feeding his mother undead blood."

She looked at him from where she stood tucked under his arm. "We didn't do any undue harm, did we?"

"No worries, little bird." He smiled, tightening his hold on her shoulders. "Close your eyes and inhale. You can taste the health spreading through both mother and baby. My guess is Emily will wake soon. Perhaps even before her mate." He laughed quietly at the sound of Ryan's soft snoring.

"He's wiped out. I know part of him wants to be in the woods hunting Delia, but Emily really needs him. If something happened to her and he wasn't there—" Lily's voice drifted off.

"Don't let the thought enter your mind, little witch. Your sister wolf will be fine."

Jenya stiffened. "Little witch?"

Before Rémy could answer, Lily gave the big vampire a playful push. "It's nothing, Jenya. Little witch is his pet name for me because

240

I'm psychic." Yawning, she stretched. "I think I better see if Kai has any coffee brewing. Lord knows I could use some. I won't find sleep until I know Sean is safe and on his way back."

Lily walked out of Catori's bedroom, leaving the door ajar. Jenya listened to the sound of her footsteps taking her into the other room.

She and Rémy were alone. She closed her eyes. So much had changed in such a short time, but then again it hadn't.

"How about a stroll in the moonlight?" He asked. "It's a lovely night, everything considered."

Jenya nodded, and the two slipped silently out the back door of the cottage. They walked side by side. The stars in the millions against a black silk sky. The clouds parted as they set upon a small clearing. The open space allowing the moon's glow to shine through an otherwise dense trees. Rémy lifted his face to the firmament, drinking it in, the moon illuminating the scars on his face in its stark, pale light.

Their past and all the pain she caused avalanched against her heart at the scarred sight. "I'm sorry. I have to go..."

"Jenya."

She turned away, ignoring his plea. Old pain tore a fresh hole in her heart, and she took off into the woods. Rémy called after her, but she ran until her tears would no longer hold. Sliding onto a toppled boulder, her body shook with sobs.

A small stream babbled in the background. The joyful gurgling mocking and intrusive. Jenya picked up a rock and hurled it at the water. Its answering plop a contemptuous laugh at her self-pity.

"That's a first. The sound of running water is usually cathartic."

She twisted around. Rémy stood just inside a copse of trees, his large frame eclipsing the moon and leaving his face in shadow.

"Why did you follow me?"

He walked toward her, his movements slow as if approaching a skittish deer. Both would be apt to bolt, but Jenya running from him again was not to be brooked. As expected, she got to her feet, her stance poised to vault toward the sky.

Lightning fast, he wrapped his arms around her waist before she could take to the trees. "When are you going to stop running from me?"

Grief rose choking her words. "It hurts too much to see you."

"Why does it hurt so much? Because of how I look?"

Familiar pain bloomed. Moments passed, measured by the rote rise, and fall of their combined breath. She squeezed her eyes closed, shaking her head back and forth. Her hands clawing at her ears and hair to stop the memories playing over in her mind.

Rémy grabbed her by the shoulders and shook her hard. "Jenya, stop! Look at me. Please!" He took her hand, laying her palm against his wet cheek. "Since you left I haven't shed one tear. I kept myself apart from everyone, allowing only logic and reason to govern my thoughts. I closed my heart to everyone and everything. Now that I have you in my arms again, I am full to the brim."

He tilted her head up, but her eyes stayed squeezed shut. "Lily was the first person in almost a century to look at me with compassion. It was she who lit the spark of hope in my heart, opening my mind to the possibility of love. The possibility of finding you again. Come home, Jenya. I won't try and change you, and I will never judge you. Just let me love you the way I have all these lonely years."

She opened her eyes, a sad refusal written in their depths. "I'm broken, Rémy. How can you love me when all I bring is pain?"

He cupped her face, brushing his lips to hers, the taste of their mingled blood-tears making it that much sweeter. "Without pain how can you know bliss? Without struggle how can you know joy?"

A tired chuckle left her mouth. "Leave it to you to answer a straightforward question with a philosophical response."

"I have something we need to bury. The choice of where we do so is yours." He reached into his pocket and pulled out the walrus tusk.

Jenya cringed, her hand flying to her mouth. She closed her eyes again, red tinged tears squeezing from the corners.

"My love, I did not bring this to stir painful memories. I brought this so we can move past the pain it represents."

Taking her hand, he wrapped her fingers around the base of the tusk, guiding the sharp tip toward his heart. "Like I said, the choice is yours where we bury this. You can bury it in my heart, and be done with me forever, or together we can bury it deep in the earth along with everything attached."

He paused, wrapping his hand over hers. "I know you've become a righteous hunter, and the thought fills me with pride."

At his words she opened her eyes. "How?"

"I'm old and I have my ways. Your deeds were clear in Emily's mind when I listened for the baby's heart. I also smell the evil on people, and if you bury this tusk anywhere but my chest, I will join you on your hunts."

Jenya's mouth fell open, and Rémy laughed at her stunned expression.

"You, my love, are no monster, and if you don't believe me then plunge this curved ivory through my heart, because it means I have failed you, again. The way I did all those years ago." His fingertips brushed her pale cheek. "*Moy angel s perebitym krylom.* My angel with broken wings."

She took a step back holding the tusk in her palm. Eyes closed she wrapped both hands around the widest part of its shaft and held it aloft, its point glinting in the moonlight. With a pain-soaked scream she crushed the ivory to nothing but dust between her palms.

Chest heaving, she opened her eyes to watch the chalky white powder drift away on the mountain breeze. Her breath hitched in her throat, and she stepped into Rémy's waiting arms. "*Protstish li ty menya kogda nibud?* Can you ever forgive me?"

He lifted her chin, brushing his lips to hers. "I already have." His mouth claimed a redemptive kiss, both of them alive with a century of unspent passion.

Weak, Jenya shivered at the onslaught of sudden heat. She slumped against him, her small frame wilting against his chest. He broke their kiss only to see the stark blue of her veins prominent in the silvery light.

His tongue swept her full lower lip. "Take your strength from me,

Jenya. All I have is yours." Sliding his hand through her dark hair he urged her forward, guiding her soft mouth toward the thick vein in his throat, a delicious mix of pleasure and pain for them both.

FRAIL LIGHT PEAKED through the shears, too faint to illuminate more than outlines surrounding the bed. Emily's eyes fluttered open, and she turned her head toward the dull glow, awareness blooming slowly.

A warm heaviness had her lifting her head from the pillow only to find Ryan's arm flung across the top of her thighs and his head nestled against her arm.

Dry-mouthed, Emily tried to swallow, but her tongue wouldn't cooperate. A soft croak was all she managed when she tried to call his name. She closed her eyes instead, trailed her fingers through his hair and relishing the thick feel.

"You're awake," he said, taking her hand from his hair and bringing it to his lips as he sat up.

Her eyes opened and she smiled. "So are you."

"How do you feel?"

"Dry."

Ryan reached behind him and poured her a glass of water. He moved beside her and held the glass to her lips, his arm slung behind her shoulders to help.

She drank greedily and then sank back against his arm and the pillow. "Where is everyone?" she asked, glancing toward the door. Her eyes went wide, and her gaze twisted back. "Sean and Lily? Are they okay? Where are they?"

Ryan ran his fingers through her hair and stroked the side of her pale cheek. "They're both fine. They're asleep in the living room. Do you want me to get them?"

"No. Let them rest." Her eyes took in Ryan's haggard appearance. The dark circles under his eyes and the two days' worth of scruff on his face. "How long have I been out?"

"Three days. Rémy was sure you'd be up and around in half a day, but..." his voice trailed off.

Too stunned to comment, Emily stayed silent. The stress of the past few days was written all over Ryan's face, and she wasn't sure what happened after she lost consciousness. Who was dead and who was left alive. Connor was dead, and so was Sam. That much she knew, but what about Kai and James? Catori? And then there was Delia...

Her eyes must have spoken volumes because Ryan leaned forward brushing a kiss across her dry lips. "Stop worrying. Everyone is safe. Delia's minions have been rounded up, and the cougars plan to deal with them their own way."

From the set of his jaw, she knew their way meant something akin to Wild West meets medieval. She didn't really care. They deserved whatever the consequences. Live by the sword, die by the sword.

"What about Delia?"

Ryan sniffed, sitting back in his chair. "I think maybe Sean should tell you himself."

The smell of fresh brewed coffee drifted in through the door, and Ryan pushed himself up from his seat to poke his head through the doorway. "Looks like everyone is up. Everyone except Rémy and Jenya. The two took to the woods days ago, and no one has heard from them since."

He smiled, and with a wink he gestured toward the hallway. "I'm going to let everyone know you're awake. They've been pretty anxious." Within in minutes she heard a flurry of feet heading back down the hallway.

"Hey! You're up! Must be nice to take a three day nap," Lily joked walking through the door with Sean.

"Hey, kiddo!" Sean murmured, leaning down to press a kiss to her forehead. "How're you feeling?"

She shrugged. "Like a Mac truck ran over my middle."

Lily stood next to Sean, slipping one hand around his waist, and taking Emily's hand in her other. "Yeah, that's going to take a few more days, but the good news is the baby seems fine. Rémy assured us his heartbeat is strong and fast."

"His?" A grin broke out across Emily's lips.

Ryan nodded coming around the side of the bed carrying two mugs, one with orange juice for Emily, the other a cup of coffee for himself. "Yup. We're having a boy."

Sean grinned, pressing a kiss to Lily's temple. "First Rissa has Braden, now another boy. Looks like it's up to us to continue the tradition."

Putting the mugs on the snack tray next to the bed, Ryan fluffed another pillow to help Emily sit up. "Yeah, but knowing Lily, she'll make sure it's a girl just to be difficult."

Laughter bubbled, and Emily held her middle wincing. "Ouch. Don't make me laugh."

"Ryan said you've been asking what happened." Sean interjected. "Do you really want me to tell you?"

She shook her head. "No. I want you to show me, but I'm not sure I should risk it. Not with my injuries."

Confused, Sean looked at Ryan for explanation.

"Emily tried to reach you across your sibling channel when we were taken. She wasn't sure it would work since you two hadn't shared thoughts in over a decade, but she tried anyway. The pain that accompanied the attempt was intolerable."

Disgust countered from Lily's mouth. "Another little gift from Edward we need to track and destroy." Her gaze swept downward, and she squeezed Emily's hand. "The story can wait until we're out of range of whatever or whoever is blocking you. You need a thorough prenatal check, and the only place a pregnant shifter whose ingested vampire blood can get that is at the Compound."

There was no need to balk. "The same thought crossed my mind as well," Emily replied.

Wearing a large grin, Ryan pressed a kiss to her forehead. "Good. Now I don't have to drag you kicking and screaming."

Catori poked her head through the door. "Can we come in?" She was tucked under Liam's arm and while she looked happy, his expression was apprehensive.

"We couldn't help but overhear. The reason you couldn't use your sibling path to contact Sean is because my dad blocked you. He followed Delia's instructions on how to do it and added a bit of his own nastiness just for kicks. He's a strong mind reader. Ethan was Edward's enforcer, and after Edward left my dad appointed himself Alpha. His ability was the only reason he was able to take over. He saw every threat before it hit."

Emily looked past Sean and Lily to the door, her eyes focusing on Liam. "It was you, wasn't it? You're the cougar that broke into my bedroom the night we were taken."

Ryan and Sean both turned, but Catori stepped in front of Liam before they could do or say anything. "Yes, but Liam is part of our underground. He infiltrated Delia's ring so he could relay whatever Delia planned. He is on our side. Your side. From the beginning."

Ryan and Sean exchanged glances. "What about your father?" Sean asked, still suspicious.

"My father wanted Delia. Everyone knew that. They were cut from the same cloth, and when she told him Edward was dead and that she carried his child, well, let's just say my father's delusions of grandeur took a huge leap." Her eyes glanced sideways at Liam. "Dad's dead. So is Cole. Liam saw to it, but the rest will stand trial, and we'll deal with them our way. The good news is your mind is free." Catori flashed a bright smile, her eyes wet. "As are my mom and James. We all are. Thanks to you."

"Where are they anyway?" Emily asked.

Catori's grin grew even wider, and she winked. "Finally doing what they've waited years to do."

A wave of awkward silence descended, and Catori and Liam made their goodbyes, leaving the original four alone in the room.

"Sean, if you're ready, then so am I. I want to know what happened, but I want to see it and feel it, so I know I didn't just dream it. If it's over I want to know it's really over."

Her brother's face was severe when he took her hand. "Are you sure?"

She nodded and she reached her other hand out taking hold of Ryan's. "You too, Lily. Take Sean's other hand."

Lily spared a look for Sean before she shook her head. "I don't need to see it again, Em. I'll make us something to eat." With a wave she walked out of the room, and Sean nodded for everyone to close their eyes.

*Frigid wind raced across Emily's skin along with the feel of moisture from sweat and damp freezing along fur.*

*There were too many scents in the air, bear, elk, mountain lion, but not the scent he sought. A howl broke from Sean's throat and was answered by brother wolves. Single natured animals that held kinship with their dual-natured cousins.*

*He sank deeper into his wolf form to help locate the scent, careful not to sink too deep or he'd lose all connection with his human side. He needed Delia's image and the reason he hunted clear in his mind.*

*Running through the dense trees, his heavy paws thundering through the loamy earth, his claws scoring deep grooves and clumps of dirt and vegetation flew in his wake.*

*Thick forest and nearly impenetrable dark from heavy cloud cover made navigating hard. The big black wolf raised his head and snout to the sky. He inhaled again, sniffing the air. The wind changed and his large head jerked toward the south. He took off, rear muscles bunching and flexing in fast twitch to aid in his speed.*

*She was there, on the far side of a deep ravine near the rock face. He sniffed the air again. Fresh blood. Delia had scraped her skin raw climbing to get away, but there was no escape.*

*He ran to the edge where the tree line dropped off and the rocks began. Snow still covered the landscape in patches, as did large melting icicles clinging to the rock along the sheer drop.*

*With a snap of bone and muscle the wolf's body reshaped to human form. "Delia! It's not worth it! The rocks are too dangerous! You're going to kill yourself and your baby! Come back! We'll talk!"*

*"Never!" Venom filled her refusal. Her foot slipped from its narrow hold, and she screamed, and this time fear replaced her hate.*

*"Hold on! I'm coming!"*

*Dread spiked across Emily's mind, and she cringed as the jagged crevice loomed large the closer Sean got. He cursed, silently wishing there was a way to summon Rémy and his ability to fly.*

*Delia screamed again as rocks broke loose from the stone face beneath her, the crushing sound a menacing echo as they plummeted into the chasm. Sean stood on the craggy precipice just past the trees. They were at a stalemate. Delia couldn't climb up, and with her footholds crumbling to the ravine floor she could no longer climb down.*

*Her eyes found his. With an evil grin she flung herself from the stone face, screams echoing as she fell. Her body smashed against a rocky outcrop.*

Emily shuddered, pulling back from Sean's mind. "Oh my God! Why would she kill herself and her baby? Was she truly that mad, or just criminal?"

Ryan hugged her closely. "I think both, but it really doesn't matter anymore."

"What a waste."

"Waste or not, Em, Delia signed her death warrant the minute she threatened our family."

Ryan's upper lip curled. "Amen, brother."

A WEEK PASSED, and Emily lounged with Ryan in bed. She was still too weak and too injured to travel, but every brought them closer to putting this nightmare behind them.

"Penny for your thoughts?" Ryan asked, stretching his long lean body alongside hers in the bed.

"Oh, I think they're worth much more than that." Emily leaned her face against Ryan's chest, snaking her hand beneath the covers to stroke his nether regions through his pants.

His arms came up to wrap around her soft, warm curves. "You're such a tease," he murmured into the hollow beneath her jaw. "And you're supposed to be too injured for X-rated thoughts."

She surrendered to his embrace, her lips curving into a smile against his hungry mouth. "Aren't you the lucky one, then," she whispered back.

"Ahem." Someone cleared their throat pulling them back from the edge. They looked up to see James in the doorway wearing an embarrassed look.

"Remind me next time to shut the door," he grumbled pushing himself up against the headboard.

"I'm sorry. I didn't mean to disturb you." The man half-turned in the doorway not sure whether to stay or go. "Maybe I should just come back later."

"Don't be silly. Come in." Emily lifted her hand to coax the older man to stay. "You'll have to forgive us. The past week and everything we've been through has given us a new lease on life."

James laughed. "To say the least."

"So, what can we do for you, James?"

Emily had to bite the inside of her cheek at Ryan's clipped tone. Down boy!

"You both have done enough. It's me that wants to do something for you." He held out his hands, gesturing for them to each join him.

*"I hope this isn't some weird tent revival prayer thing he's doing"*

*"Ryan, behave. He's a nice man, and he can probably hear you. So shut it."*

James's lips twitched making Emily's cheeks burn.

Their minds cleared and James's voice beckoned them through the mist. They could only hear the Shaman, and there was nothing above or below them. Simply a nothingness that made it clear they were somewhere not of this Earth.

"James?" Ryan called.

The Shaman appeared with a soft smile, sweeping his arm outward. "This is my gift to you both."

*The mist cleared and the scene before them washed vibrant. It was the beach in Ogunquit. Two children squealed in delight, splashing through the tidal pools while a man and a woman walked slightly behind holding hands.*

*The children were tanned and happy. Their bathing suits and hair wet with sand and salt. Their faces were too far away to be clear, though the sun was bright on the water. Suddenly, another child, slightly older than the others ran up behind, calling for them." Mom! Dad! Come see the sandcastle I made!"*

*The family turned and Emily's breath caught in her throat. It was her and Ryan, and the three children playing on the beach were theirs. An older boy, and a set of twins. A boy and a girl.*

*The scene faded and the mist returned. Emily reached for James's hand, but he stepped back shaking his head. He swept his arm out again and the mists swirled, but no scene appeared. Instead a woman walked toward them. She was tiny, with dark curling hair and the greenest eyes.*

*Ryan's eyes jerked to James, and the old man nodded. Teresa.*

*The woman approached, and her smile was so beautiful it made Emily's heart break. She came to stop just feet away. She didn't say a word but glanced over her shoulder beckoning to someone.*

*For a moment fear gripped Emily's stomach that the person beckoned was Edward, but James's sharp headshake told no.*

*Another woman, much younger, walked through the swirling vapor and stood beside Teresa. Emily knew immediately it was Terri.*

*Funny how they mother and daughter shared similar names, and Em wondered if Carl and Beverly had named her purposefully to give her a tiny piece of her birth mother.*

*Ryan stepped forward, his eyes were wet, and he held his arms out. They shook their heads. It was forbidden to touch.*

*"Are you at peace?" he asked, his voice cracking with emotion.*

*Teresa nodded. "Sí mi hijo, estoy tranquilo."*

*She spoke in Spanish, but Ryan understood, and his face glowed. "Te amo, siempre."*

*He looked at his sister. "I wish I had gotten to know you." Anger edged his voice this time, as if he blamed the fates for robbing him of what was left of his family when he had been so close.*

*Terri's eyes were soft and full of love. "Don't be angry, Ryan. It was all for a reason. I'm with mama now, and the same way we're meeting here, we will all be together one day. Take care of Lily for me, okay? She's a handful."*

*He laughed, wiping his eyes, unashamed. "That she is, but I can tell you, she's happy. She and Sean got married last week. We both wished you could have been there."*

*Terri smiled wide. "I was there, silly. I will always be with you, and with her. Mama, too."*

*James stepped forward gesturing it was time to go.*

*Ryan took a step forward but stopped. He turned, taking Emily by the hand, and then moved closer to his mother and sister. "This is Emily. My mate."*

*Both women smiled warmly. "We know. All for a reason, remember?"*

*James cleared his throat, signaling for them to leave. Teresa and Terri backed away through the mist, and Emily's heart broke for Ryan as he took another step toward them.*

*"Take care of my niece and nephews. Remember, twins just like us." Terri blew him a kiss and Teresa's hand went to her heart and they were gone.*

James let go of their hands and the spell was broken. Ryan sat on the end of the bed, his mouth open and his eyes wide. He looked from James's face to Emily and back again.

"Was that for real?" he croaked.

James smiled. Exhaustion etched on his face. "Yes. It's very draining and not something I do often, but real, nonetheless. You've lost so much, Kai and I wanted to give you something you could hold onto forever. Maybe help you find a little closure."

Ryan stood and went to hug the old man, but then hesitated.

"Come here, you big cat." James laughed out loud. "Touch may be forbidden between realms, but it's certainly welcome here on Earth."

He grabbed the older man in a bear hug. "Thank you, James. I will never forget it."

The older man wiped his eyes and then cleared his throat. "Kai's making dinner for an army, so I hope you have an appetite." With a nod, he walked out. Closing the door behind him.

Ryan slumped onto the bed, his head spinning. "Wow."

"Now that's an understatement," Emily said through a large yawn. Closing her mouth she watched his face and the spectrum emotion reflected in his eyes. "Are you okay?"

Shifting around, he nodded with a sigh. "Yeah, I guess. I'm grateful to James. I mean I'm blown away, yet at the same time I feel cheated. Two amazing women were taken from me before I got the chance to know them, or them me. It sucks."

Emily rubbed Ryan's arm, her touch light. "At least you know you were loved. Kai told you earlier, but now you know in your heart it's true."

He nodded. "At least my mom and my sister are together."

"Yup, and their dimension is different from ours. How else would Terri have known Lily and Sean were married unless she was there? I think your mom and your sister are going to be with you from now on..." she paused, a small smile on her lips. "And you can always bribe James to let them visit from time to time."

Ryan laughed. "I suppose." He ran his fingers over her cheek before pulling the blanket up, tucking it under her arms. "You look like you could use a nap. Do you want me to leave?"

Emily pushed herself up and snaked her arm around Ryan's neck, the blanket falling away. "Never," she murmured into a kiss. "I want you in my mind..." Her voice was low as she pressed kisses from his mouth down his throat to his chest. "In my heart..." she paused with her fingers splayed against his hard planes. Her eyes caught his and biting her lip, she slid her fingers down to the bulge forming at the front of his pants. "And in any other place we can think of."

He inhaled sharp and deep, his body hardening and his inner lion roaring to claim what was his. "Forever," he growled, his arms sliding around her thin frame, tightening in a possessive lock.

# EPILOGUE

The sound of muffled crying carried on the chilly breeze and the lonely moan of the wind the answering lament.

"Shush. *Te lo ruego, guardar silencio!*" One of the girls slipped her arm around another, her whispered warning more a plea as they stumbled through the dark. Every tree and root jumped out at them, heightening their terror.

"*Por favor señor, a dónde vamos?*"

Weil Davis backed handed the girl across her cheek, the resounding slap and her frightened cry sending birds winging from the trees.

"Anyone else?" He threatened, raising his fist.

Three girls shook their heads, their teeth chattering from the cold.

Davis pushed passed a low hanging branch, the snap of early spring shoots and the crunch of dead leaves a cacophony in the silence. Where the hell was Sam? Delia was a bitch stickler when it came to delivering on time.

Things looked different at dusk, and he shook his head. She'd never changed the delivery time, and she never contacted him unless she had a specific request about a girl. Something wasn't right.

The sound of running water perked his ears, and he peered through the brush. Liam said they would meet him at the waterfall near the cliff edge as usual. Well, at least that hadn't changed. Maybe there was something going on, and she didn't want to push the trade-off another day. He squashed his suspicions and licked his lips thinking about the fat envelope full of cash and the promised bonus for the inconvenience.

Pulling his flashlight from his back pocket, he flashed the narrow beam of light through the trees and found the path he cleared the last time. Except for the quiet sniffling from the girls behind him, he didn't hear anyone else. Guess they were the first to arrive.

He pointed the flashlight at the girls, gesturing with the light for them to go ahead of him through the short trail. His eyes traveled the length of them as they filed past. They were all young. No more than fifteen or sixteen. Illegals all. He reached out and grabbed one around the waist, his free hand squeezing a full, pert breast.

"No one around Chica. I just might sample the wares before my buyers get here."

"Por favor! No!"

She struggled against him, but that only made his erection harder.

"Feisty, young and spicy, just the way I like it." He licked her ear, squeezing her nipple between his thumb and forefinger.

She cried out in pain, and he let her go with a laugh as she ran up the path flinging herself into one of the other girl's arms.

"Where do you think you can go? Huh? Nowhere. He spread his arms. "*Me perteneces. Entiendes?*"

"Really, Davis? And here I thought they belonged to us." Liam said, appearing as though from nowhere.

"Liam! Jesus, I didn't hear you come up. What are you people, part cat?"

"Funny you should make that connection, Detective." Ryan walked out of the shadows along with Catori.

"You? How? Did you...? When? Davis looked from Ryan to Liam and back again. "What the hell is going on here?"

With a merest gesture from Liam, Catori nodded, telling the girls in perfect Spanish to come away from the men and follow her to safety. Davis sputtered, raising his hand to try and stop them, but Ryan let out a low, ominous growl.

Even in the gathering dark Davis's face visibly paled at the feral sound. "What the fuck are you?" he whispered, taking a step back.

"Well, since you asked so nicely..." Ryan crouched, and with a solid leap he phased in midair, letting out a bone shattering roar.

"Holy shit!" Davis pulled his sidearm, backing up. His hands shook so hard, the two shots he managed missed by a mile. "Fuck this and FUCK YOU!"

He turned to run, but massive paws hit him square in the chest, their weight crushing the man's ribs and spine when he hit the ground. Nothing and no one was coming to help. Just as nothing and no one had helped the girls he took and then sold.

The detective's screams echoed through the silent forest, but the giant lion took its time tearing flesh from muscle, and muscle from bone...

**Curious about Emily and Ryan's**
**Meet Cute in Boston?**

It was definitely more spice than sugar, LOL!
Well, wonder no more. Here's their steamy story!
Just a little something extra for my readers in honor of
the Cursed by Blood 10th anniversary!
Turn the page and ENJOY!

# RYAN AND EMILY'S SPICY MEET CUTE

The limo pulled up to the club and stopped. The outside of the Red Lantern was distressed brick, giving an almost sketchy feel to the place. Amilynn peered out the tinted window, squinting to get a better look. Laughing, she gestured to the line of wannabes freezing their asses off as they waited to get in. "Please tell me that's not going to be us."

Emily craned her neck to see out the window. "Oh, no way. I made sure we had reserved VIP status."

"Here you go, ladies! Put 'em on," Patricia teased, holding out three more boas to Lily, Rissa, and Em. "You can't pull up to a place in a pink monstrosity like this and not! It's showtime!"

"Oh boy." Rissa's eyes narrowed. "I know you Emily Leighton, and you have something up your sleeve."

"All you need to concern yourself with is having fun," Emily replied with a giggle.

Not waiting for the driver to come around, Rissa got out of the car. She wrapped the feather boa around her shoulders and struck a pose. "Oh well, let's get this embarrassment over with." She bristled, but her smirky grin took the wind out of her huff.

The six of them strutted into the club, the limo and the boas turning heads and causing whispers.

"Ah! The bachelorette party, no?" The maître d' asked as their group approached the hostess desk.

Rissa opened her mouth to say no, but Emily piped up first. "That's right!"

"And who's the blushing bride?" he asked, his eyes locking on Lily first. "You, pretty lady?"

Lily's eyebrows rose and she shook her head. "Not me."

He looked at Emily.

"Not me either. It's this one over here," she said pointing to Rissa.

"What? Em! Cut it out!"

The maître d' laughed, grabbing a handful of menus and gesturing for them to follow.

Hooking elbows with Rissa, Emily gave her a quick hip bump. "Oh, come on. It's only a matter of time before Mitch pops the question and you know it. Consider this a trial run for the real last hurrah."

Rissa hmphed. "Yeah, well he'd better pop the question soon or I'm going to do some popping all by myself," she said, patting her belly for effect.

As requested, the host sat them at a table in the bar area. The place was dotted with stone Buddhas and samurai warriors of every shape and size, and the largest Buddha was situated in the middle of a fountain at the center of the space.

"I bet there's a thousand dollars' worth of koi swimming in there," Amilynn whispered as she sat.

The maître d' smiled. "There used to be. Unfortunately, people kept throwing fried noodles into the water trying to feed them, so the owner moved them to his home."

He handed them the menus and left with a little bow. "Enjoy your-selves, ladies."

"This place is cool! I'm getting my jam on just looking at those life-size Samurai statues."

"Char, leave it to you to squirm in your pants over a guy made of stone."

"I like 'em rock hard, that's for sure."

Patty cracked up. "Who doesn't? If I wanted noodles, I would have stayed with my ex instead of hooking up with Gerry," she joked, picking up her menu. "My own personal stone fox."

The waitress walked over to the table, pad, and pen in hand. "Can I get you ladies anything from the bar?"

"Absolutely! This place is incredible, so there's got to be something amazing you can recommend," Amilynn interjected.

The waitress grinned. "Thanks, we try. People tell me this is the best place to be at the end of a cold pub crawl." She tapped Amilynn's menu with her pen. "Our Flaming Plum Shots. They hit your hot spot every time."

"Ha! What girl wouldn't want that?"

The waitress grinned even wider. "I can't tell you what's in them, but after a few you won't feel your teeth."

Emily put her menu down. "Bingo! Can we have a round of those and some rose saké?"

The waitress raised an eyebrow. "Are you going to be ordering food, too?"

Her question sounded a little too worried, and Emily laughed, meeting the young woman's concerned expression with a smile. "Of course, we are, but just appetizers because it's late. Can we still get crispy spring rolls and lobster rangoons?"

She looked at everyone before giving Emily a nod. "Is that everything?"

"For now. Just keep the saké flowing."

"Wait!" Lily called after the waitress as she headed toward the bar.

"Something else?"

Lily nodded. "Yes, bring this one a Pink Geisha." She lifted her hand gesturing toward Emily.

The waitress pressed her lips together clearly trying not to laugh.

"You got it." She turned toward the bar, glancing over her shoulder once with a huge smile.

Emily blinked. "A Pink Geisha?"

Lily winked at the others. "That drink has your name all over it."

Everyone laughed except Emily.

"I still don't get it."

"A pink cherry blossom satin blindfold?" Patty elaborated, moving her hands in furtive seduction like a Japanese dancer.

"Oh, come on!"

Lily grinned in a slow deliberate fashion. "I'm not saying anything, but your cheeks are powdered and pink, you ooze sex appeal, and you pick an Asian bar chock full of samurais as the backdrop for this little get-together. Seems to me if the kimono fits..."

"Emily brought the California kink New England style!" Amilynn grinned, moving her neck in a cool Middle Eastern head slide.

"Go ahead. Laugh it up, ladies, but you forget my memory is long... very long." With her lips poised in a devious slant, Emily took a sip of her drink, eyeing Amilynn across the table.

Ami reached for the crunchy dried edamame at the table's center but stopped, her hand hovering over the bowl. Nonplussed, her eyes darted from girl to girl at the abruptly quiet table. "What?"

Emily tilted her head, twirling a strand of her hair around her finger. "Nothing." She paused. "Lily should be grateful I don't know her as well as I know the rest of you."

"And what's that supposed to mean," Amilynn said with a laugh.

"It means I'm not the only one who breaks out the wanton sex appeal from time to time or am I the only one who remembers what happened when you and Samuel met up with a swarm of mosquitos during an outdoor quickie on a park bench."

A dusky crimson spread from Amilynn's décolleté to her high cheekbones. She dipped her head, sticking a small handful of edamame in her mouth, not saying another word.

"Hahahaha! Ami! Look at your face! You're as pink as your boa!"

Charlayne snickered, pointing her finger at the pretty raven-haired girl.

Patricia let out a loud snort. "I wouldn't go there if I were you, Char. You forget I was with you at that Alien Nation-SciFi Convention when you ended up in a ladies room stall at two a.m. with some random dude who thought he'd hooked up with Sigourney Weaver."

Charlayne's eyes widened and her jaw dropped. "Patty!"

"Well, it's true, isn't it?"

The ash blonde snapped her mouth closed with a sniff. "Yes. But that was years ago, and you know damn well that random guy is now my husband, Bruce!"

"Oh, come on, don't be that way," Patricia persuaded. "If it'll make you feel better, you can tell them about me and Gerry and the RCMP."

"RCMP? What's that, another related pack?" Lily asked.

Rissa smacked Lily with the end of her pink zebra boa making her wiggle her nose from loose feathers. "Not everything we do is pack, Lily. RCMP stands for the Royal Canadian Mounted Police."

Ami's head jerked up. "Holy crap, Patty! You had a threesome? Now that's something I want to hear about!"

Water spewed across the table with Charlayne coughing and sputtering between giggles. "Patricia certainly loves a man in uniform," she wheezed.

With a wicked smile, Patty ran her finger around the rim of her water glass. "That's not what happened, although he did have a pretty long, thick...flashlight."

Rissa and Emily groaned amid the chuckles.

The waitress brought the drinks, setting a flaming plum shot in front of each woman. She put an iced carafe of rose saké and six blue painted porcelain cups at the center of the table. "Enjoy. Your appetizers will be out shortly."

Lily grinned, picking up one of the flaming drinks. "I think I'm going to need more than mere alcohol to keep up with you wild women!"

Through the double doors the waitress brought their food, setting it on the table for everyone to share. Rissa leaned over resting the side of her head on Emily's shoulder. "I'm so glad you're home, sweetie."

Emily tilted her head, resting her temple against Rissa's hair, blinking away the wetness stinging her eyes.

"I love you, too." Rissa said, answering the unspoken sentiment in her friend's sigh.

Emily straightened, downing Rissa's untouched plum shot. "These go down like warm silk, but man do they have a kick! My teeth are tingling."

"She did warn us, right?" Charlayne said, lifting another glass of saké to chase her plum shot. "To kicking names and taking ass."

"Hey! That reminds me. Speaking of taking ass, guess what I found on YouTube?" Amilynn waggled her eyebrows and fished in her back pocket for her phone. She scrolled through her apps. "Oh good, they have WiFi." Finding what she was looking for she held the full screen out toward the table. "Britney Spears 'Work B**ch' uncut. You know, the one with the orgy scene that ended up on the cutting room floor."

"Isn't there anything that girl won't do?" Rissa asked, shaking her head at the risqué video.

"Oh, come on, she's tame compared to some of the rap videos. Besides, if it's between two consenting adults, who cares, right?" Lily said swirling the saké remaining in the bottom of her glass.

The waitress cleared their empty plates, her face not happy at how much food was left untouched. "Would you guys like some fortune cookies?"

Lily handed her plate to the woman. "Hey, do you have alternative fortune cookies, you know, the bachelorette party kind?" She made bunny eared quotation marks with her fingers.

The waitress grinned. "Yeah, we do. They're wicked funny, and some even have truth or dare questions. They're an extra charge, though."

Charlayne raised her hand, beckoning the air. "Bring 'em on. And bring another round of saké." The waitress nodded, laughing when Char yelled, "And keep 'em coming."

A different waitress showed up a few minutes later with a beautiful bamboo basket filled with golden crisp fortune cookies. They were sitting on a bed of almond cakes and were definitely not the mass produced kind you get at your local Chinese take-out.

"Who wants to go first?" Emily asked, eyeing Amilynn.

"No thanks. You put me in the hot seat once already. Swarm of mosquitos, my ass. Literally! It was awful. My lady lumps never itched so much in my life!"

"Oh my God! Ami, you're killing me...stop!" Rissa said, holding her sides from laughing.

"I'm game. I'll go first," Lily said, reaching for the first cookie. She cracked it in half and took out the narrow white paper inside. Rolling her eyes, she handed it to Emily.

"What does it say?"

"You have great legs. What time do they open?"

Five women groaned.

"Me next," Patricia said taking a cookie from the basket. She cracked it in half and then tossed the cookie part across the table.

"Jeez, Patty. Not a fan of fortune cookies?" Amilynn teased.

"I just want the fortune. With the way I've been drinking if I eat another thing, I'll end up puking."

Charlayne rolled her eyes. "I think you've got that backwards, sweetie, but hey, whatever gets you off."

"What does it say, already?" Rissa asked.

Their original waitress walked towards them carrying a double order of sake. She put both iced carafes on the table. "Courtesy of the two gentlemen at the end of the bar," she said, before moving on to her next table.

Charlayne reached over and smacked Patricia's arm. "Look at the eye-candy checking us out."

Patty looked back over her shoulder. "They're not looking at us, Char. They're looking at Lily and Emily."

Charlayne raised her hand and waved, only to have Patty knock her hand down. "You're a married woman. Cut that out."

She blew a razzberry at her friend. "What happens in Boston stays in Boston, remember?"

Rissa chuckled. "Sorry, hon. I know that was the joke on the ride down, but I think that only applies in Vegas."

"Come on, Pat. What did your fortune cookie say?" Emily asked pouring more ice cold sake into the six blue ceramic cups.

"You like cum from sum yong guy."

"No, it doesn't!" Lily laughed, holding her hand out for the paper. She glanced down at the small white strip in Patty's hand and laughed even harder.

"Guess it does," Emily added dryly.

"That's just wrong on so many levels."

The lights flickered and the place went dark, the crowd applauded, and a row of overhead spotlights snapped on across the bar. The bartenders lined up, each holding a colorful liquor bottle in their hands. Music started, and a slow, seductive beat played as the bar staff moved into a choreographed mixology routine, tossing bottles in the air like something right out of the 80's movie *Cocktail*.

Charlayne got up, her body swaying in time to the music. "I fucking love this song!"

The bar was primed for a party, and she answered. Hips grinding, she found the two guys at the bar who sent the saké and eye-fucked both of them. The beat intensified and her moves matched the erotic grinding pulse.

Patricia stood, waving dollar bills, pointing to the guys watching Charlayne gyrate. "It's all for you, baby, if you join her!"

With a laugh, one of them dropped his chin and without missing a beat moved toward Charlayne, matching her hips thrust for thrust.

Cheers erupted around the bar, and Patty squealed, "You go girl!" tossing her fistful of dollars at them.

People scrambled for the money as it fluttered to the floor. The maître d' was not happy, especially when Patricia knocked over chairs to join Charlayne on the makeshift dance floor. Sandwiched between the two girls, the first bar guy slid his thumbs under Charlayne's ass, pulling her hard against him. In a move nothing short of maneuvered sex, he spun around and did the same to Patricia.

In the middle of the commotion the waitress brought another round of drinks, but the manager shook his head catching her off guard. She stopped short and glasses crashed to the ground. Another guy joined the dance floor and swung Patty around, lifting her onto the backlit bar. She stood, grinding to the beat, her gaze traveling the length of the guy's body, lingering on the prominent bulge at the front of his jeans.

"Come to mama, baby!" she shouted.

"She's nuts! What the hell is Gerry going to say if he hears about this?" Amilynn shouted over the music and noise.

"Looks like the flaming hot spot kicked in," Rissa shouted.

Patty jumped off the bar into the arms of the guys that lifted her, wrapping her legs around his waist. Holding her by the hips he let her drop back, dry humping her against the largest stone Buddha.

The other guy grabbed Charlayne but lost his footing mid-grope and the two crashed into the empty koi fountain.

"Stop!" The manager yelled, despite the hoots and cheers from the crowd. With a muttered expletive, he pulled Charlayne out of the water, his face red and veiny with the effort.

Emily jumped up to help him while Lily and Ami pulled Patty away from the humping Buddha guy.

"Hey, where you going, sweethaaht," he slurred in a heavy Boston accent.

"Sorry, dude, but her dancing days are over." Lily tried to keep Patty steady, but the girl listed to one side taking Lily and Amilynn with her. "Come on, Patricia. Cooperate."

Patty smiled, but then her eyes widened, and her hand flew to her mouth.

"Oh no you don't." Lily rocked back on her heel, grabbing Patricia by the collar and dragged her toward the ladies' room with Ami in tow.

The manager straightened, shaking his wet hands out to the side, sending droplets everywhere. "Who's going to pay for all this?" he demanded

Emily looked up from trying to dry Charlayne off with leftover napkins from dinner.

"You!" he shouted, pointing his meaty finger at her. "You made the reservation; you're going to pay for the damage."

"Me? Why are you blaming me?" she yelled back, gesturing awkwardly with one arm.

He continued yelling in Japanese, which made his face redder and his veins more pronounced. "They are your friends. If you don't pay, I'll call the police," the manager shot back.

"That won't be necessary," a masculine voice said from behind.

Emily and the manager both turned in unison.

The guy who spoke was drop dead gorgeous in a dark, sophisticated way. He came closer. The way he moved sinuous and sexy left no question he hold his own in any situation. He reached for his wallet quickly flashing his badge.

"Good." The manager nodded sharply. "You take care of this. I have a club to run." He snapped his fingers for the waitstaff to clean up the glass and pick up the chairs before he walked back into the kitchen.

Emily moved slowly, turning Charlayne and her suddenly green pallor over to Rissa who sat her on one of the chairs at the table.

The bar returned to its normal hum, the drama fading into the air along with the sound of clinking glasses. With an aggravated sigh, Emily ran a hand through her hair. "This sucks."

Misreading her friend's upset face, Rissa propped Charlayne on the chair and then flanked Emily's side. "Officer, my friend is not responsible for all of this," she said, but stopped when Emily put a staying hand on her arm.

"It's okay, Ris. He's not going to arrest me. He's not a Boston cop."

"I don't understand." She jerked her eyes toward the dark haired guy. "You're not a cop? What kind of a creep says he's a cop when he's not?"

Emily shook her head "No, Ris. I said he's not a *Boston* cop, but he is a police officer. From New York. I read the front of his shield when he flashed it."

The guy nodded slowly, a gorgeous, crooked grin gracing his full mouth. "Quick." Approval flashed in his eyes, and his smirk took on a playful quality. "Your friends seem down for the count. Do you have a way of getting them home?"

Emily crossed her arms in front of her chest. "I've got it covered."

"Clearly." He nodded toward the door where Amilynn was pointing to the limo parked outside.

"I'll see what's going on. Be back in a sec," Rissa said, giving Emily a wary look before heading toward the door with a determined stride.

The waitress walked up to Emily and handed her the check. "My boss says whenever you're ready." She spared a glance toward the kitchen doors. "I'll be back."

Emily scanned the bill and frowned. She walked over to her chair and grabbed her purse, fishing inside for her wallet.

"Why don't you let me take care of that," he offered, slipping the check from between her fingers.

"Excuse me? Give that back!"

"I'm just trying to be nice."

She exhaled roughly, shoving her hand through her hair again, the blond strands flowing back into place framing her aggravated expression.

He smiled. "You look like a vengeful angel when you do that." When her frown deepened, he held the bill out to her. "I'll make you a deal. I'll let you pay the check if you agree to come out with me for an afterhours drink."

This was too surreal, and certainly not the way she wanted the evening to end. Two out of their original six were three sheets to the wind. *Fucking light weights*. Emily exhaled. Rissa was probably pissed to high heaven, and she hated that Lily was right and Sean was certain to explode. Maybe she could catch the red eye for California and not have to face the music.

Emily watched the New York cop's face, catching a whiff of him.

His scent tickled and the sensation of soft fur crossed her sympathetic nervous system along with the feel of sharp claws against her back. Her breath froze in her throat and wetness pooled between her legs. Her body hadn't tingled with want like this in ages. Who was he?

"You smell familiar. Have we met before?" She tilted her head, running the possibilities. The only shifters she'd run into in California had been selkies...shape shifting seals or sea lions...wild horses and big horn sheep. She'd heard about big cats...cougars...but hadn't come across one. Until now.

Eyebrows up, he gave her a strange look. "Now that's a new one. Usually people start a pick-up line with you *look* familiar."

Mouth open, Emily tilted her head considering him. He was a cat. Of that she had no doubt. This made no sense, and the way her body reacted to his scent made it all the more curious. Either he was just playing coy, or he truly had no idea about his dual nature. But how? She inhaled again. Half breed. Well, that explained a lot.

She shook her head. It was too late, and she was too buzzed to worry about his ignorant state. It was his problem, not hers. She had enough to deal with.

"Never mind. I just like your cologne, that's all."

He smirked. "Then I guess it must be me since I'm not wearing any cologne. But don't worry, I get that a lot."

"I bet."

He looked at her, his own nostrils flaring slightly. "If it's worth anything, you smell amazing yourself. I guess you could say I have a very keen sense of smell, too. Always have."

"You don't say. Listen, my friends are waiting. I'd better pay this check, and then get them to our hotel. Thanks for your help." She stopped, her words fading. "Sorry. I didn't catch your name."

"Ryan. Detective Ryan Mar—"

Emily held up her hand. "Ryan is enough."

"So, you like to travel light, huh?" An appreciative gaze swept her tall frame. "Me too.... uhm..."

"Emily. Just Emily."

He laughed. "Well, Just Emily, do we have a deal?" He held the check out to her again.

His voice held the low seductive rumble that shifter males take on when aroused. She looked at the bill in his hand and let her eyes travel from his flat, obviously muscled torso to his high cheekbones and deep green eyes. He really was gorgeous, with dark wavy hair and olive skin. His strong jaw was set off by a small cleft in middle of his chin and he had a pair of dimples that captivated her as much as the tiny beauty mark slightly above his lip.

If she left with Ryan, then she wouldn't have to listen to Rissa when they got to the hotel. And if she lingered in town long enough for Lily to diffuse Sean, she'd be golden in that department too. She knew it was a cop out, but if she had to be on the outs it might as well be with a good-looking cop. She knew she'd eventually have to go back and face them, and she would. Just not tonight.

Her eyes met his and she licked her lips. "Why not?"

"I can't believe she went off with a complete stranger. Rissa, why didn't you stop her?" Amilynn huffed, her unease climbing with every twist of her purse strap.

"Ami, listen to me. Emily is not eighteen anymore, and she's been on her own for the past five years. I can't believe I'm saying this, but we need to back off. She'll be okay."

"Hmmph. And if she's not? How are you going to explain it to Sean? How are you both going to explain it?" she shot back, eyeing Rissa and Lily equally.

Rissa shrugged. "Emily has always been a runner. Even when we were kids and in trouble she'd always manage to skip out until after the smoke cleared. She said she's been working on it. Maybe this is just her way of blowing off steam."

"Or blowing us off." Ami frowned.

Lily stood, crouching as best she could in the back of the limo to sit closer to Rissa and Amilynn, the only other shifters not passed out in the car.

"I know you're worried, Ami…and despite Rissa's bravado, she's as annoyed and anxious as you are." Lily paused, watching her friend eye her circumspectly. "And to answer that raised eyebrow of yours, no, I did not eavesdrop inside your head, Ris."

Lily crossed her legs, reaching for what was left of their flat champagne. "You both have every right to be angry and concerned, but Emily's a big girl. She has her cell phone, plus she has strength and skills that give her a distinct advantage over an average human male. I'll be the first one to admit I know what it's like to be a runner."

"I've never known you to run from anything…well except for that little incident on the manor house gabled roof," Rissa joked.

Lily nodded in agreement. "See? Like I said. I was a runner, but the only difference is I was an emotional runner and not a physical one. I never flinch or run from conflict, but I still haven't seen my family since I've been here."

Rissa reached out and took Lily's hand.

Amilynn reached up and brightened the limo's dim interior lights and closed the Plexiglas partition between them and the driver. "I hate talking in the dark and I hate eavesdroppers." As if on cue, Patricia's hand flopped over still closed eyes and Charlayne snorted, her head back and her mouth wide open. Ami chuckled. "I hope they're having some kickass dreams now because they're going to be two hurting puppies tomorrow."

"Well, at least in that department shifters aren't so different from humans. In fact, nothing those two did tonight is any different than what happens in the human world." Lily winked, tilting the edge of her glass toward the other girls. "Did either of you get a look at the guy Emily left with? Did she say where they were headed?"

Rissa shrugged. "I think they were going to the Catwalk. It's a bar in the Liberty Hotel. The building used to be a jail," she explained for Lily's sake. "Considering he's a cop, it fits."

"I was with Lily in the ladies room holding Patty's hair back while she prayed over the porcelain. You talked to the guy, Ris, what did he look like?" Amilynn prompted.

Rissa considered for a moment. "He was tall and dark. Spanish or perhaps Italian. Very good looking. Still, not someone I would bet Em to go for."

"Why not? She not into ethnic?" Lily asked.

Rissa shook her head. "No, it's not that. In the past she always went for guys who looked like Sean. In fact, we used to tease her about how creepy that was, right Ami?"

The pretty raven-haired girl nodded. "Always. Built, blond and blue-eyed, but then again maybe that's why she did a 180 degree turn. Connor was striking, with a typical hot surfer dude look, and Emily went clear across the country to get away from him."

Lily looked at Rissa again for clarification.

Rissa sighed letting one shoulder lift and then fall. "He's the guy Sean told you about. The one Emily ran away from marrying. It was bound to happen regardless of what Connor looked like. In that respect Em's very much like you, Lily. Independent, strong—but the aftermath of her action was terrible, especially for Sean after he took over as alpha."

"I get it. He's Abenaki, right? Just like Cecily and Mitch, only Cecily is holding it against Sean and by default against you," Lily said tilting her glass toward Rissa.

Rissa's answering sigh was all the confirmation Lily needed. "So, what happened exactly? Sean mentioned something, but said it was a story for another time."

"Connor's clan thought Sean's father weak in allowing his daughter to have her own head. They made the old alpha pay reparations, and when he finally died, they looked to Sean to enforce the contract. He didn't. In fact, he went so far as to annul all previous arrangements for everyone at the compound unless both parties consented of their own free will. Even now there are factions who would love to use this as a reason to start a pack war."

"But that's all in the past now, right?"

Rissa exhaled, the question hanging in the air. "I don't know, Lil. It's not as cut and dry as it should be. Connor's father took the matter one step further, blaming him for not being man enough to stake his claim. The kid was so shamed, he rebelled in the worst way possible for a shifter. He started consorting with vampires, having sex with them while they fed from his veins. He eventually drank their blood too and became addicted. No one has seen him for over a year. He sort of disappeared into the underground."

Lily exhaled. "Well, it all makes sense now."

"What does?" Rissa questioned.

"Emily's running. If it were me, I'd never come back. Listen, based on what you just told me, Emily is probably expecting everyone to make a big deal about her going off on a tryst. My suggestion is don't. As long as she stays in touch, what does it matter? As long as we know she's safe, whatever happens between two consenting adults is none of our business. Agreed?"

Rissa and Ami exchanged glances and then looked at the two women passed out at the far end of the limo.

Lily put her hand out, gesturing for the other two to do the same. "What happens in Boston, stays in Boston, right?"

The three linked hands. "Right."

Ryan's eyes swept the place as they walked into the bar. "This building has some serious history. Did you know it was formerly the Charles Street Jail?" He pointed to the iron walkways that marked each floor and surrounded the entire perimeter. "The original catwalk was used by prisoners and guards to move from cell to cell and floor to floor. Designers kept it and reworked it to circle the entire rotunda of the main hotel with the Catwalk Bar as its main attraction."

"Impressive. Are you a guest here?" Emily asked, sliding into a chair an intimate little table.

He nodded. "We couldn't be here otherwise. The Catwalk is a

hotel-guest-only retreat," he quoted, tapping the shiny information card on the table.

Emily took the laminated rack card and looked at the pictures of the smiling guests and fancy drinks. "Hmmm. It also says a place of unrestrained fun and that it closes at two a.m." She gestured to her watch. "I guess that means we'd better drink fast. It's almost closing time."

Ryan slid the information card from her fingers and laced his own with hers instead. Lifting her hand to his mouth, he turned her palm upward, kissing the inside of her wrist with a slow sexy caress.

Watching his lips against her skin and the feel of his mouth, subtle and warm, made her own water. Her pulse increased, and she knew she was throwing off fuck-me pheromones by the gallon. Dual-natured or not, there was no way Ryan wasn't feeling the effects as well.

He lifted his head and his eyes locked with hers. They were dark and dilated, and when he inhaled, she swore he made a sound at the back of his throat. He was as turned on as she was.

She slipped her hand from his and crossed her arms on the table, leaning in a bit so he could have a better view. For once she was glad she listened to her own advice and wore the plunging gold silk tunic with her winter white pencil skirt and matching knee-high boots.

"So, hotel guest, what do you recommend?"

Ryan's lips slid into a sideways smirk. "Do you really want to know?"

"To drink, wise guy. What do you recommend to drink?"

"Oh. That. I recommend the French Kiss. It's Grey Goose La Poire, Chambord, pineapple and topped with Prosecco. It's sexy and sleek... just like you. Plus, it goes down easy..."

He let the last part of his description trail off, but the innuendo wasn't lost, and heat crawled up Emily's cheeks.

"High color." He slid back from his seat and moved around to her side of the table. "There's nothing sexier than a girl who still blushes."

He kissed her cheek close to the base of her ear and then whispered, "I'll be right back."

He straightened and walked toward the bar, his stride strong and muscled. Emily watched him and let go of the breath locked in her throat. "Oh my God," she mumbled, smoothing the front of her silk blouse.

She opened her purse and took out her phone, expecting twenty panicked text messages from Rissa alone. Instead she saw only one.

*Hey. Have fun and b safe.*

*Breakfast at 10 in lobby...*

*Want details. Call if not coming.*

*xoxo*

So, everyone was expecting her to be out all night and they were okay with it. She smiled to herself. *Lily.* She'd bet her lungs she was the one who set the wolvettes straight.

"That's quite a secret smile. Something happen?" Ryan asked carrying two martini glasses filled with a hot pink mixture.

"No, just checking texts," Emily said stuffing her phone into her bag. "Guess the French Kiss is hot pink, like everything else tonight." She picked up the feather boa she carried in from the Red Lantern and then let it drop back onto the chair.

"I don't know about that, but I'm betting tonight is hot all right."

Again, with the innuendo. If she didn't do something with this guy soon, she was going to pop.

Ryan handed her one of the stemmed glasses, then held up his. "To possibilities," he said, his eyes never leaving hers.

Emily smiled and clinked the edge of her glass with his. "Definitely."

"How long have you been a detective?" she asked, taking a sip of her drink.

"A couple of years. Feels longer, though."

She nodded. "I bet. Must be hard. Are you street crime or DEA?"

He frowned. "Homicide."

"Ouch."

278

He laughed. "Actually, it's not as bad as it seems. I've seen some pretty nasty things, but I'm lucky. I work with really great people and my prospects are good. What about you?"

"I work for a newspaper. Right now, I'm just a copy editor, but eventually I'd like to be a reporter."

"So, you're nosy," he teased, pushing his drink back and forth on the napkin.

Emily choked a little. "No, I am not nosy. I just like action. I get bored easily and I like change. The news changes every day. Like you joked earlier, I like to travel light."

She took another sip and placed her drink on the napkin in front of her. Looking around it was clear there was no one left in the bar. "Should we be here? It looks like they're getting ready to close."

"It's okay. They're not going to kick us out. We can finish our drinks and then take it from there."

"Take it where?"

He looked at her with eyes full of desire. "Wherever you want it."

Emily picked up her glass and drained it in one gulp, wincing as the vodka scored her throat. "I want it here and I want it now," she said, surprised at the rough sound of her own voice.

Ryan pushed his chair back and it clattered to the floor, causing the bartender to look up from the glass he was polishing. "You okay, buddy?" he asked.

With a low rumble, Ryan shot him a look and the guy actually took a step backwards.

"Ryan," Emily said softly, her fingers turning his eyes back to hers. "Let's go."

With his arm around her waist, the two walked out of the bar and headed toward the tower elevator. Ryan pushed the up button and then pulled Emily against his chest. Arms of steel locked around her and he pressed the hard length of his body to hers. "I want to taste every inch of you," he breathed against her ear.

"Ryan..."

The elevator doors opened.

"Holy shit! Emily! Is that you?"

At the sound of her name, she turned. "Connor?" Dumbfounded, she shook her head clearing the lust from her brain and tried to find her voice

"Yeah. Funny seeing you here...in Boston...at this hour," he said, flicking his gaze between her and Ryan.

"It's been a long time," she replied, ignoring his dig. "Connor this is Ryan. Ryan...Connor."

Connor's features were as attractive as ever, but his sun kissed skin was pale, even for winter. He was dressed in a stunning double breasted suit, and the shoulder-length surfer hair had been cropped short.

"I always knew you were a bitch in heat despite what everyone said," he taunted.

His good looks she had always admired were suddenly ugly as his mouth twisted into a snarl. "Too bad I didn't get the chance to smell the sex scent on you then, the way you reek of it now," he shook his head, his contempt clear. "And with this cat, too. I'm sure your family is so proud."

Ryan stepped forward, pushing Emily slightly behind him. "You got a problem, dude? The lady is with me, so I suggest you move along to wherever you were headed."

A woman stepped out of the open elevator. A stunning dark-haired beauty with large obsidian eyes. Her skin was luminous, pale like the moon, and she was wrapped in white ermine with a matching hat that set off the wide, smoky beauty of her eyes.

One look at the woman's delicate wraithlike features and the underlying pattern of blue veins beneath her white skin and Emily knew the rumors about Connor were true. The woman was a vampire.

Emily stepped out from behind Ryan. There was no way he would recognize the woman for the predator she was.

As if she could read Emily mind, the woman smiled, the sharp edges of her canines peeking out beneath her ruby painted lips, but not enough for an innocent eye to discern. "The gentleman is correct, *moy dorogoy*. There is nothing here for you. *Poydem otsyuda...* let's go."

She turned Connor toward her. Lifting her gloved hand to his cheek, she murmured something that sounded Russian.

"Yes, Jenya. Whatever you say." Sparing a final glare at Emily, he followed the vampire down the hall, the two disappearing around the corner.

"Who the hell was that," Ryan asked, running a hand through his hair. "And how creepy was his girlfriend. I swear the hair on my neck stood on end when she smiled at us."

"I don't know who she was, but Connor was the guy my father wanted me to marry. I said no. End of story."

Emily's shrug punctuated the words. She was not about to get into it, not with her hormones still racing despite Connor's chilly exit with the vampire. It was pretty clear Ryan had no idea about the supernatural world living side by side with his, but one thing was sure, his sympathetic nervous system certainly did. His fight or flight instincts were on the money.

Not wanting to lose any more of their intensity, she slipped her arms around Ryan's waist and pressed herself against him. "Now, where were we?"

Ryan's mouth slid into a seductive smirk. "Right where I've wanted you all night."

The two stumbled into the elevator, hands grabbing at clothes before the doors slid closed. Emily fumbled with Ryan's tie, finally slipping it over his head. "Let's not lose this," she said stuffing the narrow silk into his back pocket. "We're going to need it later."

The doors closed and he lifted her against the chrome sidewall. "Push the stop button, I can't wait any longer."

He crushed his mouth to hers, and she groped for the button as he groped for the hem of her skirt. The elevator jerked to a stop, and Ryan lowered her to her feet, letting her feel every inch of his hardness the whole way down.

Her pencil skirt bunched against the elevator's decorative chair rail, and with one hand Ryan hiked it up the rest of the way 'til it was gathered around her waist. A delicate gold lace thong was the only thing separating her from the bulge at the front of his dress jeans.

Hooking one finger into his waistband, she unfastened his top button, his fly coming undone one button at a time. She gasped, at the nest of dark hair in her hand and the hard, corded mass that strained to get free beneath her palm.

"You're commando," she murmured.

"Yes. But you're not." With a single tug he tore the lace in two at her hip and pushed her thong to the side. Freeing his cock, he lifted her again, driving himself into her soft, wet folds with one stroke.

Emily moaned, digging her fingers beneath the back of his jeans, kneading his hard ass as he drove into her, thrust after thrust. The elevator car shook with their efforts, and the alarm bells sounded.

"Is everything okay in there?" a disembodied voice asked over the intercom, only to hear the words, "Holy shit, Tommy, come see this. Two people are fucking like rabbits in car four!"

Ryan swore, turning them so the only thing the peeping toms could see was the wide expanse of his back. With a rough grunt, his hips thrust harder and harder until Emily cried out in release. A guttural growl escaped his throat, and he plunged deep, his balls high and tight as he exploded inside her.

Emily slumped against the inside curve of his shoulder, hiding her face. "We should probably continue this in your room," she said, her breath raspy and jagged.

"You think?" With a laugh, Ryan slid Emily down for the second time, only now he helped her shimmy her skirt back into place. Still hiding her face, she helped him straighten the front of his pants before he pressed the up button.

The elevator doors opened at the sixteenth floor, and Ryan stepped aside letting Emily out first.

"Almost there. I'm three doors down on the left side."

They walked side by side, and heat nagged at Emily's cheeks from the squishy, wet feel between her legs. Her panties were ruined and stuffed in a wad into her purse. She needed the bathroom immediately before she let Ryan anywhere near her nether regions again.

Keycard in hand, he swiped the plastic rectangle through the digital reader above the handle, and the door snicked open. "Home Sweet Home Away," he teased.

Emily walked in behind him, and took in the expanse of the room, the fireplace and the plush club chairs and matching sofa. Around the corner were a full bar and a California king bed and an enormous marble bathroom. Floor to ceiling picture windows offered a view of the city that took her breath away. "It's beautiful," she murmured.

"It sure is," he said, his eyes taking in every inch of her.

She walked to the window and dropped her purse on the couch along with her coat. She had never reacted this way to anyone. All her previous lovers, human and shifter alike, left her satisfied, but never craving more. It was always a take it or leave it scenario, with her deciding yes or no. For the first time in her life she felt there was no decision to make, no willpower to tell him no.

There was nothing about this man that was meh. Everything, from the way he looked and smelled to the sound of his voice and the feel of his light touch on her skin, had every fiber of her being screaming for more. And she didn't even know his full name.

She knew he'd tell her everything if she asked, but her life was too complicated, and right now, all she wanted was his body on hers. There was time for more. Maybe. *Maybe not.* She had come home, but she wasn't ready to stay, here or anywhere else for that matter. Her life was in a state of flux, but regardless if it was the saké or the vodka, she was in a state of heat.

"Mind if I freshen up a bit," she asked, a little embarrassed at being caught sparing with her own inner musing.

He smiled. "Take your time. There are a couple of terry robes on the inside hook, if you want."

With a nod she snapped on the light closing the door behind, but not before she heard his phone buzz. She turned on the tap but left the door purposely ajar.

"Hello? Oh, hey. Nah, I'm still in Beantown, but I'll be home tomorrow afternoon. No, I don't have to check in with Shaw until Monday so I'm free. Whaddadya have in mind? Oh man, hockey sounds good. Listen, can I call you when I get back? I'm kinda in the middle of something." He paused. "Okay, great. See you Sunday... oh and Murph, don't cheap out and get nosebleed seats. I want to feel each crash off the boards. Okay...gotta go."

Through the crack in the door, Emily watched him press end call and toss his phone onto the chair next to his jacket.

She tiptoed toward the mirror, stripping out of her clothes and slipping on the terry robe from the hook next to the door. Dipping her hands into the running water, she pulled her fingers back the minute they touched. "Shit!"

"If you hadn't been busy eavesdropping you would have known the water was too hot," he said, coming up behind her as quiet as a cat.

"It wasn't eavesdropping. It was overhearing. There's a difference. Now if you don't mind, I'd like to clean up a bit."

She pulled the rolled collar of the terry robe tighter across her chest, and for the first time tonight it hit her how stupid and reckless this was. She was alone with a complete stranger in his hotel room wearing nothing but a terry cloth robe. A stranger with whom she just had sex within a hotel elevator.

She knew she was every shade of red known to man, and with the blotched color against the white of the terry cloth she probably looked even more vulnerable than she felt.

He smiled, backing her up until her ass hit the marble vanity. Sliding his hands around her waist he lifted her onto the crème colored granite.

"I said it before and I'll say it again, there is nothing sexier than a woman's genuine blush."

"Ryan..."

"Shh," he whispered, pulling out the tie she had shoved into his back pocket. "You did say we should save this for later, right?"

"Ryan..." she tried again, only to be silenced with a kiss.

"Relax, Emily. I'm not going to hurt you. You are so sexy and fearless. I can't get enough of you. I'm so hard I could cut diamond with the tip of my cock."

He separated the front fold of her robe and slid her knees apart, his hands running slowly from her shoulders to her thighs, grazing the taut peaks of her small breasts. Hooking his hands onto her hips, he pulled her forward, the soft fuzz surrounding her mound brushing the cotton of his jeans and the bulge beneath his fly.

At the rough feel she gasped, her breath hitching, and a fresh pool of wet, slick juice ran from her sex.

"I smell how much you want me, Emily," he rasped. "I smell my own cum on you, mixed with your own wetness."

She moaned at his words, leaning back to lift her legs and wrap them around his waist. She wanted to grind herself against him for release, but he held her knees down.

"Not so fast," he murmured. Grabbing both her wrists, he steered them behind her back and tied her hands together with his silk tie.

"You want release? You're going to have to ask for it. Beg for it."

He ran the water in the tap and when it was just the right temperature, he wet a washcloth, dipping the edge in the hot water until it was soaked. "I want you dripping wet, just like this. I want your pussy to run slick down my legs as I fuck you, slippery and sweet."

Ryan held the hot saturated cloth above her sex, letting the water drip onto her mound, wetting everything until she glistened with water and her own slickness. He teased her with the rough seam of the cotton cloth, letting the abrasive edge tickle and graze her nub until she squirmed at the slow sexy torture.

His other hand teased her nipples, rubbing and caressing intermittently between the light cloth strokes.

"Please..." One word escaped Emily's lips between gasps.

He chuckled, throaty and low. "Getting there, baby, but not quite yet." Discarding the washcloth, he took his time stripping out of his clothes, letting her eyes take in every inch of his body, especially his long thick cock, corded and red, waiting to take her.

He dipped his mouth to her lips, letting his tongue spar with hers, feeling her whimper in his mouth as his hand teased body, finally dropping his head to her nipples, his tongue rasping and licking, sucking, and biting.

Ryan slid his hand across her stomach, his fingers finding her erect nub. He slid two fingers around the taut core and pulled, earning another whimper before gliding the same two fingers inside her slick entrance. Her sex was swollen and ripe, and he knew her juices were at their peak, but he held off, watching her face as he worked her inside and out. His fingers pumped while his thumb circled and rubbed her clit until Emily pushed forward, using all her strength against her tied hands to thrust against his palm. It was time.

"RYAN! PLEASE!" she shouted. He pulled his fingers from her and she cried out in protest, but he silenced her with a crushing kiss, pulling her hips to the end of the vanity and driving his thick, throbbing member into her with a violent thrust.

Impaled on his sex, he picked her up and carried her to the bed, dropping her to the edge. He untied her hands and pulled out, flipped her onto her stomach. With a growl, he yanked her hips up and back and filled her again, his balls smacking against her swollen sex as he rode her hard.

Emily cried out, her ass in the air, grinding and thrusting back as she came. Her inner walls convulsed milking Ryan's cock dry. A snarl left his throat like none he'd ever heard, and the sound pulled from his balls as he came. The two slumped forward, spent. Exhaustion consumed them in a fog of sleep, still entwined.

Morning light spilled through the curtain sheers, and Emily picked her head up, cracking one eye open to get her bearings. "Shit!" she mumbled, looking at the spacious room across the large expanse of Ryan's back.

The whole night flooded back, and she slumped against the

pillows, her hand flung over her forehead. She muttered an expletive, trying to convince herself she was dreaming, only to feel the soft motion of Ryan's shoulders moving as he breathed.

Real enough.

She sat up, wincing with the effort, tenderness in her nether regions a poignant reminder of just how real this all was—that and the slight tenderness at either side of each wrist.

Taking the sheet with her, she wrapped herself toga style and went to find her purse and subsequently, her phone. The bag was on the chair where she'd left it along with her coat. Unzipping the top, she reached in only to find the damn thing had run out of battery at some point during the night.

"Stupid," she murmured under her breath. The clock on the night-stand read nine fifty a.m. Rissa and the girls were meeting for breakfast in ten minutes. Crap. Purse under her arm and toga in tow, she scooted into the bathroom trying not to wake Ryan. The last thing she wanted was a sticky good-bye, or worse, facing him and realizing she didn't want it to be good-bye.

She closed the door and took inventory of her face in the mirror. Swollen lips and smeared make-up. Wonderful. Add in disheveled hair and a distinct post sex stink and she'd win the prize for skank of the month. Ugh.

If she showered, she'd wake him for certain, so it was a whore's bath for her, and she grimaced at how apropos the thought. Well, at least she enjoyed herself for once. The washcloth Ryan used on her last night was still on the vanity, and just looking at it sent a crimson stain across her chest and up her neck into her cheeks. She'd never done anything like that before, not being the "tie me up, tie me down" type. In fact, she always looked a little askance at the alternative practice, thinking herself to be too independent and strong willed to ever let a man take complete control. However, last night was unbelievable, and Ryan was definitely someone who would haunt her even though she wasn't planning on sticking around to say thanks for the memories.

Careful not to let the tap get too hot again, she grabbed a fresh wash cloth and lathered it to a sudsy froth, giving her face a scrub and the rest of her a good top and tails detailing. She pulled open her purse again and tossed her shredded thong in the trash before running a brush through her tangled hair, doing the best she could with what little makeup she had in the small evening bag.

At least her clothes weren't wrinkled since she had hung them up when she slipped on the terry robe. She dressed quickly, gathering everything and stuffing it back into her purse.

"Good morning."

Emily jumped, dropping the contents of her purse in a clatter on the bathroom tile. "Ryan...I didn't want to wake you," she said scrambling to collect her spilled items.

"What you really mean is you wanted to sneak out without so much as a goodbye," he said eyeing her like a district attorney staring down a hostile witness.

"No," she replied, closing her bag and straightening. "But I do have to leave. When I checked my texts last night in the bar, my friends said for me to meet them for breakfast at ten, and as you can see, I'm already late."

He smirked. "Breakfast or a debriefing?"

She picked up her boots, holding them across her chest like a protective shield. "Don't be a jerk. We had a good time last night, but now I've got to run."

He nodded. "Yup, I gathered as much. Is that your M.O?"

She stamped her still bare foot. "Will you stop with the cop talk? I'm not running." She tried to make bunny ears with her fingers and ended up dropping her boots.

Ryan picked them up, handing them to her with a sideways grin on his face. "First thing they teach in detective school is how to read body language, and yours screams guilty and scared. What I want to know is what you're guilty of and why you're afraid."

Emily pressed her lips together. "I'm not afraid of you. If I was, I would never have allowed you to...to..." She couldn't bring herself to say it out loud.

"...tie you up?" he finished the sentence for her.

"Yes. Exactly. I'm not afraid and I'm not guilty, it's just I'm not usually one for this...this kind of thing," she added letting her arm swing wide and dropping her boots again. "Oh, for fuck's sake!" She bent to scoop them up and then pushed passed Ryan still standing in the doorway in his underwear.

"For fuck's sake indeed," he reiterated.

Emily sat on the end of the bed and slipped on her boots, lifting her leg to slide them over her calf.

"Looks like going commando is catchy," he said gesturing to the little peep show she just gave him lifting her leg.

"Not funny. Those panties are in shreds, what do you expect me to do?"

"I could give you a pair of mine," he offered, snapping the waistband on his boxer briefs. I've got a clean pair in the drawer with the rest of my clothes."

He stopped, his eyes considering her. "Actually, what I expected was for you to wake up next to me as naked as a jaybird and together we'd have breakfast in bed with a little dessert on the side." He walked over to where she still sat on the bed. "I'm not ready to let you walk out that door, Emily. You said this is unusual for you. Well, it's not exactly usual for me either. I came up here to testify in a case that crosses state lines from New York straight up to the New Hampshire border, and the last thing I expected was to hook up with someone who rocked my world the way you did last night."

Emily froze, her other boot in hand. She looked up at his face, using every shifter sense she possessed to evaluate his sincerity—his scent, his pulse, even his stance. Being on her own for so long taught her to be an excellent judge of truth or bullshit, and everything in her said he was telling the truth.

*What do I do?*

"When I said I don't do this, I wasn't just referring to the tie thing. I don't normally have one night stands."

His eyebrow rose. "But you yourself said you weren't exactly good with permanence either?"

She exhaled. "No, I'm not. Yes, I like excitement and variation, but that doesn't mean I flit from bed to bed."

"I never said that, and if you think that's what I meant, I'm sorry."

She inhaled and let her breath out slowly. "I don't think that." She paused. "I'm at a crossroads, Ryan. And I'm not sure where I'm headed."

"Why do you have to be headed anywhere? I'm okay with taking things one day at a time. In my life, my line of work it's about all you can do. I'm here now, but tomorrow I may take a bullet. I'm not exactly good with permanence either, so I'd say we're a matched set."

Her mind raced as he watched her so intently. *Am I really a runner? Is that what I've become because of Connor and my dad? What if Ryan turns out to be an asshole? What if he doesn't? What if I skip out and then regret not staying? What have I got waiting for me at the Compound or in California for that matter?*

The mental sparring was making Emily nauseous. Maybe it was time for her to take a chance. "Ryan, what time do you leave today?"

He shrugged. "I was planning to head back to New York after lunch, but I don't have to be back at work until Monday. Why?"

"Can I borrow your phone?"

"Sure. Why?"

"I need to call my friends and tell them I won't be meeting them today."

He smiled and tossed her his cell. "Does this mean I should cancel my tickets for the Ranger's game tonight?"

She laughed. "If I'm cancelling on my friends for the rest of the weekend, then yeah, I think it's a safe bet."

He picked up the house phone, but instead of calling his buddy Murph, he ordered room service—a pot of coffee, orange juice and everything they had on the breakfast menu.

Emily laughed. "Getting a little pushy aren't we there, big guy?"

He looked at her outfit and the tiny evening bag. "Before you call your friends, shouldn't you at least tell them we'll be stopping by to pick up your clothes and toiletries? I've got no problem driving you over."

She shook her head. "Nah. I didn't bring much with me anyway. I think this is a weekend for me to treat myself all the way around, but Ryan, that's all this is for now. One weekend. I have a very complicated life and I'm not in the market for long term attachments. Whether you think I should be headed somewhere or not, I meant it when I said I was at a crossroads.

"It may not seem like much, but this is actually a big step for me— staying, I mean, so that means baby steps. I'm giving you 'til Sunday night when you have to head back to New York, and I have to go home. Cell phone numbers—that's it. First names and cell phone numbers. Nothing else. Okay?"

He shook his head, chuckling. "Sneaking out before the one night stand wakes up, saying upfront you want no commitments, only first names and cell phones...are you sure you're not a guy?"

Emily unzipped her skirt and let it fall to the floor. Unbuttoning her blouse, she let it float to the outer sides of her breasts as she laid against pillows, propping her legs open wide with just her boots on. "Let me refresh your memory."

He crawled onto the bed, leaving his underwear on the floor with her skirt. "I'm all yours."

She lifted her hips and let him slip inside, her legs turning to jelly as she wrapped them around his back. "For now, anyway. For now..."

Ryan's suite was luxurious, but the shower was amazing with its ultra-contemporary fixtures and seamless floor to ceiling double shower. The glass was so perfectly set it created the sensation of showering in the open. Of course, the minute Emily stepped into the steam her wet body on display was all Ryan needed for round three.

Her lower belly spasmed in delicious aftershocks at the memory of slick soap and her even slicker sex as Ryan took her against the heated tile, hot water jetting over hard nipples and down to her already swollen clit.

"Do you want to head over to Newbury Street and do some shopping or did you have other plan in mind?" Ryan asked, snapping the damp towel at Emily's smooth, taut butt as she dried her hair.

She jumped at the unexpected sting. "Don't do that!"

He dropped the towel and slid in behind her, his hands skimming the sides of her bare waist. "I only wanted to get an idea of how you planned for us to spend the afternoon."

She turned in his arms, hairstyle forgotten. "How I planned? Does this mean you'll do whatever I want?"

He chuckled, kissing the tip of her nose. "Not a chance. But I am willing to take you shopping. You need clothes, right? Or are we spending the next twenty-four hours in the buff?"

"That's one plan, but I think we need fresh air and something other than room service."

With a laugh, he stepped back from her. "Whatever you say, boss. I am at your fashion disposal," he teased inclining his head in a mock bow.

Ryan left to get dressed and Emily exhaled, letting her breath out slowly as she raked her brush through her hair. "Oh boy," she muttered, turning the hairdryer on low.

Despite the cold, Newbury Street was crowed even though the Weather Channel called for late afternoon snow showers. The wind had picked up and Emily shivered inside her coat, the brisk gusts along the street making her panty-less state all the more acute.

"Where to?" Ryan asked, looking at the rows of shops and restaurants along both sides of the street.

"I need a department store. I don't want to waste the rest of the day flitting in and out of storefronts. One stop shopping. Then we can do something fun."

Ryan pulled a business directory from his pocket, complete with a Newbury Street map and schematic of the all the shops. He unfolded the flyer and ran his finger along one of the color coded guides. "One block up there's Lord and Taylor as well as Saks Fifth Avenue. You should be able to find what you need there."

She shook her head wearing a sideways grin. "You look like a tourist."

"Come on," he said, slinging one arm around her shoulders. "This tourist is treating you to a shopping excursion. You refused to let me pick up the tab last night, and don't forget I'm the reason you don't have any panties this morning. It's the least I can do."

Emily elbowed him in the ribs, deliberately ignoring the wide-eyed stare from the woman standing on the corner five feet away. "Keep your voice down. The wind and this skirt are making my bare bottom uncomfortable enough without you broadcasting it to the world. While I appreciate the offer, I can buy my own clothes...thanks anyway." With a sniff she took the tourist map from his hand.

"Relax. I was just trying to be nice—again." He shook his head, pulling a pair of gloves from his pocket and slipping them over his hands. "Haven't you ever had a guy want to spoil you? I would think with your good looks and sharp wit you'd be used to the royal treatment."

Emily looked at him, her annoyance draining at the genuine interest in his eyes. "Thanks for the compliment, the answer to your question is no, not really." She hooked her arm with his as a peace offering. "Let's walk, my legs are starting to ossify, they're so cold. I'll make you a deal. I won't let you pay, but I will model for you. You can play Caesar and decide thumbs up or thumbs down on what I buy."

"Sold. You got a deal."

Ryan cocked his head giving her a sideways glance as they walked. "What about the dipshit from last night? Didn't he treat you right? Or was that the reason you broke it off."

Curiosity was written all over his face, and she had to smile. No big surprise there. "Your detective side is showing. Better tuck in that bad boy or I'll start to think you're a narc. First names and cell phone numbers. We agreed, remember?"

He sighed. "I remember. Then again, we have to talk at some point, and I can't believe I'm about to say this, but we can't just have sex."

She laughed out loud at the astounded look on his face as the words left his mouth. "I bet that was a first!"

He shook his head, laughing. "You got that right." His chuckle turned into a soft sigh as he glanced across his shoulder at her on his arm. "I don't know, Emily. You're a game changer, I think."

She didn't answer, and it was obvious when he quickly looked away that he was just as self-conscious. His words hung in the air like white wet clouds from their breath, yet Ryan tightened his hold on her arm underscoring their potential.

Two hours later Emily waited at the register, her arms overflowing with clothes. The store was hot and crowded, and she exhaled up blowing a few loose strands out of her eyes.

"Let me help," Ryan offered, reaching out to take some of the clothes from her overburdened arms.

"No, I got it," she said, shifting her bundle onto her other hip. "If you take something it will throw the entire balance off and I'll end up dropping garments in a trail all the way to the register."

He chuckled, putting his hands up in surrender. "Whatever you say, Gretel."

Ryan was certainly pouring on the charm, and Emily smiled at his clever clothes-to-breadcrumbs analogy. He went back to the cheap seats, waiting for her by the base of a post-holiday sale display when a toddler ran past dragging a Batman scarf and hat set behind him. His mother's panicked yells from two aisles down set Ryan in motion as he helped her corral the runaway tot, securing him safely in his stroller.

Emily blinked at the sudden wetness in her eyes; her cheeks warming in a sappy awkward pride as she watched the woman thank

Ryan for his help. Emily squeezed her eyes closed tamping down the threatening emotion. What the hell was going on with her? She turned away, looking at anything but Ryan.

He tapped her on the shoulder. "That little guy was something, huh?"

Emily nodded not trusting her voice at the moment.

He looked toward the exit and then back again, one hand in his pocket and the other holding his coat. "Listen, do you mind if I step outside? I need to make a phone call." He took his coat from his arm and slipped it on. "Remember my friend with the Ranger tickets? I never called him to cancel. I guess you could say I got a little side-tracked."

His tongue-in-cheek smirk was just what she needed to break the odd discomfort holding her hostage. She met his eyes, grateful for the shift in gears "Go ahead. I won't be long...I hope," she added hopefully.

"I'll wait for you across the street at the Starbucks. Do you want anything? Coffee? Tea?"

"No, I'm good."

He leaned down and kissed the side of her jaw. "Yes, you are." With a wink he turned and walked toward the exit doors.

"What have I gotten myself into," she muttered.

"That's exactly what I've been wondering since last night."

Emily whirled around in line to see Rissa standing in the aisle off to the side holding a pair of leggings in her hand.

"Rissa! What are you doing here?" Emily stopped short. "Wait a minute. Please tell me you're not tailing me around the city."

"Ha! Like I have the time or the inclination to follow you around on your exploits, and from what I caught of his profile and his broad shoulders he is some exploit!"

Emily sniffed. "What's wrong with having a little fun?"

Rissa gave her friend a knowing smile and a quick chin pop in the direction of the exit. "Not a thing. And?"

Emily laughed shaking her head. "And nothing. I don't kiss and tell."

"Party pooper."

Emily grinned at Rissa's amused expression, gesturing for her to follow as the line moved up. "Where are the girls? Didn't they come shopping with you?"

"No. They slept in. Charlayne and Patricia have wicked hangovers, as you can imagine. Wicked even for us." She raised her eyebrows for emphasis.

"I'll bet. So, who needs the leggings, then? Did one of them get sick all over their suitcase?"

Rissa laughed. "No. The leggings are for me," she said, holding them up to show her the cut and the waistband. "I think they're just what I need after being in party clothes all night, plus the idea of driving home tomorrow in jeans makes my nether regions hurt just at the thought." She eyed her friend. "I guess you're not coming with, then?"

Emily shook her head. "I'm not sure yet. I know Sean is going to have kittens, but I'm a big girl and can make choices for myself, good or bad. I wish one of you could make him see that."

Rissa looked at her watch and then glanced at the door. "I'll mention it to Lily. If anyone can set him straight, she can."

"You mean like she set all of you straight last night?"

Jerking her eyes around, Rissa frowned. "What's that supposed to mean?"

"*Hmmph.* Oh, come on Ris. Lily must have said something to make you relax. Otherwise you and Amilynn would have scoured the city for me."

"Well...maybe not the whole city."

Emily wrapped one arm around her friend, dropping a pair of jeans and a blue ombre blouse in the process. "And I love you for it."

With a sniffle, Rissa stepped back, wiping a tear from the corner of her eye. "This line isn't moving at all is it?"

Eyes soft, Emily smiled. "At a snail's pace. Listen, if you're in a hurry I've got a pair of leggings just like that in my overnight case with you at the Fairmont. Just take those," Emily offered. "I'll buy these and trade you when I see you tomorrow." She paused. "Did anyone remember to tip the limo driver last night?"

"Of course, and Amilynn reserved a rental car for tomorrow. We're leaving after breakfast if you want to hitch a ride." Rissa eyed her friend. "No pressure, but I think it would be better all-around if you came home with us. I mean, we left together we should come home together. It would leave a lot less for people to question, if you get my drift."

Emily didn't answer, just took the leggings from her friend's hand, giving her cheek a peck in the process. "I'll let you know."

Rissa's eyes narrowed assessing if she should push the issue or not. "Okay. My cellphone is on." She hugged Emily goodbye and turned to leave but stopped, looking back over her shoulder. "At least tell me where you're staying...just in case."

Emily laughed. "I'm staying at the Liberty Hotel. And his name is Ryan."

"Just Ryan?"

Emily shrugged. "For now."

Looked like those two words had become the mantra for the weekend.

The two walked into Ruth's Chris Steakhouse a few blocks from Faneuil Hall. The temperature had dropped but the snow held, leaving the streets dry but frigid from the breeze off the harbor.

"Have you been to this steakhouse before?" Ryan asked, taking Emily's coat.

She shook her head. "I'm more of a fish kinda gal, to be honest. Though I do like a good steak now and then."

He handed both his and Emily's jackets to the girl at the coat check and stuck the paper receipt in his pocket. "I like fish too, but I've always been a meat eater.

"I bet," she said, ticking off another mental marker that he had no idea of his dual nature.

He nodded. "It's odd. Ever since I was young it's like a craving, but I attribute that to growing up poor. You always want what you can't have." In that moment his eyes skimmed Emily's face, traveling the length of her body. "You look beautiful," he murmured.

"Thank you, sir. You have very good taste." She turned, modeling the clingy knee-length black knit dress. The boat-neck style cut across her collarbone but fell into a deep 'V' beneath her shoulder blades ending just above the two dimples gracing her lower back.

"That dress is the perfect marriage of elegance and sex. The back is amazing." He turned her again but stopped her mid-twirl. Stepping closer, he pressed a kiss to her the nape of her neck and skimmed his hand the length of her exposed back, sliding the tips of his fingers beneath the top edge of the zipper just above the small of her back. "If you're commando under this dress we are not going to make it through dinner."

She turned in his arms. "Then I'll have to wait to tell you until we're ready for dessert."

He groaned, but before he could slip his hand further beneath the fabric of her dress, the maître d' cleared his throat.

"Your table is ready, Mr. Martinez."

Emily's eyebrow shot up.

Ryan shrugged. "Oops. Couldn't be helped. But now that I've told you my full name...sort of...you've got to tell me yours."

"No, I don't."

Ryan took her elbow and steered her along to the table. The host held the chair out for Emily to sit, but Ryan waved him off. "I've got it, buddy. Thanks."

Emily slipped into the chair, and Ryan took her cloth napkin placing it on her lap, deliberately grazing his thumb across the sensitive juncture between her legs. "Oh, yes you do."

Her breath hitched at the sexy tone of his voice and the dangerously sensual feel of his hand on her sex in plain sight. Dangerous. That was the right word.

He sat, his green eyes smoldering and dark with unspoken desire.

He said they wouldn't make it through dinner. Hell, they'd be lucky if they got past the appetizers.

"Um. Ryan..."

The waiter walked over. "Can I get you anything from the bar?" he asked brightly.

"Can I see the wine list?"

"Certainly," he said, handing Ryan the slim leather bound book. "I'll be back in a moment."

Ryan nodded, opening the book to the center page. "How about a nice Pinot Noir?"

"Ryan."

He looked up from the wine list. "Emily."

She folded her arms on the table in front of her. "Put the list down for a minute. We need to talk."

He made a face but did as she asked mimicking her folded arm stance as he watched her face.

"My last name is Leighton. I'm twenty-three years old and I currently live in northern California. The Bay area to be exact. As I told you before, I'm a copy editor. I work for the San Francisco Chronicle. That's all I'm going to tell you for now. When I agreed to spend time with you until you left for New York and I left for home, I don't think it occurred to you that home might be on the opposite side of the country, or that we might be geographically undesirable to each other."

He laughed out loud. "You didn't draw breath once. Did you think if you paused, I would pounce, demanding your blood type and the rights to your first born? Miss Leighton, this is not a test, nor is it a race to see who can google who faster. I want to get to know you. All about you, and not just in how many octaves I can make you scream. Although I do think we need a little more research on that front."

She exhaled, but the glint in his eyes and the tantalizing smirk on his face made the argument easy to drop. For now. "I see why you chose your line of duty. You are relentless, Detective Martinez. Now can we eat?"

~

The food came and Ryan dug into his medium rare porterhouse, savoring each bite. Emily ate slowly, the scent of her petit filet and sautéed mushrooms making her mouth water with each forkful.

"Don't you like your filet?" Ryan asked, gesturing with his fork.

"It's delicious. I'm just a slow eater." She put her fork down and picked up her glass of wine. They were on their second bottle and her head started to spin.

"I probably should have eaten when you suggested the hot pretzel in the commons earlier. I'm a little buzzed."

He chuckled, picking up his glass of wine. "That's okay. I promise not to take advantage of you later."

She swirled the ruby liquid in the wide mouthed glass. "You won't have to. I have a surprise for you."

He put the glass down and pushed his plate aside. "Oh really?"

She nodded. "Interested?"

Slanting his arms on the edge of the table he templed his fingers, leaning closer to her across the small rectangular table for two. "Depends on what you have in mind."

She put the wine glass down and reached behind her chair to unhook her purse. Opening the front snap, she took out a small black hard plastic box. "This is for you."

He held out his hand and looked at the black rectangle she placed in his palm. "This looks like a miniature remote control."

She tilted her head suggestively. "Exactly."

"What does it do?"

She shrugged, picking up her wine again. "Only one way to find out, but you'd better swing your chair around and sit next to me first."

He gave her a questioning look but slid his chair around to sit catty cornered at the table, their knees touching under the tablecloth.

Giving him an encouraging smile, she flicked her eyes to the box. "All systems go."

Ryan pressed the on button and a low muffled buzzing rose from beneath the table linens.

Emily inhaled sharply and slid her hand onto Ryan's thigh. "I think you'd better switch that to low or I'm going to reenact the diner scene from When Harry Met Sally...but for real."

"Holy shit!" he whispered. "Is this thing connected to something in your panties?"

Her breath hitched again, and she nodded squeezing his leg.

"Where did you get this? When?" He turned it off and Emily's shoulders slumped.

Her body was on fire, and the heat from Ryan's close proximity combined with his scent and the wine left her moments from climax. "I found it while we were walking around town at a shop called Good Vibrations. Murph called you back about the tickets, so while you were on the phone, I ducked in to see if they had anything fun."

Stunned, his eyes searched her face, and he leaned down to brush his lips across hers. He discreetly ran his tongue along her bottom lip, nipping it with his teeth, sucking it in softly before breaking their kiss.

Their eyes locked for a moment and Ryan pushed his chair back.

"Check please!" he yelled to the waiter.

The main hurried over. "Is everything okay? Do you want me to wrap your food?"

Ryan shook his head, taking the bill from the man and tossing three hundred dollars on the table. "Everything was wonderful. We just need to go. Now."

Pulling Emily from her chair, Ryan pocketed the remote control and fished out a five dollar bill and the coat check receipt. "Let's go."

He was like a man possessed and heat crawled up Emily's neck, a combination of unspent need and wanton desire, but also the satisfaction of knowing she'd topped anything he could have planned for tonight.

They climbed into the back of a cab, Ryan's eyes never leaving hers as he fingered the remote in the front pocket of his pants. He turned it to the lowest setting, and Emily sighed. A soft warm tingle spread from her lower belly through the perfect 'V' between her legs and down her thighs. She snuggled closer to Ryan, letting the warmth of his body fuel the sensation.

"That's nice," she said, her voice a soft purr.

"We're just getting started," he uttered, and turned the remote up a notch.

The cab stopped at a red light, the hotel within sight. Emily leaned up and licked the tender flesh beneath Ryan's jaw, her tongue rasping along the cropped stubble to the soft skin under his ear. She nipped at his lobe. "If you keep this up, we'll be fucking in the lobby men's room."

With a groan he turned the remote down.

The driver pulled in front of the hotel and Ryan handed him twenty dollars for an eight dollar fare. He got out of the cab, holding his hand out for Emily before tossing her over his shoulder and carrying her into the hotel, her squeals of laughter turning heads almost as much as the Neanderthal move.

He stalked across the lobby toward the elevators, and as if fate decreed an express car waited empty and open for them. Minutes later the elevator pinged and the two fell into the hall outside Ryan's suite, clothes half off and arms and legs entwined.

Emily slipped her arms around his neck and jumped, wrapping her legs around his waist. The remote in his pocket went to full throttle and she threw her head back moaning, grinding against his belt buckle.

He got the door open, and as it slammed shut, he ripped the dress from her body, the soft knit puddling on the floor around Emily's feet. She kicked it aside and stood in her thigh high stockings, black leather boots and black thong. Her hand slid down her stomach, but before her fingers reached the top edge of the satin and lace, Ryan caught her hand.

"That's my job."

He spread her legs and knelt in front of her. "I gotta see how this works."

Lowering the remote speed, he pulled the front of the thong forward and Emily moaned. Inside a discreet inner pouch was a tiny silver cylinder. A magic bullet. With a wicked smile, Ryan flicked the remote to off.

"You are so ripe I smell the orgasm ready to rip from your pussy. You're dripping and I want to taste you before I fuck you."

He pulled the thong the rest of the way down, helping Emily step out of it before tossing the wet satin to the side.

Ryan leaned up and licked her clit, his tongue laving in short quick strokes. He spread her thighs wider, letting his fingers delve inside the soft, moist folds, her juices running down his palm while his hand worked her spot.

His tongue moved in time with his fingers, and Emily fisted his hair, grinding her pussy farther into his mouth. She cried out, her hips thrusting as she rode his hand, his mouth sucking her clit until her climax rocked her off her feet and she fell backward.

She landed on the floor with an audible huff, but didn't blink, instead scrambled to her knees, her fingers already unbuckling Ryan's pants.

She freed his cock and pushed him onto his back. She gathered his long, corded shaft into her mouth, sucking in his throbbing head, licking and swirling her tongue as she worked her mouth around him. He growled, and with strength she didn't expect, he lifted her up and onto his thick cock, impaling himself in her pussy. She rode him hard, his hips bucking and thrusting upward until they both exploded, wet and limp.

They lay there panting, Emily's blond hair a curtain of yellow around them. After a minute she leaned up, resting her elbows on Ryan's chest. He took her face in his hands and pulled her down for a soft kiss.

He lay back, taking in the different shades across her flushed cheeks and neck. "After this, how am I ever going to let you go?" he said, running a hand through his damp hair.

With him still inside her, she sat up, ignoring the dull pain from the rug burn on both sides of her knees. "Why do we have to do anything at all? I go home in the morning and so do you. Whatever is between us, it has to run its natural course. It's got to feel easy, Ryan... effortless, or it won't work. Let's wait and see. You got me to stay for now, and that's a lot."

Emily pushed herself off his lap and climbed next to him on the floor, tucking herself under his arm. "Considering we're on opposite sides of the country, what else can we do?"

He exhaled, scooting onto his side so he could see her face. "So, it's to be a long distance love affair," he teased, brushing the tip of her nose with his index finger.

"For now..." she answered.

His eyes met hers. "For now," he whispered back, folding her in his arms as he slipped between her legs...

*Like I said! A spicy meet cute that ties into the Lion's Den! I hope you enjoyed the little extra!*

*XOXO!*

*Marianne*

# ACKNOWLEDGMENTS

It's hard for me to thank everyone who has helped me along the way. It takes a great deal of time and an even greater amount of patience to write, and for those of you who know me, patience is not one of my strong suits.

Let me start with thanking God for all the blessings in my life. My husband, Bill, and our three kids. They inspire me every day with how much faith they have in my endeavors and how they forgive my short-falls and grant me the gift of patient tolerance.

And most importantly, I need to thank my readers. You are the lifeblood in this author's world. Without you, none of this would be possible. You guys ROCK!

# About the Author

Hi everyone! I'm Marianne Morea. I write Paranormal Romance, and Paranormal Romantic Suspense. You might also know me as Marianne Dambry, or even my young adult alter ego, M.A. Morea.

I was born and raised in New York, and there's nothing like the city that never sleeps to inspire this writer's imagination.

I began my career after college as a budding journalist, and later earned a master's in fine art, from The School of Visual Arts in Manhattan, but it's my lifelong love affair with words and books that finally led me to do what I love most. Write.

I'm always interested in chatting with readers, so check out my socials and tag me in a post. Or send me a direct message!

### Have you joined my Newsletter?

It's easy peasy lemon squeezy! Just type the link and boom! Done! Lots of book news and fun tidbits, and special email-subscriber-only specials! And don't forget to do an author solid, and leave a review, because every little bit helps!
www.mariannemorea.com/contact

# Also by Marianne Morea

**The Cursed by Blood: Vampires**

Blood Legacy

Collateral Blood

Condemned

Of Blood and Magic

**The Cursed by Blood: Shifters**

Hunter's Blood

Twice Cursed

The Lion's Den

Power Play

**Club Vampire: The Red Veil Diaries**

Choose Me

Tempt Me

Tease Me

Taste Me

Bewitch Me

**Shifter Romance**

Her Captive Dragon

Taming Their Tailfins

The Siren's Mate

The Wolf's Secret Witch

Never Cry Wolf

The Demon Hunter's Wolf

The Wolf and the Rose

Torn Between Two Alphas

**Syndicate Clan Series**

The Vampire's Daughter

Lady Wolfe

Queen's Gambit*

Rebel Witch*

*Releasing in 2025.

**Whisper Falls Holiday**

A Little Mistletoe and Magic

**The Blessed**

My Soul to Keep

**CIA Rogue Operative**

Dangerous Law

Like to binge read? **I've got SPECIAL EDITION BUNDLES** for an even better reading experience!

**CLUB VAMPIRE**

*Special Edition RED VEIL DIARIES Bundle*

# BOOKS BY MY ALTER EGOS

## MARIANNE DAMBRY!

### MARIANNE DAMBY

*(PARANORMAL WOMEN'S FICTION)*

*Jeepers Reapers: There Goes My Midlife Crisis Series*

Jeepers Reapers

Where'd You Get That Keeper

One Scythe Fits All

### M.A. MOREA

*(YOUNG ADULT FICTION)*

*The Legend Series*

Hollow's End

Time Turner

Spook Rock

www.ingramcontent.com/pod-product-compliance
Lightning Source LLC
Chambersburg PA
CBHW072107020726
47501CB00003B/739